Also by Les Pendleton

FICTION

PRIDE AND PRIVILEGE

TREASURE

EVENING

DISINTEGRATION

THE SEA LES TRAVELED

THE SEA'QUEL' LES TRAVELED

NON-FICTION

THE DEVIL, ME AND JERRY LEE

SEA OF GREED

Widow Walk

LES PENDLETON

Essie Press

Palm Coast Services, Inc. dba *Essie Press*
901 Sawgrass Court
New Bern, NC 28560
www.essiepress.com
EMAIL: essie-press@lespendleton.com

ISBN for Print: 978-0-9823358-3-3
        Ebook 978-0-9754740-0-6

Second printing

Cover by Damonza

Published in the United States of America
February 2015

This book is dedicated to my family, who have added so much joy and inspiration to my time on the planet.

My Wife
Susanne Harrison Pendleton

Our children
Alan Howard Pendleton
Christopher Matthew Pendleton
Kelly Pendleton Nossiter
Stephen Christopher Curtis
Shannon Curtis White

My brother and sisters
Stuart Pendleton
Eileene Pendleton Cresawn
Amy Pendleton

My parents
Howard Pendleton
Anne Pendleton

Acknowledgments

Thank you to my editor, Betsy Barbeau, for all your dedicated efforts.

Thanks to the historic seaport of Beaufort, NC for providing the authentic setting for this novel.

Prologue

Boston was never his favorite town. It was cold and dark in the winter. Certainly, it offered all the amenities that money could buy. But money had never been his problem. His concerns were worldlier, more basic. They had more to do with his needs than his wants. This particular evening he was all about taking care of his rather "unique needs."

It was just after two in the morning. The high end bars at hotels had all closed up hours before. It was the low end dives and their clientele that intrigued him. He was especially interested in the working girls who visited his favorite joint, Sinclair's Tavern. As late as it was, the place was still alive and packed with his kind of people. She came in and sat with friends in their usual corner table, away from the blaring speakers on the juke box.

"Hey guys. Sorry I'm so late. I thought I'd waited my last table two hours ago and then this pack of drunk attorneys came in. They'd been to some kind of meeting and visited at least two bars before they showed up the restaurant. And of course, nothing they wanted was ready. So while they continued to drink beer, we had to round up their food and basically kiss their butts. I hate lawyers. They all want to pinch my butt and make filthy remarks about my boobs. I'm personally very fond of my girls and I want them treated with respect. So, what's up with you guys tonight? You ask Shelia to be your bride yet, Tony? You said this would be the week."

"Not yet. I will. I'm just building up my nerve. You know, she still has a thing for her last guy. I still think I may be her plan B if you know what I mean."

"You are nobody's plan B, Tony. If I were in the mood for a new man, you'd be the first guy I'd jump on. How 'bout you, Ceps?"

Ceps was a large, muscled product of the gym whose large biceps earned him the moniker. He looked like a pro wrestler but was actually the stereotypical gentle giant.

"Nothing much happening in my world, Barb. Job sucks. Ex-wife constantly screaming for money, and I'm tired of being cold. I need a vacation. I want to go somewhere warm, maybe the Keys or Bahamas."

"Count me in. Of course, you'll have to pay me to go as I have exactly no money. Want to get some nachos and another beer with me?"

"We can't Barb. We were both just getting ready to head out when you came in. I got an early day tomorrow at the slave ship."

"You too, Tony?"

"Yeah, I'm afraid so, Barb. Hey, let's get together this weekend."

"Sounds good. See you guys Friday after work. Same time, same channel."

"You're on."

Barb finished a beer and started out the door. Her unseen admirer put out his cigarette and set his unfinished beer down at the bar. He thought it was a great break that she didn't leave with the two idiots. This would not be a dry run like the previous evenings when she had company on the way back to the train she rode home. The steam shot out of the sidewalk grates in silky plumes and headed toward the streetlamps. Half of them had burned out making the steam look more like fog over the Scottish moors. She pulled her overcoat up around her shoulders and walked briskly down the almost deserted sidewalk. He pulled up ever closer to her. She noticed his closing footsteps and instead of turning back to see who was there she picked up her pace. He followed suit. When she reached the end of the block she would wait for the light to change so she could cross over to the station. Just as she reached the corner, the light turned green instead of red as she was hoping. This dark stretch always made her nervous. Tonight she had reason to be nervous. It was now just Barb and him. He bumped into her back as he came up to her. She turned with an exasperated look on her face. "Excuse me might be in order here."

"Sorry, Barb, but you're not excused. I need your help tonight."

No one heard the quickly stifled scream as he covered her mouth with his hand and showed her the glint of polished stainless that protruded from his other hand. Her eyes expanded and opened with the unmistakable terror that is only seen during the last seconds of life.

* * *

The two detectives had seen just about every imaginable horror that Boston had produced over the past quarter century. As they looked down at the limp figure on the alley floor, the older man offered up his thoughts about the scene.

"No question, we have a serial killer working the streets. That's two women in less than four months. Same calling card and MO. I'm sorry, Max. I just never get used to this. It's unbelievable to me that there's people out there, just walking around that are capable of doing something like this. To carve up a young girl who just wanted to get home from busting her ass in some dead end job. It's unfair. That's exactly what it is. Nobody deserves an ending like this."

Max walked over and gently pulled back her blouse to reveal a word carved on her chest with what must have been a very sharp knife.

"The word Fear. Nothing else, just 'fear' cut into her chest. It would take a really sick bastard to do this. You know he'll do this again if we don't find him."

"I know, finding him is on the top of my list. I haven't had a good night's sleep since the first girl."

A state crime lab van pulled up to the alley entrance and a team of four forensic technicians came over to the body.

"If you fellas are through with her, we'll get about working the scene. You seen enough?"

Max looked at Barb's frozen eyes as he said, "I've seen enough of this to last two lifetimes."

None of the crime scene technicians, the two detectives, or the street cops guarding the crime scene noticed him just across the street in the gathering crowd watching them work. To anyone else he was just another face. It was a very satisfied face, at least for the moment. He was no one they would ever catch or even suspect. He was far too smart to have a collection of morons like these unveil him. That said, it was time to move on. You can only throw a knuckleball so many times before the great hitters figure out your pitch. It was time to make the move. Boston was very cold but for him the heat had just been turned up. He would make that long awaited trip down south.

1

Alan Kelly studied the albatross as it tailed the ship, hour after hour, mile after mile. Surely, this solitary traveler, so far away from any perch, just wanted to know there was another voyager close by. After all, an albatross was just a bird, no different in the broad sense, than a robin or a bluebird. Perhaps if a sparrow had been seen on the rail of the Titanic, it too would instill fear in latter day sailors.

"Superstition," he thought, "What an odd invention of man."

Wind Trader moved swiftly with a graceful rise and fall. Silently she moved across the face of smooth Atlantic swells responding to a freshening, fifteen knot breeze. Out of Boston, she was a vintage Alden schooner built for an affluent New England banker back in the thirties. Time had treated the old boat kindly. Each successive owner had appreciated her lines and abilities enough to maintain her with the respect due her pedigree.

Irving Monroe was last in this proud line. Twenty years in the insurance business had claimed most of his hair and filled his brow with wrinkles. He was short and stocky, covered with the markings of a self-made man. His tight fitting polo shirt, white shorts and Rolex spoke volumes about his values. He had plenty and was damn proud of it. He left his family and divorced his first wife, leaving her well set in a mansion in West Orange, New Jersey. He sold his business and set sail to fulfill many years of dreams.

His associates told him he was suffering from middle-aged madness and it would pass. His response was always the same. "I'm not going to let it pass; I'm going with it." Along with "it," he picked up a younger wife, much younger, with an unquenchable urge to sail the tropics.

On this day he was taking his dreams south. They were a hundred miles off the east coast of North Carolina. This put them beyond the Gulf Stream, a powerful, mid-ocean current that moves tirelessly northward at two to four knots, an insurmountable counter force for even the swiftest, southbound vessel. *Wind Trader*'s crew could see only the dark blue Atlantic and a clear horizon this beautiful August evening. She was making seven knots easily as she headed for ports along the eastern seaboard. Eventually, they would make for the Caribbean and spend the winter. *Wind Trader* was built entirely of the best and most exotic woods available. Her decks were Burmese teak and her trim was African mahogany. She had twelve hand-rubbed coats of varnish on her bright work and a glistening, bright white finish on her hull. A quick glance and one would swear she was new. Any knowledgeable sailor could take one look at her lines, her proud bow, the narrow hull and recognize her for what she was, the best of her generation.

The crew handled *Wind Trader*'s twelve hundred square feet of sail with skill and the eighty foot vessel completed a seascape with her majestic surroundings. She possessed an aura that only those who love the feel of wind in the sail can ever know and appreciate.

Irving's wife Sherrie sat on the companionway hatch. She watched her husband work the old mahogany wheel, holding the ship on a broad reach. She was about thirty, fifteen years the junior of her husband. Her dark hair laid down the middle of her back and her olive skin needed no coaxing from the sun to shine. Careful attention to her makeup and clothing, along with a seductive smile and personality, made her a sexy woman, especially to a man with Irving's tastes. Sherrie set her sights on Irving the first time she met him. It was a gut wrenching time for Irving as he was breaking up with his wife. Sherrie could start his heart racing with one well-placed touch. She was what every middle-aged woman hoped her husband wouldn't find, a female bold enough to do the things they weren't willing to do to keep their men. She knew what Irving's friends thought of her and couldn't care less. The poverty and strain of her youth made her a survivor. She worked her way into this position and would remain there, no matter what anyone thought. Sherrie admired her husband's knowledge of sailing and his enthusiasm for adventure. She had a desire to know what lay beyond the horizon, something a small town upbringing had fostered in her. With Irving, she'd find out and in style.

Irving was comfortable at sea, though he was aware of the precarious nature of ocean voyaging. This wasn't his first offshore adventure. He'd participated in numerous ocean races over the years. Earlier, he'd crewed on a friend's boat in the Newport-Bermuda race. That event put him in virtually the same area they'd covered on this trip during the first three days. His experiences taught him to carefully put together a proficient crew. He had the utmost confidence in his second in command. Should he take sick or, God forbid, suffer an injury, his first mate, Jason Aldridge was a particularly fine sailor. He glanced toward him, standing by the starboard rail, studying the horizon.

"It doesn't get much better than this, eh, Jason."

Still staring at the horizon, he replied. "I ain't so sure, Cap'n. There's some thunderheads back there and the way the wind's blowin' one of 'em might wind up staring down our bowsprit."

Jason was salty looking by anyone's standards. Irving thought him the perfect choice. Should the voyage become perilous, there were those on board who were up to the task. If that was the primary requirement, Jason would be your man. He was fiftyish, bearded with a mostly hidden face that was weathered enough to testify to many years under a broiling sun. A sailor of character, his presence was a tribute to *Wind Trader*, a master seaman for a stately ship.

Irving trusted him, though he knew Jason liked to throw a little scare into the rest of the crew. He'd recall events from some past adventure and the rest of the crew would be chilled by his well-told tales.

There are not a lot of sailors today who can identify all the rigging and lines on a vintage schooner. The trend on modern yachts for many years has been to simplify them, to make them as user friendly as possible. *Wind Trader* had almost a mile of rope and cable that made up her standing and running rigging. To the untrained eye, it would be a huge task to make sense of it all, though every inch of line had a specific purpose. Jason knew each of these like the back of his hand. He needed no book on seamanship to understand what was happening on board every minute. He knew boats and he knew the sea. This summer afternoon found him preparing to administer a knot-tying lesson to the youngest member of the crew, Stephen Woods. He left his

post by the rail secure that the distant clouds posed no threat. Jason would effortlessly tie an appropriate seafarer's knot and ask his pupil to duplicate it. If he accomplished this, Jason would take the dull edge of his razor sharp knife and untie it with one or two well-placed insertions and tugs on the line. More likely than not, his apprentice would end up with something quite different than what he'd been shown. So it continued for over an hour, with a lot of interesting sea tales interrupting the lesson.

Stephen, also from New England, was tall and lean with boundless energy, a pleasant demeanor and a good hand on the harmonica. This added a desirable touch to the movement of the boat, a sea tune with a rhythm to match the steady rolling of the swells. For a true voyager, it was like being rocked to sleep. With the boat under a steady trim, Stephen gave up on mastering the double bowline and began going through most of his repertoire to the enjoyment of the rest of the crew. Thanks to his new, three-day growth of facial hair they teased him about how he could find his mouth. He had always wanted to see what he'd look like with a beard. This six month trip would offer him the perfect opportunity. Prior to this, the restraints of his profession had demanded a clean cut appearance. The old warriors of the financial establishment still had their stereotypical picture of what a responsible employee should look like. He had fulfilled this requirement to a "T" for the past eight years. Alan Kelly had been kidding him about his attempt at bearding all afternoon.

"This is only a six month cruise, Stephen. Why don't you just try for sideburns this time? Go for a beard when you're looking at a year off."

Alan stood out from the group in both his appearance and bearing. Alan Christopher Kelly was true to his name, a third generation Irish American. Nothing about him spoke of a sailor. Small framed, thin and introspective, he would have appeared more at home in the library of a college or pounding numbers in the back of a bank or accounting firm. His hair was sandy and thick, neatly trimmed and his face framed by round, wire rimmed glasses. He was quiet with an unobtrusive manner. His piercing, hazel eyes betrayed his calm exterior. Looking into them revealed a mind that examined and evaluated everything occurring around him. His intellect and upbringing was easily read. Always polite and thoughtful, he tended to avoid idle chatter. His teasing, such as with Stephen, was good-natured. If anything stood out in his manner of speech, it was his New England accent and the absence of profanity under any circumstance.

He watched other crew members go about their tasks as if he would be asked questions regarding their duties upon arrival at port. On more than one occasion, this characteristic got under the skin of Jason. However, just before Jason said anything about it, Alan would instinctively go about a needed task. It was as if he knew an explosion was coming and he'd defuse it. On this afternoon he sat perched on the bowsprit that protruded just over fifteen feet from the boat's proud hull. Only a webbing of rope and line under this precipice prevented passengers from taking an unwanted ocean swim. Alan realized this and kept one hand securely anchored to a support line. He watched the waves run tirelessly under the bow and studied the horizon as a new infusion of scarlet indicated the approaching sundown. "Always more beautiful at sea than on shore," he thought.

The captain and crew kept *Wind Trader* southerly bound on a true course and trimmed her for the maximum speed the wind allowed. She was far too stable to succumb to small variances in the wind or waves. It took better than twenty five knots of wind to get her to hull speed. Another ten knots would be needed to bury her rail. She heeled gently to port as a westerly wind slowly increased in velocity. The crew was enjoying the stronger conditions. Since leaving Boston, they had encountered only light winds and flat seas. She had been sailing upright and slowly until this welcome change occurred. She was now rising and falling, heeling moderately as she raced over the building swells. This was what they'd all been waiting for. If the wind held, in three days they'd reach the northern-most islands of the Caribbean.

This symphony of nature was halted by a weather alert on the VHF marine radio. It was mounted just inside the companionway, directly in front of Irving's position at the wheel. The stoic voice brought a frown to Irving's tanned face.

"Pan Pan, Pan Pan, Pan Pan. Hello all stations, this is Coast Guard Station Fort Macon. The National Weather Service has issued a severe weather alert to mariners for offshore waters east of Cape Hatteras. Severe thunderstorms have formed along a line parallel to the Gulf Stream with reports of two water spouts. The probability of severe weather exists for the Atlantic coast until eleven p.m. Frequent lightning, severe winds and waterspouts are possible. Seek shelter if possible. Boats offshore should prepare for dangerous seas and gale force conditions."

Irving looked at his wife. "Damn, wouldn't you know it. Two days out and we've already got bad weather headed our way. So much for the five day forecast. We're probably going to get hammered out here." There was growing concern in his voice.

"Jason, damn it, looks like you guessed right. Bad weather on the way. Force eight or stronger. Shorten sail and secure the deck for heavy seas."

His commands seemed unnecessary with the moderate seas *Wind Trader* was riding at the moment. But they all knew how quickly a storm could blow up in the Gulf Stream.

Irving turned back to his wife. He could see the worry in her eyes. "Sherrie, babe, you better go below and make certain everything's secure down there. When you're done, come back up and see to it that everybody's got a life vest on. We've got a while to get prepared. Let's take advantage of it. Thanks, sweetie. Look, don't worry, this old boat's seen many storms out here and she's definitely up to whatever is thrown at her."

Irving then directed his commands to the remaining crew members. "Stephen, you and Alan give Jason a hand and then space yourselves out where you can work the lines. You guys better put on a harness and tether to the jackline before it gets too rough."

Distant flashes of light were beginning to punctuate the brilliant sunset. Jason said out loud to the group, "Red sky at dawn. Should'a seen it coming."

Quickly the sails were lowered. Only a small storm trysail was left up to help the boat maintain steerage. That way, she could be kept with her bow properly into the seas should they build to a dangerous level. No one spoke of it but they all felt a growing anxiety creeping into their minds. They were experienced sailors in a strong ship but there were a lot more desirable places to be in a storm than Cape Hatteras, the "Graveyard of the Atlantic."

The seas began to build, along with the increasing darkness. They reflected the sharp flashes of lightning that filled the sky. The old ship began to rise and fall more rapidly as the space between swells shrank and their crests turned a frothy white. With the noise of an approaching freight train, rain began to move across the water's surface all around *Wind Trader*. So strong were the pelting drops that they stung as they struck the crew's faces. Every couple of minutes a large cresting swell would break over the bow and wash over the teak decks. The wind increased dramatically. As predicted, the weather was becoming severe.

Irving shouted above the roar of wind and rain, "Make sure your lifelines and harnesses are secure! I don't want to lose anyone overboard. These storms don't last long but they can get pretty damn nasty 'til they pass."

All were prepared. They were in the thick of the storm in moments, the bow of the boat punching holes in black twenty foot waves. Each joust brought the boat nearly to a stop as the sleek hull drove itself into tons of water. It seemed she might completely bury herself but then, she'd suddenly rise from beneath the white mountain and leap forward, propelled by a forty knot wind in her shortened sail. Irving knew she'd probably move just as fast with bare poles in these conditions. If it worsened, a sea anchor would be dropped from the stern to slow her down so she wouldn't dive under a wave and be unable to rebound to the surface. Green water was sweeping across the deck with each giant swell that smashed onto the bow. The port and starboard running lights cast eerie red and green reflections on opposite sides of the deck. The water rolling across the teak planking picked up their color and added a surreal effect.

Stephen had never experienced a storm at sea. He'd already gathered this was no time for a missed step or lost grip. A storm at night turns imagination into reality as the crew envisions huge, unseen, cresting waves barreling down on them. A strong flash of lightning illuminated the horizon and Stephen could see that his imagination had not over-dramatized the situation. Perhaps, he thought, total darkness might be better.

A burst of light fell on the deck in front of Irving as the companionway suddenly opened. Sherrie appeared, with a death grip on the handrails. There was unmistakable anguish on her face as she shouted, "There's water coming in below. I don't know if she's bursting her seams or what's happening, Irving--you've gotta' come see."

Irving looked to see who could take the wheel. He realized in these conditions, no one should try to disconnect their lifelines and attempt the treacherous walk to the wheel. Seeing no other alternative, he directed his wife. "Sherrie, just hold the wheel where it is for one minute and I'll see what's happening down below." He moved toward her. "Here, connect to my lifeline and I'll be back in a moment." With that, he disconnected his harness and connected Sherrie's to the jackline. As he moved forward, the bow raised up as if pointing to the sky and a monstrous wave went under it. Free from his only security, Irving slid backwards, falling, grabbing at everything he passed. Several loose ropes gave way as he grabbed for them. Just that quick, he was gone, swept overboard into the boiling, dark sea. Sherrie screamed at the horrible sight unfolding before her, knowing he was lost. *Wind Trader* was moving away from him at ten knots and who could even get a line to him? What could be done?

As terror filled her every pore, Alan appeared at her side, with Jason close behind. Forgetting their own safety, they'd disconnected from their lifelines the moment Irving was swept overboard. Jason screamed to her, "Go below and secure yourself in the main cabin! Forget the water down there for now. We're coming about!"

With that, he spun the wheel hard to starboard in what all aboard knew was a dangerous attempt to slow the ship's movement away from its fallen captain. As the bow turned into the wind, the ship lay powerless at a ninety degree angle to the huge seas. This was a dangerous undertaking and they all knew the possible consequences. The boat could broach and be rolled over so far that she'd take on water from her leeward side, a potentially fatal event. However, Jason knew this was the only chance to try and save Irving.

He shouted orders to the crew, "Hold on to anything if you're not tethered to the jackline! Stephen, can you get a spotlight on the water and see if you can find him? Watch the crests and pan the spot on them."

Stephen plugged in the high powered searchlight they normally used for spotting channel markers. It could put out a concentrated beam of light for a hundred yards. In this driving rain and with the vicious tossing of the deck, its usefulness was less than half that. They would have to get very close to Irving to spot him. There was also the risk of a wave smashing him into the hull of the boat if they got too close. The chances of saving him in these conditions were very small. Three successive waves crashed into the now-depowered ship, hitting her broadside as she floundered with her side into the wind and sea.

"He's there!" Stephen yelled, pointing the beam of light at the struggling form twenty yards away. As each wave passed, he disappeared from sight. "No way we'll ever get a line to him in these seas."

Seemingly, with no discussion or thought, Alan grabbed a length of line and handed one end to Stephen.

"Secure it!" he yelled over the howling winds. "I'll get it to him." With that he leaped over the stern into the raging ocean.

"You idiot!" screamed Jason, "Now there's two we're gonna lose. Follow him with the spot. Try and keep him headed right."

Stephen replied, "How do I know which way is right? I can't see a damn thing."

As the seconds ground by like an eternity, nothing appeared on the water other than the glow from the tiny spot and flashes of lightning still ripping the skies all around the ship. With each passing moment, they both knew all hope, whatever there had been in such a desperate attempt, was fading. The ship could not remain in this precarious position much longer. Now lifeless and at the mercy of the sea, she would have to be turned before the wind and repowered in order to save the vessel and her remaining crew.

"One more minute," Jason said, as much to himself as to Stephen. "Then we've got to come about or we're all going to the bottom."

The seconds dragged by ever more slowly. When he could wait no longer, Jason spun the wheel. Then he and Stephen saw it at the same instant.

"The line!" Jason said. "He's pulling on the line! Stephen, take the wheel."

Jason inched over to the rail. With the certainty of an experienced hand, he knew what must be done. He strained at the secure end of the line holding Alan and got enough slack in it to wrap a length around a winch on the rail. Immediately, he cranked at the winch, hauling in the line as fast as his powerful frame could work. Slowly, surely, the angle of the rope increased until it was straight down off the side rail.

"Hit them with the spot!" he screamed at Stephen. He quickly shone the light on the water at the end of the rope. There they were, Alan holding tightly to Irving. Amidst the fury of the storm he had retrieved him from a certain, watery grave.

With great effort on all parts, the pair of men was plucked from the boiling ocean. Jason helped them to the companionway.

Inside the main cabin, Sherrie sat in a semi-coma awaiting the news confirming her worst fears. She not only foresaw the end of the only decent life she'd ever known, but a lonely path back to her pathetic past. She'd rather drown with Irving, she thought.

The companionway doors in front of her swung open with a rush of water and then she saw the drenched presence of her husband. She ran to him. "Oh My God!" she screamed as she embraced him. "You're alive! You made it!"

Too exhausted to even respond, he collapsed on the water-soaked floor in a pile as Alan did the same. They were spent, but they were alive.

"She's still sound," Jason said. "Rain just overloaded the bilge pump. I'm going topside."

They could all feel the motion of the boat settle as she came about now running before the wind. *Wind Trader* could let the storm pass without a victim this night. Such an unbelievable event would stay with them the remainder of their lives--the fury of the storm, the terror of a man overboard in a raging sea. The storm passed as quickly as it arrived. Most of all, they'd remember a show of unequaled courage in the face of overwhelming danger. A courage so fierce it enabled a man to risk his life to save that of another, a man he barely knew. They all realized they had witnessed a rare and special act.

2

Taylor Creek is deep and affords some of the best, most protected anchorages on the Atlantic coast. Located about a mile from the wide ocean inlet at Morehead City, North Carolina, only Shackleford Banks separates it from the Atlantic Ocean. On the inland side is the beautiful seaport town of Beaufort. The water is deep right up to shore. It's a tidal creek whose surface rises and falls about three feet between high and low tides. The current flows swiftly, whether incoming or receding. When setting an anchor there, sufficient slack has to be allowed for the boat to reverse its direction each time the tide changes. Otherwise, it will drag or foul the boat anchored next to it.

Though dark, the water is clean. Flounder rest on its sandy bottom and native shrimp are always plentiful when the weather's warm. Even dolphin play regularly in the smooth water. Only the strongest of weather conditions can bring a slight chop to the water's surface.

There are those who are inclined to venture out in these waters in boats of every type. They find the creek a perfect place to moor their craft. The widest part of the creek had been adopted many years before as a perfect nesting place for seafarers.

The streets, as few as there are in Beaufort, were busy very early. Being a seaport and a major layover spot for yachts and workboats headed north or south on the Atlantic seaboard, a number of crews and watermen were trying to catch the morning tide. Shrimp boats had been working for hours when the sun's first light reflected on the horizon. The warm, coastal waters just offshore offer some of the best fishing in the world. The locals were hard-working people, fifth and six generation watermen. They wouldn't change places with any of the more prosperous vacationers that frequent their hometown.

The watermen's boats were about fifty feet long. They were mostly open so their cockpits could be used for work. Their bows rose sharply out of the water, but the decks taper quickly to a more moderate height so that nets could be worked without struggle. Generally, they had a small cabin forward to accommodate the steering wheel, offering shelter from the weather and a warm spot for a shrimper with frozen hands to escape the elements.

These workboats could be seen offshore, working in weather that would keep the most ardent sport fisherman camped at his favorite bar or tied to the dock telling fish tales. A day at the dock meant a day with no money for working watermen. Their hardworking old vessels were maintained as best as the locals could. They got painted at least once a year, and anything pertaining to safety or mechanics was kept in perfect working condition. These men didn't have to be reminded of the temperament of Cape Hatteras and the Gulf Stream. The old cemetery in the center of town was all the proof they needed.

In sharp contrast, sport fishing yachts were mainly fiberglass, not too far removed from a new sixty foot microwave oven from stem to stern. Their cabins covered two-thirds of their length and their interiors compared easily to the most expensive condominiums. They were literally floating palaces and many were never untied from their slips. They were often used as floating beach houses, where their owners could get sloppy drunk or conduct wifeless interludes under the pretense of fishing with the guys. Costing hundreds of thousands of dollars, they looked as though they would be able to weather any condition at sea and probably could. But more often than not, their weekend skippers had the good sense to stay inside when small craft advisories were posted. After all, if you could afford a toy of that magnitude, you certainly didn't have to risk your neck to catch a fish.

The town itself looked like it did when its founders brought great sailing ships to the waterfront. The old white, framed houses still looked out on the broad expanses of the Atlantic. The homes weren't restored. Though many were two hundred years old, loving owners had maintained them with pride since they were built. Widow-walks remained on the tallest gable of each roof. These roof-top decks were built so that anxious seafarer's wives could get an early glimpse of their husbands' ships returning. A four hundred foot square rigger's tall masts and thousands of feet of white sails were the first indicator that signaled their safe return from months at sea. For the wives whose husbands didn't return, the name widow walk was born.

Though many seafaring men were buried in the old churchyard cemetery bearing testimony to the harsh and dangerous way they earned their living, there were others who found an untimely death at the hands of Mother Nature. There was the grave of a young girl who died at sea on the way over from England. The ship's crew, afraid her family would suspect foul play had been involved in her death, brought her body home pickled in a whiskey barrel. The locals swear to this day she was buried as she was delivered, still in the whiskey barrel, for practical reasons.

The sea was bountiful and generous to some, making a fortunate captain wealthy as the stately homes clearly illustrated. But the sea was a treacherous partner and exacted a heavy toll from many families. They remembered and told the sagas of woe-begotten ships which perished on Diamond Shoals, a few miles out to sea off their coast. The Cape Lookout lighthouse still stands ever stately, casting a beam of hope to the approaching ship. Directed by this powerful light they could avoid the shoals and make safe harbor in this welcoming, beautiful town.

There were also stories of ships being misled by false lanterns and lured to their doom on the shoals so they could be looted the next morning. However, old photographs and newspapers documented the many brave local seamen who lost their lives trying to save crew members of foundering vessels. These glimpses into her seafaring heritage are proudly displayed in Beaufort's Maritime Museum.

Though many of her residents still toiled on shrimp and charter boats, the town was attracting a new type of citizen. They were the wealthy yachtsmen who appreciated what the town stood for, its heritage and it's fondness for boats of all types. New docks had been built along the length of the town's waterfront to attract these affluent travelers to their town. The seafood processing plants and the smellier end of the industry had been moved to less conspicuous sections of the city. On any day there were hundreds of yachts and boats of all descriptions anchored in and around the town. The scenery and spectacle also attracted landlubbers who came to gawk at the yachts and prowl the gift shops, restaurants, and antique stores that seemed to be multiplying daily. All said, no better place existed to rest your crew and vessel for a while.

Sarah was headed to Sam's for a cup of coffee before opening the Water Dragon. She was deep in her thoughts and didn't hear the car taking the corner behind her and then accelerating straight toward her. The elderly woman driving the dilapidated Buick was slumped over at the wheel experiencing a heart attack. There was no horn to warn Sarah and it was too late for her to even react. With not a second to spare a strong pair of arms grabbed her and tossed her to the sidewalk just off the street and out of the path of the car which ended its journey plowing into a parked Town truck. Sarah looked up to see Eddie Fitch, the town's dock master standing over her. Somewhat disoriented she asked him, "Eddie, what happened?"

"Mrs. Moore just crashed her car and almost you with it. I didn't mean to throw you so hard but I really didn't have time to think about it."

"You must have saved my life. Is Selma alright?"

"I'm headed her way right now. You sure you're okay?"

"Just a few scrapes, nothing to worry about. Thank you so much, Eddie. I owe you, big time."

"You don't owe me a thing, Sarah. I've got to go over here and check on Mrs. Moore. Can you call 911?"

Sam, the grill owner had come to Sarah's side and was helping her up. "Already called them, Eddie. They'll be here in just a minute."

Eddie went to the car and checked the elderly woman's pulse. Several other townspeople came to help as well. Eddie gently leaned her head back and saw a large gash on her forehead. Her color was pale and he feared she might not make it, but he nonetheless stayed with her 'til the paramedics and the sheriff got there.

The crowd that had gathered started to disperse and go back to their routines. Sarah, visibly shaken and in need of a first aid kit and a cup of coffee, headed to Sam's.

The Grill was a local institution. Every morning, the locals and tourists would fill the place for a good, home-cooked ham, eggs, and grits breakfast and many cups of coffee. Even the greenest newcomer could quickly separate the locals from the visitors. The permanent residents wore hip boots or waders with flannel shirts and stocking caps. In the summer, they still wore blue jeans and work shirts, but the stocking cap was generally replaced by a dirty ball cap. In the worst of the winter season, their heavy rubber, foul weather gear was a dead giveaway. If you were still in doubt, their thick beards, windblown hair, and skin turned to dark brown leather by the sun, would convince you of their identity.

The interior of Sam's Grill had remained the same for over thirty years. There were rows of booths running down both of the side walls and the center was filled with small, square, formica-topped tables, sporting a chair on each side. Were it located on a major interstate, as opposed to the waterfront, it could easily have passed for a down-home truck stop. What it lacked in cleanliness and style, it made up for with good home-cooking and local flavor. The walls were papered with black and white photos of the town, its citizens, and newspaper stories of interest. Some were old and yellowed and dated back to when the place was new. Others were as recent as the wedding and graduation announcements from the past spring.

Conversations invariably revolved around local gossip and the fishing conditions. Sarah had heard it all a thousand times but enjoyed the atmosphere and the company each morning before work. This morning she found her usual seat near the window by the check-out.

"That was some accident!" exclaimed Jean, a seventies retro waitress. She was rarely seen without gum, and a pencil stuck behind her ear.

"Yeah! Do you happen to have a first aid kit? I am a little scraped-up. Eddie pushed me out of the way just in time, but I landed on my knee and elbow. Oh, and a large coffee."

"Holy, shit! I'll be right back with both." Jean ran off in search of the band-aids, leaving Sarah to dab at her wounds with a napkin.

The men seated at nearby tables nodded good morning to her, and Sam, who owned the grill, came over to check on her. He needed a shave, as usual, and his dirty apron looked more like a tablecloth as it laid out over his protruding beer-belly. He was the son of the grill's founder and grew up working there. It was his now that his father had died. It never occurred to him to consider any other way to make a living. Just as the area fishermen were the sons of fishermen, he had followed his father's footsteps as he always knew he would. That's just how it worked in this simple, but highly structured existence.

"You alright, Sarah? You want me to call Miss Myrtle?"

"No, don't do that, Sam. It would just upset her. She is just now getting around better. Warm weather eases her arthritis."

"Do you think she might like one of the girls to run her a biscuit to the house when it calms down a little in here?"

"I know she would, Sam. Let Jean take it, 'cause Myrtle keeps asking how she's getting along."

Jean walked up just in time to hear her name.

"What am I going to have to do now?" Jean said, handing the first aid kit to Sarah.

Sam nudged her, "How 'bout taking a couple of biscuits up to Myrtle in a bit?"

"You got it." Turning her attention back to Sarah she said, "How's the gift shop doing? I heard Floyd say he was expecting this to be a big year since he added all the greeting cards and stationary."

"I don't want it to get any busier than it is right now, unless Floyd is going to come in and work some himself. He's the laziest man in the county."

There is general agreement on this assessment, but not in a mean way as they all like Floyd. It's not a crime to be a little laid-back "down East." A lot of the tourists were particularly pleased with that trait. It was the opposite of what they faced at home most of the time. Sarah doctored herself and finished her coffee, said her goodbyes and headed toward the door. *"Time to go to work,"* she thought.

The table closest to the door held an assortment of locals who watched her walk past them. The youngest of the group, Zed, offered loudly to his companions. "One night with me and she would be cooking fish for my table regularly."

Sarah overheard the none-too-quiet remark and shot back at him, "Zed, you smell like you don't do anything but clean fish yourself. If you need help with something, it's taking a bath, not cooking fish. Besides, from what I hear, if it weren't for those friends of yours, you wouldn't have any fish to clean." She then winked at the older men with him, whom she had known all her life, and said, "He doesn't know how feisty I can be when I want to, does he fellas?"

They all roared with laughter as she left. Zed, embarrassed by her response said more quietly to the group, "From what I hear, ain't no man gonna be touching that piece."

Immediately, one of the older men shut him up. "Zed, button it up, you hear? I knew her momma and daddy. She comes from as fine a family as ever lived here. She's been given a lot to handle to be so young, and she's doing pretty damned good."

Another at the table said to him, "At least we haven't been going home drunk a couple nights a week, Zed. You know what I'm saying?"

Zed gave him a sneer and took the last swig of his brew.

* * *

Sarah had lived in Beaufort nearly all of her twenty-three years. Even though the town was a place of beauty, she added to it immensely, not just by her appearance, which was admired by everyone who saw her, but by the warmth and charm she shared readily. Sarah worked in the Water Dragon, a gift store with cards and stationary for tourists and visiting sailors. She loved to pass the day talking with visitors and encouraging them to tell her more about the places from which they had journeyed. This was a wonderful spot to meet people from all over the world as they passed through on their small ships, headed to exotic places she'd only seen in photographs.

She loved to explore the beaches around Cape Lookout; to take a dinghy and row through the anchored yachts across Taylor Creek and over to the Outer Banks. There she hunted for sea shells and sand dollars for hours on end. As many times as she had been there, she never tired of watching the seagulls soar without moving a wing as they rode the strong ocean winds, looking for the minnows that flourished in the surf. Once their prey had been spotted, they'd dive down in the fashion of a vintage dive bomber and rip the free meal from the water. To Sarah, there was no better way to pass a day than walking barefoot in the surf, feeling the grip of warm beach sand on her toes. She delighted watching the wild horses which lived on the small barrier islands. These horses were the descendants of Spanish mustangs, brought to the new world hundreds of years before. When their ships were lost on the shoals, some made it to the beach and took up residence on the barrier islands. They were the last of their kind.

Sarah had another great love in her life, the young children in town that came to her home every day after school. They were delighted to just be with her, to explore, to talk and share their secrets with this special adult. She was grown, but she still had the gift of childhood, the innocence of youth that only children know. Many afternoons, she'd get out brushes, water colors, and finger-paints for the younger children and together they would try and capture the wonders of their world in simple paintings. Many of them hung from the walls of her small home. They were the children of friends. They loved their children, but the long hours of working watermen and their wives, who worked in the shops and restaurants, left little time or money to spend on them. It was good for the children and their parents to have Sarah there filling this void. To many of the children, this was the high point of their day and Sarah was part of their family. The children were sweet, well mannered, and respectful. Many wore clothes from the thrift shop or hand-me-downs from an older sibling. To Sarah, they were all equal, all deserving of the same care and attention. Their laughter helped to make her home a very special place.

Though very old and built by her great grandfather, the quaint house was maintained almost as a tribute to family members who had lived and laughed there for generations. Sarah appreciated this and always felt no other place could ever be as much of a home as this was to her. In a world full of violence and trouble, her little friends added just that much more happiness.

Sarah's world needed as much happiness as possible. Her mother had died when she was a child and her father passed away when she was seventeen. Only her invalid grandmother, Myrtle, who Sarah attended to much of her waking hours, lived with her.

There was a trade-off, however, as Myrtle told Sarah all the great old tales, both fact and fiction, about Beaufort and her family. These she would listen to for hours on end, both to the satisfaction of the elderly woman, who loved her company, and for Sarah. They gave her a feeling of family and roots that she found comforting. Most of the stories were about people that Sarah had never met. Yet, her grandmother's gift for embellishing a tale made her feel as though she knew each character personally. Myrtle would take great pains to not leave out the smallest detail when undertaking one of these wondrous tales.

There was a story of particular interest to Sarah and she never tired of hearing it. With ever so much enthusiasm, her grandmother told of a man she'd met over sixty years earlier and with whom she'd become enamored. His name was Ernest Galloway. He was a sailor back when the last remaining sailing ships sailed the oceans and called on every port. He was strong and handsome and, for a brief period, called Beaufort his home. Myrtle and he spent a summer she'd never forget, sailing in a small dinghy and exploring all the secluded beaches around Shackleford Banks.

These escapades were told so expertly that Sarah could envision herself as a witness to the events. To have them occur in a setting she knew so well, and so delighted in, only made it that much more fascinating.

Myrtle described how she was so infatuated with the young man that she ignored all the advice of her family and friends to stick to a local boy, someone she could relate to. However, what struck her the most about Ernest were his beautiful photographs. They were magnificent pictures of the ocean and the people who lived along it. "They were haunting, almost alive," she would say.

"Many people have a special talent, something they do better than most folks can. And a few, a very few, are touched by the hand of the Creator. Leonardo Da Vinci, Albert Einstein, and Enrico Caruso surely were blessed by God to be more than most men. Ernest had this gift with his camera. I always told him he had the Van Gogh touch. He would set up his camera down by the shore. He would take pictures of the fishermen at work, and the ships resting at anchor in the channel. Anyhow, he left that fall on a freighter to South America, said he was going to make this one trip, just for the money to help us get a foothold. Then he'd be back for me. I had this terrible feeling the day he left that I'd never see him again. I cried for days. Since then, I've learned to trust these feelings about things like that.

"There was a hurricane, a bad one. The ship had no warning and was lost with all hands. Still got the newspaper clippings in a box. Ever show them to you, dear?"

Sarah would nod in agreement.

"I used to think that somehow he might have survived and one day he'd come back home. But, I'm eighty four now and it never happened.

"There was the letter though. I'll never understand. Over a year after he died it arrived, just out of the blue. It must have been left in a port, somewhere where the mail only got picked up a couple times a year. He spoke in the letter as if he were already dead and promised that he'd be watching over me no matter what. It sure looked like his writing. I would hate to think someone would be cruel enough to fake it. And why would they? It was just strange, that's all.

"A few years after that, I met your grandpa. We fell in love and married. Fifty two years we were together. All said, it was a good life. Sometimes though, I can't help but wonder what might have been if he'd returned."

Myrtle would generally drift off in thought for a while and then fall asleep. Sarah thought this to be a beautiful tale, almost like one of the novels she liked to read. "It would certainly make a fine book," she would tell her grandmother.

Myrtle would always reply the same. "One day, Jean is going to write it all down for me. Remind her about that when you're down at the grill, Sarah."

"I will."

It was nearing the end of summer and the town was full of Snowbirds, the northern sailors who took their boats south in the winter, mostly to Florida and the Bahamas, and then back to their home ports in New England for the balmy summers off Long Island and Cape Cod. Many of them held a particular fondness for Beaufort and would arrange their schedule to spend as much time there as possible. Such interest had given Beaufort busy restaurants, gift shops, and even the latest fad in tourist accommodations to appear in the area, the bed and breakfast inns. A lot of the old sea captains' homes were offering a pricey rest to visitors. They were popular with the tourists, offering a glimpse into yesterday. Most still contained the old furnishings and pictures of the families that built them. It was like staying in a museum. The businesses that catered to sailors were always full. An especially busy lot were the shipwrights and woodworkers who had learned their craft from their fathers before them. These hardy craftsmen had built many a fine shrimp boat or Harker's Island sport fisherman. These vessels had earned a reputation among fishermen worldwide as high quality, seaworthy craft. They were still being built of juniper and other local woods instead of the more modern materials, such as fiberglass.

* * *

As she walked down the street on her way to the Water Dragon, Sarah passed friendly faces along the way and noticed an increase in the number of boats in the harbor.

"Looks as if it's going to be a busy day," she thought. She reached the door of the gift shop and had to push several boxes of supplies that had been dropped off earlier in the morning by a freight service, not an unusual occurrence in Beaufort. Crime here was almost non-existent. The locals were far too proud and, for that matter, too happy in their work to ever think about stealing. Besides, there was nothing there that their neighbors wouldn't give to them if they really needed it. There was an occasional outboard motor stolen and the town rowdies, such as Zed, had to sober up in the jail some nights. But, for the most part, it was a peaceful place. The tourists and yachtsmen came to town, expecting to leave with less than they came with, so the elements weren't there for a problem to start.

Sarah opened the door and cut on the lights. Then, she immediately turned on the stereo which furnished background music for the store. She kept it tuned to a soft FM station that played the classics, jazz and opera, one of her passions. She always joked that if Pavarotti ever came to town, she would kidnap him and force him to sing for food. As usual, she adjusted the volume a little louder in the mornings before customers arrived, listening intently while unpacking the new deliveries, pricing and displaying them as she worked. She went to the small bathroom and looked in the mirror at the injuries she suffered during the incident that morning. She realized only too well if it hadn't been for Eddie being close by and coming to her rescue, she would not be here right now. She said a silent prayer for the old lady in the Buick.

The Water Dragon was built on the waterfront. Located in an old fish-house building that had been upgraded for the tourist trade, it still retained much of the old timber and flooring. The back wall had been opened up with large windows that looked out over the docks. Only the boardwalk, about ten feet wide, actually separated the window and back door from the decks of the visiting boats. This assured that almost every day the view would be different. One day, she might be looking across Taylor Creek through the rigging of an old sailboat. The next day she would be looking at the side of a brightly finished motor yacht, with its nattily dressed, professional crew moving about, performing their appointed chores to keep the yacht in Bristol condition.

This morning, the slip adjacent to the shop was vacant, a condition not likely to last very long. Sarah quietly sang along with Pavarotti on her favorite, "Nessun Dorma." She was interrupted by the bell attached to the front door as her first customer came in. Sarah quickly turned down the volume on her private concert.

"Good morning, come in and make yourselves at home," she instructed the thirtyish woman who was dragging her two young boys and husband behind her. "We have some great ship models already put together over here that the boys might like to look at, so you can browse in peace."

The boys, about seven and nine years old, attacked the model counter over by the rear windows. "Alright," the older one said. "These are great, David!" he called to his younger sibling. "Look at these boats! Mom, can we..."

He stopped dead in the middle of the question as something more exciting had captured both of the boys' attention. "Holy shit, Mom! Look out the window. A ship is pulling in. Look at how big it is! Can we go outside to see it, Mom? Please?"

"Watch your mouth!" she responded. The mother looked out the window and was also taken by the size and majesty of the ship. She motioned for her husband, "Bob, take the boys outside, would you. I'll stay in here for a while and meet you there shortly. Let the boys see the ship, but don't let them get too close to the water." She turned to Sarah. "Neither one of them can swim at all. I know we should get them swimming lessons but there's just not a lot of water in Knoxville, where we live. We haven't been as concerned about it as we probably should. I guess all the kids here swim before they can walk, right?"

"Well, not really that early, but with as much water as we have here you better teach them soon or they'll learn the hard way. Most of the local kids help their dads on the water and can swim like ducks. It's just second nature to them." Sarah turned to see the boat slowly approaching the slip, its ragged looking crew standing ready with the lines.

It was *Wind Trader*, bearing the scars of her battle with the storm. There was a lot of torn up rigging and equipment strewn out across the deck, the crew too beaten up to secure and reorganize properly until reaching port. Beaufort was for them the closest shot to a safe inlet from where they'd been during their encounter with the storm. They'd limped to port under auxiliary power, an old diesel that smoked and belched, but nonetheless allowed a direct course when the wind wouldn't cooperate. At last, they'd made safe harbor.

Wind Trader would spend a few days here, re-rigging and repairing the damage. The crew was anxious to touch solid ground again, and Irving was already considering the possibility that some of them might choose not to continue the voyage after so close a brush with a watery grave.

Sarah's customer left through the back door to join her family and the tourists on the docks. They were enjoying the sight of *Wind Trader* being tied up. Compared to the modern cruising sloops which filled the harbor, she was a page out of the past. Her tall masts and extensive rigging, coupled with the antique-looking waterfront buildings, made that section of the town dock look like it had gone back in time a hundred years.

Sarah forgot about the sailors and continued with her chores in the shop. Several hours passed peacefully and, as she was working a counter display, the back door opened. The wind from the creek extracted music from the wind chimes, hanging by the back entrance. She turned to see if the strong sea breeze had opened the door as it had a thousand times before. Instead, there stood Alan, looking like a refugee, covered with sweat and dirt on his face. His clothes looked as if he had been cleaning a bilge. He spoke politely, "Miss, I am with the crew of *Wind Trader*. We've just docked here, right outside your door." He noticed that she was staring at his appearance. "Please excuse how I look. We've been securing the boat and she's quite a mess right now. I guess I am too. Looks like you had a little accident."

Sarah replied, "Yeah, this morning I almost got hit by a car. What can I get for you?" There was an edge of distance in her reply but Alan was used to a rather clannish aspect in the small ports they visited.

"Boy, I am glad you didn't! Are you okay now?"

"I'm fine. Still a little shaken by the whole thing. So, what do you need to know?"

"I just wondered if you might suggest a good place to get cleaned up and maybe a good meal. I don't like tourist traps too much. Where do the locals eat?"

Sarah didn't have to think to answer the question. "Sam's Grill, next block down on Front Street. Tourists and locals eat there. It's cheap and the food is good. There's a restroom with a hot shower at the end of the dock. If you dock here, the dock master will give you a key. He's probably asleep in his office right down the wharf there." She pointed out the window in the direction of the dock master's office. "His name is Eddie Fitch. He's the guy who saved me this morning. He pushed me out of the path of the car. Just yell Eddie and he'll eventually wake up." Sensing that he was not as rough as he looked, she added, smiling as she did. "You're wise for considering the shower before you go to the grill, in case you haven't looked in a mirror recently."

"That bad, huh?"

"I've seen worse, but not this week."

"Thanks," Alan replied, departing quickly toward the dock master's office. As he walked down the waterfront, Alan was taken by the beauty of the town. It was not large, just four blocks along the waterfront. There were shops, restaurants, and taverns conveniently arranged to be accessible to those arriving at the modern docks. There was a pier-like boardwalk along the entire length of the town. It separated the waterfront shops from Taylor Creek, the deep water channel running several miles beyond the town. There was a combination of sailors, tourists and locals lending a busy, friendly atmosphere to the place.

The shops were quaint, mostly with nautical themes. Even though they were modern and well appointed, the buildings were old. They were the original structures, maintained with dignity and authenticity to the present day. It was a beautiful town. No wonder so many sailors passed the word that it was one place you should not pass by when heading down the Atlantic coast.

Alan arrived at the dock master's office. He knocked politely several times on the door to no reply. He was about to yell, as Sarah had suggested, when someone came up from behind.

"What do you need buddy? Are you docking?"

"Yes, I'm crewing on the old schooner that just arrived. I'd like to find out what services you have."

"You mean like showers?"

"Exactly."

"Well, come in the office and let me get your name and information. We try and keep the facilities for just our visiting boaters. Lots of tourists here. They would use the toilets continually if we didn't keep 'em locked. Where you from?"

"New York, but the boat and her owners are out of Boston. They'll be by shortly to check in, but I'd really like to get cleaned up. A hot shower would make my day right now. *Wind Trader* is the boat's name. I'm Alan Kelly."

"Alright, Alan. I'm Eddie Fitch, the dock master."

Eddie was the kind of brash, hard-speaking northerner that usually generated animosity in southerners. He was short, fat and sloppy looking. His untucked, wrinkly flowered shirt made him look like a reject from a Jimmy Buffet concert. He wore rubber flip flops instead of deck shoes and he seemed to be an unlikely candidate for his job. Reeking of beer and stale sweat, he needed a shower as badly as Alan, maybe worse.

"Beaufort ain't much but a lot of folks seem to like it here. You'll probably enjoy it for a while. Gets a little small after a few weeks though. Look, I don't know much about sailboats, so you guys secure the thing yourself. They don't pay me enough to bust my ass, so I pretty much just hand out keys and keep track of the parties. When you get cleaned up, come on back over and I'll point you to the action. A lot of these rich broads come down here with their husbands and are bored shitless. The old geezers go fishing and me and their old ladies, we go spend their money. Perfect job, heh?"

"Sounds interesting anyway."

"I'm a Yankee too. Came down on a boat a couple years ago and just fell in love with the place. Took this job and haven't left since. Ain't a bad place to live. How long you gonna be staying?"

"Just long enough to make repairs. We got hit by a bad squall out in the Atlantic. No structural damage, but everything got pretty rattled. We'll have to straighten her up and re-tune her lines. Probably take a week."

"That's great. Glad to have you in town. Come with me and I'll show you where the restrooms and showers are. Don't forget now; come back later if you want to find out where all the partying is."

"I appreciate it, Eddie, but right now, rest seems to be the only thing I can think of. Maybe later."

"You got it, man."

They walked off toward the far end of the waterfront.

The day passed quietly and Sarah prepared the shop for closing. All done, she locked the front door from the inside and exited from the rear as was her custom. Usually, she walked along the wharf on the way home, looking at the new arrivals tied up in the slips. She enjoyed the feeling of festivity that descended upon the waterfront as the musicians started playing and tourists began gathering along the docks to enjoy the entertainment and beer. As she locked the rear door, she turned and almost tripped over Alan. He had come up directly behind her.

"I'm sorry. Did I startle you?"

"Yes you did, but I'm okay. We're closed now. If it's an emergency, I could open back up." She moved back closer to the door and started to insert the key.

"No, I just came by to thank you."

"Thank me for what?" His voice was familiar. He had an accent that sounded like Ted Kennedy, she thought.

"For the information on where to eat, and the shower."

It then dawned on her who he was. He certainly had improved his appearance since the morning. She hadn't recognized him at all. Embarrassed, she said, "I'm sorry. I didn't recognize you. You look a lot different now."

"Better I hope."

"A lot."

There was an awkward pause as both Sarah and Alan were at a loss for where the conversation should go from there. Finally Sarah spoke. "Well, goodnight. I have to go home and fix supper for my grandmother."

Finding her interesting, Alan boldly threw out to her, "Maybe you'll go to Sam's with me tomorrow for lunch? My treat."

"Maybe, ask me tomorrow.

Then, deciding that she might want an "out," she added, "Sometimes it gets pretty busy at lunch."

"I'll do that. Oh, by the way, what's your name?"

"Sarah. Sarah Turlington. Well, goodnight."

"Mine's Alan. See you tomorrow."

Sarah turned and started down the wharf, heading home. Alan watched her as she walked away. There was an obvious attraction here, and they both felt it.

3

He followed them down the wharf, just far enough back to not draw their attention. Down the streets and alleys, through the darker edges of Beaufort, he shadowed them. As quaint as the little town was during the day, and at night in its tourist-filled watering holes, it became dark and quiet elsewhere in the town, when the sun receded into a sea of sparkling red rollers. Fishermen had to rise early as did the shop owners that took care of the tourists. By nine p.m., all but the waterfront taverns was quiet.

So it was this night. He would pick a lovely young woman and watch as she left a tavern, hoping she might be unescorted as she walked to her car. There was great skill, he thought, in not rattling the woman as he followed closely. His head was pounding, pummeled with adrenaline, generated by the thought of the challenge, the struggle, and then his eventual conquest. So many times before, and yet, the thrill was still there. Yes, even better he believed. You couldn't appreciate the complexities of these matters until you had attempted them countless times in a variety of settings. This was a new place, a different challenge, and even though the prey was similar, everything else had changed. The thought of all of it excited him greatly. And there she was, his first selection.

Bev kissed her companion goodnight at the tavern door. She implored him, "Let Tom drive you home, sweetie. You don't need to get behind the wheel after all the beer you've had." She yelled to their mutual friend, "Get him home, will you, Tom?" With that, she turned, swinging her purse and crossed over to the dark side of the street, the shortest path to her car parked two blocks down the waterfront.

"Such vanity," he thought. *"Newspapers are bursting with nothing but crime, murders and rapes, and yet this woman feels safe on an unlighted street at night by herself. She's asking, no begging, to be an example to all the others. Better that a few suffer so that the rest will understand. And here she is, literally forcing me to choose her. I hope she at least attempts to get free. A struggle is necessary. There's no glory in hitting a dog crossing the street if it doesn't see you coming; that would just be a statistic. There's no meaning, no message there. The struggle is so very important; it gives meaning to the message. So very crucial to the whole episode."*

She heard it behind her, the footstep on gravel, but when she turned to look, there was no one there. Her pace quickened and she began to look for anyone's presence she might know as she moved farther into the dark, toward her car and home. She couldn't help but remember the warnings where she worked to not go out alone after dark. She thought of her reply to the warning. "I'm looking for a man to want me that bad, honey. He'll never know what hit him."

She laughed at their squeamish behavior. Yet, here she was wishing she had heeded those warnings. She continued to walk faster toward her car.

The music was getting faint behind her. *"Why didn't I wait for someone to walk with me?"* she thought, growing more concerned.

She had always been leery of walking alone after dark, but she reasoned it was all just her imagination. Beaufort was not a dangerous place to take an evening walk.

There it was again, to her side, in the alley between two shops across the street. Now she was aware of just how nervous she was. Beads of sweat were running down her face. How much darker it suddenly seemed. Only a block away from the brightly lit tavern and the lights coming from the warmly lit interiors of all the yachts and yet, she felt like she was walking in a cave with unseen predators watching her every move. Someone was following her, it was clear. It had to be one of her friends. Get ready, some jerk would surprise her any second, and take great satisfaction if she were frightened. There it was again, much closer.

"David, is that you. I can hear you, you know! David, you son-of- a-bitch, if that's you I'm getting really pissed off. Stop it! I'm warning you."

No reply. She was almost there. If this was David or Tom, they would pay. Almost at a jog, she quickly reached her car. She reached in her purse, fumbling desperately for her keys. "Why do I have to lock the doors every time I get out," she asked herself. "There's nothing in it to steal and the only time it needs to be locked is when I'm in it." She found the brass apple with the key ring attached to it in the bottom of her purse and quickly brought it out, shoving it toward the door of the vehicle. As she thrust it in the direction of the slot, a gloved hand slid in the way, covering the spot on the door where she'd aimed

"Need some help?" a voice from behind her asked.

"Who are you?" was the best she could blurt out in reply. She recognized neither the dark shadow of a person or the voice emanating from it.

"I'm the man you're going home with tonight, sweetie," he said mocking the way she had addressed her boyfriend moments before. "You might say, I'm the new man in your life, and probably, no, certainly the last."

Over the loud music that blared on the waterfront, her muffled cry would be heard by no one. She struggled hard to get free. It didn't happen.

4

Morning came, the same as any other in Carteret County. Before the sun put the first touch of orange on the surface of the ocean, many red and green lights gave away the presence of shrimpers pulling their nets through the shallow coastal waters. They were working just beyond the breakers, hoping to find the small, tasty creatures that had made their livelihood possible for generations.

The shrimp trawlers were generally white and bore the names of girlfriends or family members. The names were always unique and very readily distinguishable from those given to pleasure craft. The workboats had names like *Two Sisters* or *Emily Moore*. The sport fishermen usually carried less personal, more tongue in cheek names, like *Sea-Duction* or *Offshorgasm*. The decks of the shrimpers were generally in need of paint as the continual barrage of equipment and nets kept them scraped to bare wood.

The back third of the trawler was occupied by one or two masts that supported the outriggers. These extended up to twenty feet above the hull on each side of the boat and fed the lines to the shrimp nets. Once the nets were filled, the center masts would act as a winch support to hoist in the heavy, woven material and its catch. Once the nets were raised into their resting position on the ends of the masts, with the other end looped down onto the deck, from a distance, the whole affair resembled a large butterfly sitting on top of the boat. That, however, was as much beauty as could be found on these craft. This was tedious, physically demanding, and often dangerous work. It was risky, not just from the heavy equipment and hundreds of feet of line needed to undertake the tasks required, but also from the turbulent, rolling swells that could turn their workplace into a violently pitching platform. One slip could mean a quick exit into the swarm of hungry, frenzied sharks that trailed the shrimpers. They were always there, picking up the scraps being thrown overboard as the nets were retrieved.

Sheriff Morris Stone arrived at his office in the four wheel drive Jeep the County furnished him. It was a necessity in making his rounds since a large amount of his time was spent patrolling back roads and beaches. Beaufort was the County seat and his office was located beside the antique red courthouse in the town square, just across the street from the old cemetery. As usual, he was the first to work. He cut on the lights and got the coffee pot going, a ritual he enjoyed. It made him feel he had a jump on the day, if he had these small matters secured before everyone else showed up.

Esther, the secretary who handled incoming office calls for the Sheriff as well as the County, arrived just a few moments after him. Grey headed and pleasant, though bordering on obese, she loved her job monitoring the incoming calls. Having this access to information made her feel important. She knew who beat their wife, who drank too much, and which kids had been caught with their pants down on the beach or, better yet, with a joint. Knowledge was her power. Having the good sense to not relay such information around the town, she jealously guarded the juicy facts and enjoyed knowing that she was privy to most of the town's secrets.

"Morning, Morris. Bet you get a call in the next two minutes. Bet me?" She walked over to the coffee pot, grabbed her cup and Morris proceeded to fill it for her.

"What makes you so sure, Esther? Course, I know better than to bet against you about anything."

"There's a crowd down at Francis' Seafood House, running around like crazy. Your deputy, Thomas, was just pulling in when I passed. You know he won't go to the toilet 'til he calls you."

Morris acknowledged her by suggesting, "Well, last time he called in it was the lady who had the heart attack and almost killed Sarah. If it is about Archie's, this would be the third time in as many weeks that his stockroom freezer has been hit. If seafood gets any more expensive, they're gonna have to keep it in a refrigerated vault. Archie Francis knows better than to leave his locker full over the weekend. It's like asking..." He was suddenly interrupted by the police radio monitor.

Esther said smugly, "I win."

"Sheriff Stone, you in yet? This is Thomas, down at Francis' Seafood. You need to get down here ASAP."

"Another B&E?" Morris quizzed.

"Not hardly, Sheriff, there's a body in his freezer. You need to come down right now. It's the most sickening thing you ever saw."

Morris, aware that many of the townspeople monitored the police radio on their scanners for amusement, reminded his deputy.

"Not on the air please, Thomas. Save it 'til I get there. I'm walking out the door right now."

Obviously shaken, Morris told Esther. "Listen for calls, and radio for a state coroner to get down here. Better yet, ask if they want the body sent to Raleigh. Damn, I've never investigated a murder here. Not in fourteen years. You better get somebody from the SBI too, before we even move the body. Shit!"

Sheriff Stone grabbed his western style hat and ran to the car. In a single motion, he spun the patrol car around and laid rubber with all four wheels as he sped to the scene.

By the time he arrived, there was a crowd gathered in the seafood plant parking lot. He pulled right into the crowd which stepped aside only enough to let the vehicle in. He could see Thomas standing just by the door to the locker along with Archie. Morris didn't really know the proper order in which he should conduct the investigation, but he did know that the crowd was of no help. His presence seemed to calm them. They all knew and respected Morris. He was fair, honest, and treated everyone like a friend. He was tall and thin, with a thick head of white hair and an untended gray mustache. He moved slowly and deliberately as if walking required special thought. There was a slight stoop in his lanky frame. It sometimes seemed like he might be a little self-conscious of his height. His uniform was always pressed, shoes polished and he kept an air of authority about him. No one ever questioned his decisions or actions in his capacity as Sheriff. He wouldn't do or say anything that he didn't think was correct. He followed several good ole' boy Sheriffs who had held the job before him. They used the position to strengthen their status and incomes as well as that of their cronies. Morris ran for the office on a promise of putting an end to such abuses. He had done exactly as he said he would for three terms. There was no doubt; the appreciative townspeople would keep him in office as long as he chose to run. With a tone of deep concern and seriousness, he spoke to the group.

"Unless you know the victim, or have some information that's relevant here, please leave the area. There are other investigators on the way and we're going to need this space left open. Please go about your business. As soon as I know something, I'll let you all know what happened."

They walked off slowly in small groups, discussing the situation among themselves.

"Alright, Thomas, where's the victim?"

"Just inside the door Sheriff and it's the worst thing I've ever seen. If you don't need me, I'll just wait outside here."

"That's fine, Thomas. Keep spectators out of the parking lot. Don't let any vehicles move and for God's sake, don't you or anyone else touch anything until the SBI gets through here."

"The SBI! Shit! You're kidding. Right?"

"No, I'm not. Who else here knows what the hell to look for? Not me or you."

"I guess you're right. Damn! The SBI!"

Morris slowly entered the locker. It was dark, with just a single light bulb hanging from an extension cord to light the room. He pulled a flashlight from his belt and shined it on the body lying by itself in the center of the floor. She was totally naked, already covered with a thin, white layer of frost. Her face was frozen in a contorted look of absolute terror. Her body was smeared with blood, but not enough to conceal the grotesque pattern to her wounds. The scene was so disconcerting that Morris could barely force himself to look, though he knew he must. As the flashlight illuminated her face, Morris realized the worst. It was a local girl he'd known all her life.

"Oh, damn. Damn it all. Bev Schroder. Who in God's name could do something like this to such a beautiful young girl?"

The word "fear" had been engraved on her skin with what must have been a knife or scalpel. There were many other, open, gaping wounds that also appeared to have been made with a knife. Her eyes were covered over with a thin film of frost as were the dark smears of blood over most of her body. It seemed as if the killer had stabbed her where he knew she would bleed profusely, careful not to strike a major organ and cause a more rapid death.

Morris thought to himself, "God, I hope she was already dead when this was done," though he doubted that was the case. Other than the body, obviously left there to be found quickly, the seafood locker was undisturbed. There was no sign of a struggle or blood anywhere except on her body. This indicated to Morris that she had been tortured and killed elsewhere and brought to the locker so that she would be found fresh. He thought to himself, "What kind of sick pervert was loose in his town? This didn't look like the work of a jealous husband or jilted boyfriend, and robbery had to be the last thing whoever did this was thinking about. How would he find the killer before this happened to someone else?"

"Archie, leave everything just like it is. Lock the door and stay in your office until I come back with the SBI, okay?"

"Yes, sir, you can count on it."

Morris exited and told Thomas as he went back to his car, "Stay here with Archie, and tape off the entire area. I'll send down a couple of guys from the fire department to help keep people away. I'll be back shortly. I'm already dreading it but I'm going to have to go tell her mother what has happened. I'm almost sick thinking about having to do it." Morris quickly proceeded back to his office to make sure the proper calls had been made.

By the time Sarah entered Sam's for breakfast, everyone in the grill was spreading the story of the gruesome murder. Already, fiction and fact were so entwined, that the actual details would be impossible to glean until the paper came out. One thing was certain, however, a woman had been killed and in a very bad fashion. This was the first Sarah heard about it and as she listened, a chill went completely through her. Flashbacks of her own night of horror played vividly in her mind. Very few could ever guess the personal turmoil she carried inside. After high school, she had gone to college at a university near Raleigh. She'd take long walks through the city, sometimes at night and almost always alone. On one such occasion, by herself and out way too late, she was brutally attacked and raped. Emotionally devastated, she returned to the security of her home, but there were scars buried deep that made it hard for her to respond to any man that might have an interest in her. The few who knew of this incident feared she would live out her life as a spinster.

As she went to find a booth to sit in, a man's voice called out to her.

"Over here Sarah. Join us will you?"

She turned and saw Alan and another man from the crew of *Wind Trader*. They were already eating but the scene she had just heard about was quickly killing her appetite.

"I really need to get on to work, I'm not sure I feel like breakfast anymore."

"That was really horrible" Stephen said. Alan added, "Just a cup of coffee or tea and then we'll walk back to the shop with you."

The offer of company back to the shop sounded good to her, so against her natural instinct, she sat down with them.

"Just coffee, please. I don't want anything to eat this morning," she said to Jean who had come over to take her order.

"I know, Sarah. That was horrible about that young woman. I hope when they catch who did it, we can all go watch them hang him."

Jean chewed gum as she took a small towel and wiped the table and seat for Sarah. With her hair up in a fifties' French twist, and her pencil sticking out of it, she was quite a flashback for Alan and Stephen. Even though there was a lot of gray showing in her hair and more than a few wrinkles had taken over her face, it was easy to see that most of them had gotten their contours from adjusting to the directions of her smile and laughing eyes. That touch of devilishness could still be seen right under their bright blue exterior.

"Him?" said Alan. "That's a little unliberated don't you think?" He was trying to lighten the moment for Sarah.

Jean replied, "No woman ever did that to another woman. I guarantee you it will turn out to be some creep that she wouldn't go out with. You wait and see. I know one thing for sure; no woman in her right mind needs to be out walking these streets alone after dark."

She brought back a cup of coffee to Sarah. She quickly lowered her head and took a sip. Alan changed the subject as he could see she was really upset.

"Sarah, this is Stephen Woods, he came in on *Wind Trader* with me. He's one of the world's truly great harmonica players and a good friend. You are having the privilege of seeing him clean shaven. On shipboard, we called him Blackbeard." He reached out and touched Stephen's freshly shaved face.

"Pay him no mind, Sarah. He's just jealous of how distinguished I looked with a beard. It's a pleasure to meet you. Are you from here or are you a transplant like everyone else we've met?"

"I was born right here. Except for a year while I was away at college, I've lived just down the street. If you go check the news-clippings on the wall over there, you'll find a picture of my high-school graduation class."

She pointed to a collection of articles on the wall of the grill.

"That's really great. In Boston or New York, all you would find on the wall of a restaurant would be a poster reminding everyone to have safe sex. I think this is a lot classier. When we get back to Armani's, we need to suggest this to him, Alan. What do you say?"

"I don't know. Back home, the safe sex warnings are probably more applicable to their customers." Alan continued. "Do you sell painting supplies in your shop? I didn't notice them while I was in there."

Sarah, still distracted, took a moment to answer.

"I'm sorry. Yes, we have a few. Some of the children I know like to paint. I always order a few colors and paper for them. Do you paint?"

A smile came over his face. He began to gesture with his hands and enthusiasm radiated as he responded to the question. "My first love. Just ahead of the ocean. A lot of times I combine them by painting the sea or boats. As a matter of fact, after spending the morning looking over the town, I see a lot here that would make great subjects. I don't think I'm going to continue with *Wind Trader*. It's beautiful here and it looks like there's enough tourists that I could sell my paintings to. I think I'll stay awhile, at least until the fall."

This was the first mention Alan made that he would be staying and it took Stephen by surprise. "Well, if you don't go, I think I might stay too. After all, if I fall overboard, I want to make sure you're close by. Sarah, did you know he dove into the ocean at night in the middle of a horrible storm and saved our boss, Irving?"

Embarrassed, Alan interrupted, "Cut it out, Steve. She doesn't want to hear that."

Sarah smiled at Alan, "A hero, huh? They're always supposed to be modest. You never hear them telling their own stories, unless they're retired soldiers. They're all heroes."

"You got it," Stephen agreed.

Sarah looked at the clock on the wall. It was ten minutes 'til eight. She stood and started to reach in her purse for change to pay for her coffee.

"I've got to get going" she said.

"Let me pay," Alan said and he and Stephen quickly rose to walk Sarah to work.

Jean met them at the cash register to take their money. They were surprised when she reached under the cash register and grabbed a small handheld calculator. She studied the keys as she carefully pecked in their order.

"That'll be two fifty-six."

Stephen could not contain his curiosity. "How come you don't add it up on the register? Is it broken?"

The office I work in carries this brand of computer and they come repair them the hour we call. I bet they would come right over."

"Can't do that. This one is almost brand new and works fine. It's just a Tuesday."

"What does that matter?"

"Tuesday and Thursday are what Sam calls free trade days. Nothing in, nothing out. Get my drift?"

Alan looked at Stephen like he couldn't believe he didn't get it. "Taxes, Stephen, taxes."

"Oh, I get it now. Jeez, that's a little risky, isn't it, Jean?"

"Not when the district tax officer is your first cousin and borrows your boat every weekend." She put her finger in front of her lips.

"That's confidential. Right, Sarah?"

"That's right, Jean. Only me, you and everyone in town knows what's going on. Probably in every store in town. Let the state make it on what the rich cities pay."

"Amen."

They left Sam's Grill and started walking down the street. There was a light breeze blowing in from the ocean. The pale blue sky was so clear, that without an occasional cloud to compare it to, it would look white. Seagulls played alongside the docks as they passed. They made no attempt to get out of the way. It appeared as if they expected bread crumbs to be thrown their way. A pelican sat on the tallest piling in sight. His movements were so slow that unless one studied him carefully, he could easily be mistaken for a wooden statue, much like the smaller versions Sarah sold in the Water Dragon.

As they approached the gift shop, Alan spoke to her. "I'm going to tell Irving that today's my last day. *Wind Trader* is almost ready to sail again and I'm about 'sailed out' of the cruising frame of mind I was in. I'm going to leave work a little early today so you can help me get my paint supplies together. All right?"

It was plain to Sarah that Alan wanted to get to know her better. She did and didn't want any male involvement just now, but she did find him pleasant company. She was particularly interested to see why he thought he could paint well enough to sell them. And of course, there were those hazel eyes to consider.

"Come by after five. It's pretty quiet then and I can take time to help you. Whatever you want that's not in the store, I can get overnight with express service. So, see you then." She proceeded to unlock the door to her shop and Alan and Stephen continued on to the deck of *Wind Trader* where Irving and Sherrie were already working on preparations to resume their cruise. Irving welcomed them onboard.

"She'll be as good as new, fellas, and rigged even stronger this time. With the repairs we've made and you guys and Jason on board, we're ready for anything, right?"

Alan realized this was the moment.

"She's ready all right, Irving, but I'm not. I'm not going on with you. I really like the looks of Beaufort and I think I'm going to spend the rest of the summer here."

The disappointment showed on Irving's and Sherrie's faces.

Fearing this might have been related to their last night at sea, Irving added, "I promise I'll keep a closer watch on the weather from here on out. Hell, we can even take the inside route down the Intracoastal Waterway if you want. I hate to lose you after all that has happened. This could be a great trip."

"I'm sure it will," Alan responded, "But I have other reasons to stay here that have nothing to do with the storm. I know you're a good captain. That's not a concern at all. If I were going to sea again, you would be my first choice to go with. Really."

Alan looked out across the creek and saw several sleek sailboats heading out to the inlet. He knew he would miss being on the cruise, but he had made his choice.

"Well, let's at least have a farewell party tomorrow night so that we can toast one another's future without having to get up at sunrise the next morning. Deal?"

"You got it," Alan replied.

Stephen, hating to hurt Irving's feelings, realized that he must tell him now also, he would be staying in Beaufort with Alan.

"Irving, I'll need a goodbye drink with you tomorrow night too."

"Not you too, Stephen."

"I'm sorry Irving, but when it comes to being a good sailor, I'm a good harmonica player. I'm just not ready to face Mother Nature again this soon. She made a believer out of me."

"Well, this has been a hell of a morning so far, hasn't it, babe?" He turned to Sherrie who had been listening to all this.

"I'm still going with you, sweetheart, even if it's just you, me and *Wind Trader*. You're my captain." She gave Irving a reassuring hug, an exaggerated kiss, putting a lot into it for the benefit of Alan and Stephen. As usual, it was more than the average wife would lay on her husband out on the public docks in front of friends. Irving, proud of her affection for him, slid his rough, diamond clad hands slowly down her back, exploring every inch as they traveled south. Their journey ended with each palm firmly pressed against one tight bun. A quick squeeze of her cheeks, they concluded their extended kiss and Irving turned to the mutinous crew.

"Well, let's finish up early today. There's not that much left to do." They all proceeded to go about the few remaining tasks.

The last customers left the Water Dragon and Sarah looked at the old banjo wall clock. "Six o'clock," she thought to herself. She didn't want to work late anymore, at least until the previous night's murder had been solved and the killer arrested. There was also her grandmother at home by herself to consider. Though Myrtle didn't get out much, she watched the television and read the papers regularly. That meant anything Jean didn't hear at Sam's Grill and pass on to her, she would find out in the news later that day. Sarah thought to herself, "Grandmother is pretty much on top of things and spry for all her years." She hoped she would be so fortunate. As Sarah started to leave through the back door, she was startled as a hand touched her shoulder from behind. She turned to see that it was Alan.

"I'm sorry. Did I startle you? I'm sorry I'm late. We can look at art supplies tomorrow, okay?"

"No, it's fine, come on inside and I'll show you what we have. Believe me; it won't take long to see what small amounts we carry." She cut the lights back on as they entered. She locked the door behind them so other customers wouldn't think they were still open for business. "Right over here is all we have. They're mostly basic colors and the brushes are fairly cheap. Very few real artists come in."

"Well," Alan replied. "Reserve the word real for a while until you see my work. I just like to paint. I don't kid myself that my work is all that good." He looked at the few supplies. "There's enough here to get me started. I have a few colors with me. It's enough to please the average tourist, I hope. I guess we'll find out tomorrow. Speaking of tomorrow, Irving and Sherrie are throwing a little goodbye party on *Wind Trader* and I wish you'd come with me. It's going to be just a small group and probably won't last 'til very late. When you close up, just walk over to the slip and come on board. I'll walk you home when you're ready to leave."

Sarah thought for a moment. He was an interesting man, but did she really want to get involved with a stranger she knew so little about? "I don't know," she said. "I'd have to get someone to watch out for my grandmother if I was going to get home late. I'll think about it tonight and let you know tomorrow. Is that all right?"

"Well, it's certainly better than no. I'll be painting on the boardwalk during the day, so just look for me when you take a break. And thanks a lot for opening back up. What do I owe you?"

"I'll figure it up in the morning and tell you when I see you. I've got to get on home now. Goodnight. See you tomorrow."

"Goodnight," Alan responded. They turned in opposite directions, Sarah toward home and Alan moved slowly down the wharf toward *Wind Trader*.

* * *

He watched her leave, her long hair swinging with her natural motion as she walked down the street. There was still a lot of day left. She was a beautiful creature he thought. *"She's nervous. You can see it in the way she walks. It's amazing how just one example can get them all thinking again. Fear is such a powerful force."*

She continued down the street as far as the boardwalk followed the shore. From there she crossed the street and walked the narrow sidewalk down the remaining block to her house. This would be a difficult woman to work with he thought. *"If she were walking to a car, she would have to pause when she got to it and get her keys out. Then she would be in a car all alone. At a home, if she made it that far, a simple knock or cry could sound an alarm. But, then again, a challenge can often be exciting. Nothing worth doing is ever easy."*

5

Morris walked up the worn sidewalk to the front door. He knew he had to steel himself to deliver the kind of news that no parent is ever ready to hear. The door opened slowly and Molly Schroder smiled at him.

"Why, Morris. What are you doing here this morning? I haven't seen you in forever. To what do I owe the pleasure?"

"Can I come in, Molly?"

"Certainly. Why such a glum face?"

"I don't know how to tell you this, Molly, but Bev has been killed. I'm so sorry to have to be the one to bring you this news."

The old woman put her hands to her face and without a word the tears began to pour without measure. After almost a full minute of gasping she gathered herself just enough to ask, "How, what happened? Was it a wreck? I told her to drive slower. I thought she was over at Mary's last night. She said she might go stay over with her. Oh my God, Morris. What happened?"

"This is going to be hard, Molly. Let's sit down and talk."

They both sat on the couch and Morris told her as much detail as he felt was warranted at the time. There would have to be more questions later as the investigation moved forward but now was not that time.

"Morris, can I see her?"

"Are you sure you want to? You might not want to remember her this way. She's gone. It might hurt more than help you."

"I have to. I have to see my baby one more time. I have to say goodbye to her. And Morris…"

"Yes?"

"You know there's no man around here since her dad died. I hate to ask this but can you help me with her funeral? I don't have hardly any money but I'll get what I need from my brother, I guess. But I don't have the strength to put no funeral together. Would you help me with it some?"

Morris went over to her and hugged the broken woman and assured her that whatever help she needed would be there. When he left her, still crying on her front porch, he felt as weak and depressed as he was capable of being. He'd have Esther alert some of the other women in town to go stay with her. He also had a strong resolve building to find and punish Bev's killer like no other criminal he'd ever gone after. He wouldn't rest 'til he was brought to justice.

* * *

The morning passed quickly. Sarah locked up the Water Dragon and put a sign on the front door reading "At Lunch, Back at Two." She went into the bathroom and looked at herself in the mirror. She got a brush out of her worn hand bag and proceeded to brush her hair. She realized she never worried about how her hair looked before walking along the windswept boardwalk. Embarrassing herself, she smiled and put the brush back in her bag.

"Damn, get a grip," she said to herself.

"He's just another guy", but she knew that was not how she felt at the moment.

She exited to the boardwalk and briskly proceeded to look for Alan. The docks were full of sailors and tourists looking over the many yachts tied up at the town docks. She had decided to stay a short while at the party. It had been several years, ever since she had returned home from Raleigh, that she'd been to a party or out anywhere socially with a man. Not that any other man ever hurt her before or after the attack, but trusting was hard for her now. Jean agreed to stay with Myrtle for a couple of hours until Sarah got back. She had to admit she was excited about the prospect of the evening and yes, being with Alan. She was anxious to see his paintings and continued to walk down the boardwalk looking for him. Near the north end of town, just outside the Seaview Cafe, she spotted him seated in front of an easel with his back to her. She approached quietly, wanting to watch him work for a while before making her presence known. He was sketching the crowd seated on the waterfront under the cafe's awning. It was pretty well roughed in and obvious he had done this before. His strokes were sure and each added something new to the canvas. For fifteen minutes she sat a few yards behind him watching him work. A waitress from the cafe approached him. "Want something to drink?" she asked.

"If you don't mind, I would love a glass of ice water, and see if the lady behind me would like something too."

Sarah laughed at this revelation. "How long have you known I was here?" she asked.

"Look in the front window of the cafe."

Sarah immediately noticed her reflection as well as that of the whole channel full of boats behind her. She had been so intent watching him paint she had not yet turned in that direction.

"I hope you don't think I'm really that stupid."

"Nope, I knew you weren't looking because I was looking at your reflection the whole time. I love watching people when they don't realize I'm studying them. That way, I can capture them better in my paintings. What do you think of this one?"

She walked over close behind him and studied what he had been working on. It had a definite style and presence. The people seated in the cafe seemed to be alive. Even their personalities were evident. "You're very talented," she said. "I had no idea you would be this good. I'm impressed."

"That's just what I was hoping you'd say. Now, you're not going to hurt a sensitive artist's feelings by telling him you're not going to the party with him, are you?"

"I guess, since you put it that way, I would be offending the whole art community if I didn't go for at least a short while."

"Alright, that's great! Want to walk down the dock a while?"

"Okay, but not too long. I'm just on lunch break."

They started to walk down the boardwalk saying very little, just looking at the boats and all the people on and around them. The sun was heating up full blast. Carolina in August is a hot, humid location. The boardwalk was thinning quickly as everyone found an awning or air-conditioned shop they needed to be under during this part of the day. There was an old, gray hound dog, curled up under one of the stone park benches alongside the dock. He was breathing heavy and making no unnecessary movements that might get him out of the shade.

"Hey, Bosley," Sarah directed to the old hound.

He knew her well and during a more cool moment, would have fawned all over her for just a few gentle strokes from her soft hands. Today, all she would get was the slightest wag from his long slender tail.

"I don't blame him. It's an oven outside today."

As they continued toward the gift shop, Sarah eased into a conversation that covered some sensitive ground.

"Do you think I'm a little stand-offish? You know, a little cold? Some people say that about me. I try not to be that way, but I'm shy around people I don't know all that well. I like people; don't get me wrong. It's just that sometimes I kind of 'freeze up' even if I want to get to know the person."

Alan realized this was a sincere question and she wanted to know how he saw her. "Well, I've never been the life of the party myself. Sometimes it's better to let people open up to you first. That way you can tell who's really interested in getting to know you. I'm a firm believer that still water runs deeper. That's true you know. Even in the ocean, in a storm you should always head for deep water. Shallow water means breakers and shoals, trouble for sailors. I can see you're a warm person by just looking at your eyes."

"You're putting me on."

"I never put people on, and I hope they won't do it to me either. I like people who are up front. I'm a simple guy and I try to live my life that way. Most people are so wrapped up in finding some ill-conceived measure of success that they overlook all the best things around them."

"So, you're a philosopher?"

"Not really, I just have certain subjects that I dwell on from time to time."

Before long, they wound up back at the Water Dragon's rear entrance.

"I guess I better open back up. This is the longest lunch I've ever taken. Thanks for walking back with me."

Alan smiled and reminded her. "Don't forget the party tonight. Just come on over to *Wind Trader* when you close up. I'll see you there. Bye."

He turned and walked away. After Sarah unlocked the door and hit the lights, she stuck her head back out the door and took a quick look at Alan walking away. She was very attracted to him and didn't deny it to herself. He was the first in quite a few years that she had let herself try to get to know.

Sarah then turned to the business at hand, waiting on customers and minding the shop. All through the day she watched the activity aboard *Wind Trader* just outside her back window. They were going to a lot of trouble to decorate for the evening's affair.

Sheriff Stone entered the police station in a very hurried and businesslike fashion, both of which were as unlike his usual manner as they were for the entire town. Esther left her customary post by the phones and came to meet him. "He's here," she whispered to Morris. "He sure doesn't look like a big wheel from the SBI to me."

Slightly more lighthearted, Morris responded to her observation about the visitor. "There you go, Esther, judging someone by their appearance. Let's hope he isn't doing the same with you and me."

Esther turned and walked back to the desk. Her muffled "humph" didn't elude Morris. He proceeded to his office where the borrowed expert from the SBI was waiting to discuss the murder with him.

Esther had already helped the visitor to a cup of coffee. He was short and stocky but dressed just as the other visitors from upstate that had come to see Morris before. He had on a white starched shirt, a bright paisley tie, and plaid suspenders holding up expensive slacks. Morris assumed that apparently, the new style must be to wear slacks that went down over the shoes and pushed themselves into several prominent folds of material. He couldn't stand to think of wearing his own pants that way. His always had a sharp, well starched crease that stopped before his black brogans could even think about breaking the line. Of course they were held in place by his oversize western belt with its polished silver buckle. Style, if that's what they called it, could go to hell. Morris took great pride in maintaining the status quo in his appearance.

"Good morning, Sheriff Stone?"

Hand extended, Morris warmly greeted him. It was a relief to have someone help him deal with this murder. His normal investigations usually concerned such things as the theft of someone's fishing tackle or a runaway.

"Just call me Morris. I'm certainly glad you're here. This is new territory for me and I can use all the help you can give. Has anyone told you anything?"

"Esther gave me the file and photos. I've been looking at them for a few minutes. Pretty gruesome stuff. I've seen a lot of these over the years and I'm still not used to it. I guess that's probably good though. If it didn't bother you, you probably need to get out of this line of work. By the way, I'm Don Ellingwood, supposedly the state's forensic expert, to blow my own horn."

"Nice to meet you, Don. See anything in the file that jumps out at you?"

"One thing is pretty obvious."

"What's that?"

"This is not a one-time event for the killer. He's thinking about the victims, how to kill them, where to dump the bodies and sickest of all, how this will appear to the public."

"You mean like a serial killer?" Morris was startled by this revelation he hadn't previously considered. That was definitely not what he wanted to hear. "You think there will be more of these here?"

"There will definitely be more, at least until he's caught. This could be the last one here or maybe not. But for certain, he won't stop on his own."

"You keep saying 'him.' How do you know it's a man?"

"Well, there were not enough bruises on the victim to indicate that she had been able to fight back at all. She was overpowered. Also, if she was on her way to her car when she was attacked, as her boyfriend stated, then she was carried over two blocks through the alleys to the fish house. The weapon that was used was most likely a filet knife from the shape of the wounds. This means we should consider fishermen, sportsmen, anyone who would use a knife like that. I guess you probably know all the locals here. Are there any zombies you can think of we should talk to about this?"

The Sheriff walked over to his desk, laid his cowboy hat on its cluttered surface and sat down. His chair was a gray metal swivel type with a black, padded seat and head rest. The padded parts had black electrical tape used for patches in several spots and the padding was so thin, it offered almost no more comfort than the metal itself would have. However, he was used to it and leaned back, placing his hands behind his head and stretching out his long legs 'til his boots rested on his desk. Morris studied Ellingwood's question for a moment and then replied. "I've been thinking about that for two days now and I really can't think of anybody I'd suspect at all. We've got a few drunks and roughnecks that get into trouble pretty often, but I've known most of them all their lives and this is just worse than I think any of them would ever do. There's a lot of tourists and visitors here this time of year, probably double the locals. They're only here a few days and then leave. If our boy is one of them, he's probably long gone."

Ellingwood moved continuously around Morris' tiny office while he talked. He picked up personal photographs and memorabilia as well as papers lying in the basket on his desk. He studied these items, turning them over in his hand, setting them back down and moving on to the next. After he surveyed the desk, he moved to the walls where he examined everything from the autographed picture of the governor to the wanted posters papering every blank space. None of this seemed to bother his train of thought at all. He had a profound curiosity; surely a prerequisite for his job. He continued his thoughts on the murder as if he were staring Morris in the face while he spoke.

"No, I don't think he's gone yet. You don't carve a message into somebody's chest unless you want to create an impression on the people here. He'll stay and watch what happens. That's his turn on. He's not killing for a turn-on. His motive is more likely the scare he puts on everybody. That's a form of control."

Don moved across the room and sat on the edge of Morris' desk. He picked up the prism paperweight, held it into a beam of sunshine coming in through the window and rotated it over and over. He examined every possible color combination he could make it generate while he spoke. He was young and bright. His slow, studied voice sounded rather casual, but his piercing eyes and rapid thoughts betrayed the hot fire that burned inside. Thirty-two years old and he already had a strongly receding hairline. The furrow on his brow showed the machinery inside was working overtime. This was his element. He was on his own "high" when in pursuit of a deviant criminal.

"I think it would be a good idea to check all the motels, restaurants, marinas and any other places someone might visit who is not a local. Try and get guest lists and names before they're discarded. Maybe we can establish who was here during the time frame. Also, you better beef up patrols in the evening and put out the word to not go out alone after dark until this is over. Where's a good place to stay while I'm here?"

Morris arose slowly. He walked over to Ellingwood, put his arm around Don's shoulder and moved him toward the door. Standing beside one another, the difference in their height became very apparent as Morris towered over him.

"Come on, I'll take you on a quick tour of the town. It won't take a half hour. You can get a feel for the town and we can get a bite to eat. Then, I'll get Agnes to put you up over at her bed and breakfast. It's real homey and she'll put ten pounds on you while you're here. Best cook I ever knew. If she weren't seventy years old, I'd marry her. Let's get going." They left together to examine the town.

6

Bev Schroder's funeral brought out everyone in the town. It was a tight-knit community and Morris was proud that at times like this, everyone pitched in wherever needed. A group of women stayed close to Molly throughout the service. It was a hard two hours to sit through. It was one thing to have a family member die but a totally different matter when they had been violently removed from their existence. Until whoever committed this heinous act was apprehended, there would be a palpable cloud of dread hanging over the town. Morris and his deputies had visited every beauty salon, store and restaurant in the area asking questions about any new faces or strangers in town. He told them to keep an eye out for anything unusual and reminded them to not go out alone after dark. Until the case was solved, no one could even feel safe in their own homes.

Sarah waited on the last of her customers. She locked the door so no one else could come in before they left. She felt a rush of excitement she hadn't experienced since prom night. "This is so silly" she thought. She surprised herself with her own giddiness as she told the customers goodnight and locked the door behind them. Quickly, she cleared the cash register, put the day's cash in a bank bag and locked it in a drawer under the counter. This would never work in a metropolitan area, but in Beaufort it was a common practice. She cut off the lights, her opera of the hour on the radio, and locked the back door behind her as she left. Ten steps across the dock was a brightly decorated *Wind Trader*. The day's labor by Irving, Sherrie, and the crew had turned the old ship into a floating gazebo with streamers and balloons strung from her rigging. There were hundreds of Christmas tree lights to be turned on after dark. Already, vibrant Jimmy Buffet tunes were blaring from the deck-mounted speakers. Passersby were smiling and congratulating them on their efforts. For the past hour, Alan had been sitting on the roof of the main cabin, blowing up balloons and surveying strings of lights to see why they weren't coming on. Invariably, it was a single bad bulb causing the entire strand to remain dark. He'd take a new bulb, exchange it with each one in the light strand until he found the culprit. Once replaced, he'd hand the rejuvenated lights to Stephen who was stringing them around the ship. Once they tested positive, they'd be shut off so they could all be cut on at the appropriate moment later that night. As he worked, Alan kept glancing at the lights in the Water Dragon, waiting for the store to be shut down. He was strongly attracted to this quiet, unaffected young woman. He wondered what it was about her that drew him to her. She was considerably younger than him. Their backgrounds touched nowhere. She was unworldly and not nearly so well educated. She was attractive, but there had been many women he'd known before her who were equally so. What was it then?

Perhaps the answer lay in the questions, he thought. The fact was, he needed to understand these things. Maybe it was just chemistry. Perhaps he was only a part of something he had very little say in.

Alan saw Sarah and rushed to welcome her aboard. He extended a hand which she grasped as she took a long step from the dock to the deck. *Wind Trader* was finally shipshape. Her decks and rigging were organized and new varnish on the bright work glistened everywhere. Sarah was duly impressed with the little ship. She'd probably seen thousands of beautiful yachts in the harbor but this was the first she had ever been aboard. Unless the locals were working on them, they were seldom invited to visit the vessels in port. Looking around, it was apparent this massive conglomeration of wood, brass and canvas was an independent island of its own. It floated and moved under its own power. It required nothing of anyone it left behind. Once at sea, it was a world to itself, furnishing everything its citizens needed until they arrived at another parcel of land. It was more carefully laid out and organized than anything on shore she thought. There was no need for cars, lawnmowers or even roads. Life onboard was back to a very basic Spartan existence. Alan moved quickly to introduce her to everyone. Sherrie and Irving came to greet her with Stephen and Jason close behind.

"Everyone, this is Sarah." You already know Steve. This is Sherrie, Irving and Jason."

Sherrie gave her a quick warm hug and Sarah was relieved that everyone was so friendly. You didn't have to get to know any of these people to like them, she thought. Alan put his arm around her waist for the first time.

"Let me show you around our proud old schooner. These boats are still more beautiful than anything built today. Fiberglass will never have the feel, the look or warmth of teak and mahogany. They are some of the most spectacular works of art that man has ever made."

These were expressions from the heart, Sarah realized. They weren't said just for her benefit. Alan really loved this sailboat. She followed him and delighted in his enthusiasm. Irving brought them both a glass of wine and they all settled in for a pleasant evening. Sherrie came over to Sarah.

"Alan tells me you're a local. I love your town. It's nice to live in a place small enough to know everyone. I was raised in the country too; Freemont, Ohio. I miss it sometimes, but I want to see the rest of the world before I even think of going back home. It's nice to know everyone though, don't you think?"

"It can be. There's a good and a bad side. Everyone knows everyone, but they also know everything about everybody. This would be a hard place to mind your own business, if you know what I mean. Not that there's all that much happening. At least 'til recently."

"Oh, I heard about the murder. How horrible. I hate it for the town. In large cities, someone is killed every day it seems, but you just don't expect it here. Well, let's don't even think about it tonight. We're going back to sea in a couple of days and I want to have fun tonight so I won't think about things like *storms.*" She looked at Irving.

"We can't possibly hit another one that bad in the same trip, babe. We're disaster-proofed for the rest of the voyage."

"I hope you're right. My heart couldn't stand another night like that. Sarah, did Alan tell you about how he jumped overboard in the middle of the storm to save my man here?"

"Stephen tried to, but Alan said it was nothing and didn't let him finish. Tell me what happened."

As Sherrie related the story to her, several visitors walked up the dock and stopped alongside *Wind Trader.* It was Zed. He was accompanied by a couple of roughnecks from the shrimp boat he worked on.

"Ahoy there. Request permission to board and join the party. Don't worry; we've got our drinks with us. You can keep yours.

We just want to be friendly, kinda like Sarah there is doing. All us locals is friendly."

He grabbed a line and started to climb aboard. He was apparently drunk and no one wanted him or his friends to crash the party. Jason stepped forward.

"Friend, this is a private party. I'm sorry, but we don't really have room on board for more quests. Too many people and someone could trip and get hurt. You know what I mean, don't you?"

"I know exactly what you mean, 'friend.' You people don't want anybody that has to work for a living on your damn boat, right?"

He stepped one foot onto the deck. Jason stepped in front of him keeping him from boarding.

Jason reaffirmed, "It's private, I said."

Zed was obviously not used to having his demands challenged. "We'll damn well visit if we want to. I don't take no shit off nobody. You understand me, asshole?" The words were not even out of his mouth when Jason grabbed him by his collar and pushed him back toward the dock. Off balance, his forced step fell short and he plummeted into the water between the boat and the dock. He came up quickly, as every man from Beaufort could swim in any condition. His curses rained upon the entire waterfront. Irving stepped behind the wheel, hit the ignition switch and fired up the engine.

"Cast off," he yelled to the crew, a hint of laughter in his commands. Jason, looking at Zed as he cast off the dock lines over his head, threw biting comments to him as the boat backed out of her slip.

"Sorry we couldn't wait for you, friend. Tide waits for no man and all that, you know."

Furious, Zed responded, "Have a nice time with the local bitch. I'll be here when you get back. You'll wish you never saw this place. Sarah, don't let me get hold of you when you come back. I'll be waiting."

Alan, incensed by this attack on Sarah, shot back at him. "You touch her and it'll be the last thing you do. You don't know what trouble is until you bother her."

Sarah moved over beside Alan and tried to defuse him. "Don't worry about him. He won't even remember he was here tomorrow."

Stephen walked over to the rail beside Alan and Sarah. "You don't know what trouble is? Give me a break. I'm going to have to teach you some fighting words. You sound like Hop-Along Cassidy on a Saturday morning western. With a guy like Zed – my God what a name – you have to say something like, 'Back-off lizard breath, or I'll eat your liver for supper, raw.' How's that?"

"Very impressive, Steve. You talk like that at board meetings, do you?"

"No, they're never that formal or well mannered."

"Well, before my next bout, I'll get you to tutor me on the basics of redneck linguistics."

Wind Trader pulled out into the channel as the sun started to fade into the sea in a bright orange ball. Zed reached up to his friends on the dock for a hand. The hand up he got was not from his buddies. He stared into Sheriff Stone's somber face.

"A little late in the day for a swim, don't you think, Zed?"

As he reached the dock again, Zed, expecting a lecture, quieted down. He knew where the blame lay for his bath in Taylor Creek. "We was just playin' around, Sheriff Stone. No harm done."

"Do you know those folks you're playing around with, Zed?"

"They're from up North. The small one's got a shine on for Sarah. I think he's just takin' advantage of her not being 'all there' is what I think."

As Zed walked away, Sheriff Stone looked out at *Wind Trader* moving gracefully down the waterway. There were over a hundred yachts visiting the town at any one time, coming and going every day. How would he ever get a handle on all these different people to link someone to the killing?

Wind Trader moved effortlessly, weaving in and out of the anchored yachts. Since the sun was going down, Irving yelled out, "Time for the running lights, Jason."

As Jason moved to the electric panel beside the companionway, he replied as salty as possible, "Aye, aye, Sir." He hit the switch.

Much to everyone's delight, not only did the red and green running lights come on, but also the hundreds of white Christmas lights. They were strung up and down the rigging to the tops of both masts and the length of the boat, down both rails. Applause could be heard from shore as the tourists on the dock and at the taverns enjoyed the beautiful addition to their evening. From shore, she looked like a giant Christmas tree, sliding slowly down the channel. As the ship continued moving, Sherrie turned up the stereo so that a soft ballad filled the entire moment. Sarah was touched by the beauty of the scene in front of her.

"I've seen lots of boats do this, but I never knew what it felt like to be out here. The town looks so beautiful from the water at night."

The waterfront was brightly lit. There were people all over the docks and laid back on the decks of the yachts tied up to them. There were bands playing in several clubs along the wharf. As they moved down the waterfront, one band would fade into the other as they approached. There were people in suits and dresses and others in bathing suits and tank tops. Every night was a block party and everyone was welcome. The reflection of lights from the town flickered across the ripples on the creek and raced out to join those from *Wind Trader*, which met them in the center of the channel.

Alan moved beside her and looked into her eyes. "Sarah, it is beautiful, but I have to tell you, on my word as an artist, you are far more beautiful than anything else I see right now." Sarah, embarrassed and at a lack of words for Alan's remarks, did not resist when he gently kissed her and put his arms around her. She warmed to him and then responded with all the pent up emotions she had been keeping locked up inside for so long. She could not believe that she had gotten involved so quickly, and yet it all felt right. *If ever a match were made in heaven, this was it*, she thought.

It was a magical trip down the waterway as they talked and touched for hours. The music, the lights, and the night all played their parts as if by command to add to the already beautiful evening. The hours passed all too quickly.

Wind Trader eased back into her slip as gently as she had left it. Each of the crew was performing their tasks expertly. They were all familiar with the lines and tasks necessary for docking. Everyone wished each other a good night. There was a final toast to the future, as they would all be going separate ways in a couple of days. It was a wonderful conclusion to an already wonderful party.

Sarah stepped ashore, knowing she had gone well beyond the two hours she had told Jean she would be gone. *"Well,"* she thought, *"I'll just have to make amends with her when I get home."* She told everyone goodnight, kissed Alan one last time, and started the short walk home.

* * *

He was close by and watched as she got off the boat. This was particularly exciting as she had been selected previously as a perfect candidate. These tasks were not quickly undertaken without forethought and planning. And now, ignoring all the warnings and even the recent example, she was walking home. This time, she was alone and in the dark.

She was preoccupied with how late she was going to be. It was for that reason her steps were quick. He didn't know the reason for her haste and could only assume that there was fear in her. All the better. Now, just follow close. Ease up behind her at the darkest spot just ahead. It would have to be a quick move to be effective, as she was just across the street from several homes with their lights still on as if the owners were awake. Ever so close now, one quick movement, grab her around the neck. Perhaps gagging would be required. He was prepared for whatever might be needed. He had dealt with almost every possible situation in the past. Nothing could get by him now. He started to move closer. She sensed a presence behind her. She felt the hand on her back and jumped with horror, the recent murder coming into her mind in an overpowering burst of realization that she should not be alone out here now. She turned to face the villain and stared into the eyes of Alan.

"Easy, it's just me. I remembered you were walking home and I thought you might feel a little better if I walked with you."

Sarah caught her breath. Relief could be read on her entire face. "You scared me. I had just been thinking about that poor girl the other night. I'm glad you came. I just live another block down the street."

They walked off together, Alan's arm around her shoulder. This was the most secure she had felt in years. She would not be afraid of anything if he was beside her.

He would wait. Patience and wisdom were all a part of a successful plan. Another night for her. He knew where she lived now and how she went home. But the night was still young, too young to not keep moving around. The task was too important to not keep working.

7

The morning sun was brighter than usual, thought Sarah. She had not slept this well for a long time. Even the lecture from Jean on responsibility, that she had expected, did not occur. She couldn't wait to get dressed and down to Sam's Grill.

"Goodness, Sarah, I don't believe I've ever seen you in this big a hurry to get to work. Where's the fire?"

"Good morning, Grandmother, I didn't know you were awake yet."

Myrtle, using her chrome-plated walker, slowly made her way into Sarah's room. "And lip gloss! Must be a devil of a sale at the store today."

"You can quit being cute Grandmother. I like the guy I went to the party with last night. A lot. He's different from anyone I've ever met. He's from New York, an artist, and very talented. I'm going to get him to help me with the children after school. You can take the opportunity to grill him."

"You know that's not my nature, dear. I just feel people out. If you ask a few of the right questions, the rest just seems to come out. People can't hide who they are, least not from me. Always could tell if somebody was a straight shooter. Sometimes your father, rest his soul, would sneak off from school. You know, play hooky with a couple of other fellas, and try to keep it from me.

Why I could see it in his eyes the minute he came through the door. He always thought somebody was ratting on him but it wasn't so. I can just tell about those things. You bring him by. I'll tell you what kind of man he is."

"Please Grandmother, don't scare him off the first time he comes over. Give him time to realize on his own that we're strange."

Sarah threw her bag over her shoulder and hurried to her grandmother. She gave her a kiss on the cheek and headed toward the kitchen. With black and white checkerboard linoleum on the floor, and an old white ceramic gas stove, it looked like an advertisement out of a 1940s magazine. Myrtle liked it as it was and would not consider the smallest change.

After taking care of her grandmother's needs for the day, Sarah made her way down the street toward the grill. Alan would be there to meet her for breakfast. The clouds were high in the sky. Seagulls danced in the air, celebrating the warmth and beauty of the day.

About a block from Sam's, she was passed by Sheriff Stone, roaring by in his patrol car. The siren was blaring and the blue lights were flashing. Not a common occurrence in Beaufort, the sight brought only one thought to mind. She hoped she was wrong.

The stainless steel grill was almost black. It suffered from success. Given the choice, clean it or cook on it, the choice for Sam was easy. Besides, any good short-order cook or housewife who ever used a cast iron skillet could tell you if you washed and scrubbed it clean, you'd ruin it. The buildup of baked on grease made it cook much more effectively.

On the dark hot surface, bacon and homemade sausages sizzled around the clock. A mixture of scrambled eggs and pancakes alternated on the other side of the grill. Just to watch Sam in action and his skill at turning out high cholesterol, high fat, high calorie delicacies, would quickly tell you why the place was called Sam's Grill.

From four a.m. 'til midnight, the smell of coffee and home cooking permeated a two block area around the grill. If you stayed in town more than a day, you'd try the food and before long, become addicted to the ritual that was eating at "Sam's."

Sam's was more crowded than usual and groups of customers were everywhere engaged in loud conversation. Alan was sitting with Stephen in a booth near the rear. He spotted Sarah and motioned for her to come over. Eventually she heard her name over the din of noise in the grill and went to the booth to join them.

"What's all the excitement about this morning?" Sarah asked.

Alan spoke, concerned but trying not to scare her. "There was another girl murdered last night, just like the other one. They found her in the hold of one of the shrimp boats this morning. I think it was the boat that moron Zed works on."

Sarah stunned, replied. "Oh my God, I can't believe this is happening here. Why would someone come to a place like this to kill people?"

"What makes you think they had to come here? Couldn't it be someone from here doing it?" Stephen asked.

"I just can't imagine that anyone here could do this. I know just about everyone in town and I can't see anyone I know doing it."

"One thing for certain, you shouldn't go out alone after dark. If you need to go anywhere, call me night or day. I mean it," Alan added as if he were her father speaking.

Stephen took a sip of coffee and stated, "I hear they took old Zed down to the police station for questioning. If nothing else, it makes me happy to know they are ruining his day."

They all laughed quietly as it would be out of place in the grill this morning.

Stephen was on a roll. "Let's hope they don't ask him any tricky questions like what state he lives in or how to spell Zed. Or, better still, where do baby shrimp come from?"

With that one, they all fought off choking on their coffee and smothered their laughter as best they could. A few tables of locals turned to see what the commotion was. They straightened up. Sarah turned to Alan. "I need a favor from you."

"You name it, I'll do it. Better yet, let's swap favors. *Wind Trader* leaves in the morning and I need a room. You help me and I'll do your bidding. Just don't get kinky on me."

"You won't be that lucky. I need you to visit with the kids this afternoon and show them how well you paint. Maybe you could give them a quick lesson. In return, I know where there's a quaint old loft that you would love. It's a little dirty, but we could clean it up."

Alan was enthusiastic. "You have a deal, sister. Where's this quaint little room?"

"Above the Water Dragon. Floyd stores some junk up there but it's mostly open space. A couch here, a chair there, a painting or two, and you're in business. Speaking of business, it's time to get to work. Don't forget our deal, five-thirty at my house. Don't be late."

"Yes, Ma'am. Here, Stephen and I are finished. We'll walk with you to work."

As they got up from their table, Zed entered. He looked a little flushed. He'd been answering questions for Sheriff Stone for two hours and was not in a good mood. Several of his cronies were sitting at a table near the door, their usual spot. One called to Zed as he entered.

"What happened, Zed? Are we going to be able to use the boat at all?"

"Probably not for the rest of this week. They want to check it for prints and the guy from the SBI said they'd be holding it, looking for leads, at least a couple of days. So, I guess we're supposed to forget about making a living 'til they're done with it."

"Shit! I got bills to pay, man. My old lady is gonna have a cow!"

Zed saw Sarah, Alan and Stephen leaving. "The problem is, they're just not looking in the right place. At least they weren't. I think I helped point them in the right direction." He looked toward Sarah and company. "Seems a few drifters come into town and people start dying."

They knew Zed was bad-mouthing them but they attempted to pass by him quietly. It didn't happen. As they opened the door and exited, Zed and two companions followed them outside to the sidewalk. The three shrimpers made Stephen and Alan look like children. They were all over two hundred pounds and, even though they supported healthy, beer bellies, there was no question that their years of toiling on shrimp boats made them as hard as steel. They were always looking for a good fight. Stephen and Alan wouldn't even make them break a sweat. They didn't like the newcomers, and they had already run through most of the locals. This would be a little morning exercise. Zed put a hand on Alan's shoulder and turned him around. Alan turned quietly to face him. He listened but there was no fear in his eyes. Zed tried to provoke him. "You know I'm talking about you, don't you, wise guy? You know what I think?"

"I think," Alan interrupted him. "Be careful, Zed. You shouldn't use the words 'I' and 'think' in the same sentence. Could cause a real credibility problem with people who know you."

Sarah and Stephen started to laugh under their breath. If he wanted a battle of words, Zed was poorly equipped to match skills with Alan. He realized this also. "I think you killed those girls is what I think, smart guy." He pushed Alan back trying to start a fight. "You might be real tough with little girls but you ain't nothin' but a wimp to me, pal. I think I should show Sarah what a weak..."

Alan interrupted him again. "I thought we covered that 'I think' stuff, Zed."

Zed drew back his fist to level Alan but dropped it quickly. They all turned to see Sheriff Stone pulling in the parking space directly behind them. Don Ellingwood was with him in the patrol car. They were coming to the grill for breakfast. Zed sensed he should leave but they all knew this would not end here. Zed gave a parting sneer. "You and I are going to have a "heart-to-heart" real soon."

Alan knew it killed Zed to not be shown respect so he said to him as he left, "Bye, Zed. Come have coffee again with us real soon. Always a pleasure to hear your attempts at thought."

Sheriff Stone and Ellingwood walked up beside Alan and his friends. "Morning folks. That Zed is a real character, isn't he? Had a long talk with him this morning. He sure doesn't speak too highly of you, Mr.... What's that name again?"

"Alan, Alan Kelly, and you must be Sheriff Stone, the town marshal."

"That's right, Alan. And this is Don Ellingwood from the State Bureau of Investigation. And your friend here?"

Stephen spoke up. "I'm Stephen Woods. Nice to meet you both. Please don't judge us by what that guy says. He doesn't seem to function quite right to me. I think it must be some sort of a genetic problem."

Sheriff Stone looked very carefully at the pair with Sarah. "Don't worry. I'd have to qualify 'most anything Zed would say. Maybe you all would like to come have a cup of coffee with us."

Sarah responded, "Some other time, Mr. Stone. I'm late to open the shop already and they're walking with me."

"That's a good idea, Sarah. You need to be real careful right now. There is obviously a very sick person in town."

He looked at Alan and Stephen. "How long have you fellas been here?"

Stephen answered. "About three weeks. How come?"

"Just curious. You haven't seen anyone you would consider unusual in the area, have you? We don't want to overlook any possibility."

"Well, no one any stranger than Zed."

"Okay fellas. Have a nice morning. Oh, and please don't get away from here without letting me know how to get up with you. I have to do background checks on everybody in town that I don't already know, especially people that have been here during these killings. Nothing serious, just a formality, right, Don?" Ellingwood nodded in approval.

They were a little shocked that Zed might have cast some doubt over them. Alan said to Stone, "Sure Mr. Stone, anytime you want. I'm going to be staying in the room over the Water Dragon."

"Have a nice morning," Sheriff Stone said as he and Ellingwood walked away toward the door of the grill.

Alan, Sarah and Stephen turned and continued their walk to the gift shop. Sarah tried to reassure them that Sheriff Stone was just doing his job. "He didn't mean anything by it, I'm sure. He's just nervous because things like this don't happen here and he's overly concerned about doing a good job."

Alan was not convinced. "That felt a lot stronger than just doing a good job to me. I guess he figures that since we're new here, we'd be prime suspects. He's probably right. I'd be suspicious of any strangers in the area too." He then added a little lightheartedly so as not to part on a bad note. "Especially when they look like Stephen here. I told you to get a haircut." He jokingly reached out and grabbed a handful of Stephen's shoulder length, brown hair.

"Ouch, don't pull it. Hey, I'm a sailor. All sailors have long hair and beards. Haven't you ever seen a picture of Blackbeard? I don't even have a beard. I'm actually a clean cut sailor now."

They all laughed. Sarah said to Alan as she walked into the shop, "I'll speak to Floyd today and get you a key to the loft. And don't you forget our deal, my house at five-thirty."

"I won't. I never go back on a promise. You can always count on anything I tell you."

Alan and Stephen walked away, back to the dock to visit with Irving, Sherrie and Jason. They were laying in supplies on *Wind Trader* to continue their journey. Stephen and Alan were more than a little disconcerted about the morning's events.

"You know what I'm thinking, Alan?"

"Let me guess. We should forget about staying here and leave with *Wind Trader*?"

"Wrong. I would never let an idiot like Zed influence anything I did."

"I was thinking a little more about being a murder suspect, Stephen. Not Zed."

"No sweat. You've got a great lawyer. No, buddy. I was thinking that you are falling pretty much head over the proverbial heels for this beautiful young lady named Sarah."

"Think so?"

"Aye, matey, I can tell by the cut of your jib and the bright light in your fo'castle. You're hooked."

"Maybe so. You might be right. She is beautiful though, isn't she?"

"That she is, laddie; that she is. Hey, I'm pretty good with the sailor jargon, aren't I?"

"That ye are, Cap'n; that ye are."

The breakfast crowd at Sam's was thinning down as Sheriff Stone and Don Ellingwood entered. Word of Ellingwood's arrival had already made it to the grill. As they crossed over the worn, heart pine floor, those remaining in the place took a good look at this big city detective. They could both feel the stares as they passed.

"I'm beginning to feel like a parade float, Morris."

"Just small town curiosity, Don."

"Well, I hope I didn't disappoint them. I kinda get the feeling they were hoping for someone a little more like Dirty Harry."

They went to a rear booth where they could talk privately over coffee. Sheriff Stone had come to admire the investigative prowess of his new associate and continued to quiz him, to learn as much as he could during the investigation.

"What do you think of those two? They've been here during both murders. They don't seem like the type, do they?"

Don took a big swallow of hot coffee that Jean brought over to him and replied, "If I've learned anything about these kinds of cases, it's got to be the fact that you can't rule out anybody. Hell, I had a case a few years back where two grade school kids disappeared on the way home from school. We started checking everyone that was remotely connected to the place. This went on for over a month without a break. We brought in anybody with a prior arrest for child molestation within a hundred mile area. I talked to more weirdoes than you'd even believe existed. Still, we couldn't tie anybody to it. Then, as luck would have it, there was a kitchen fire in an apartment of one of the teachers from the same school. Guess what? His apartment had enough child pornography in it to wallpaper this whole grill. Turns out the guy was a big time pedophile. I swear to you, he looked like one of Santa's Elves. You'd never guess.

"And the kids? Morris asked, already knowing the answer."

Ellingwood took a studied breath and replied, "Buried in his basement, and there were others alongside of them. I was stunned. I'd talked to this guy at the school. Hell, he led one of the search parties for two days. Listen. Suspect everybody and then rule them out slowly, not the reverse. And…"

"And what?"

"Pray for a little luck. Sometimes that's the only thing that works."

Morris, though not really suspecting him, asked Don, "What about Zed? He's certainly mean and definitely strong enough. He didn't seem to be lying. Even when he was small he was always in trouble, but I could always look at him and tell if he was guilty."

Don nodded in agreement. "As stupid as he is, he wouldn't be dumb enough to dump the body in the hold of his own boat. But, that does bring up an interesting point."

"Go ahead. What point?"

"Once again, we're talking about someone with strength, who knows how to use a knife, someone who knows that a shrimp boat has a hold and that it's usually filled with ice everyday. His work would be quickly found and in a fresh state. Not to mention that he might want to cast dispersions or anguish on Zed."

"You mean like those two guys with Sarah? Zed's been bothering them for a week now. My guess is he's got a thing for Sarah himself and he's upset that she's spending so much time with one of them."

After another sip of coffee and a drag on a Camel, Ellingwood added, "They certainly warrant watching, just like a lot of others here until we figure this out."

"I know one thing, if they keep on antagonizing Zed, he's eventually going to hurt one of them, maybe both."

"I'm not so sure, Morris. They seem pretty bright to me."

"Well they're breaking one of the rules to live by that my father passed on to me. One that has served me well."

"What rule is that?"

"Pick your enemies more carefully than you do your friends. You'll probably be seeing more of them."

"That is very thought-provoking, Morris. I'll have to remember it. I'll tell you the old words of wisdom that I live by."

"Okay, go ahead."

"Things are very seldom as they seem and almost never as simple as they appear. When I'm investigating a crime, that's the rule I live by. And let me tell you one more thing, we need to come up with some solid leads on these killings. And it better happen fast."

"Why is that, Don?"

"Well, whoever it is, knows a lot of people are trying to find him. My guess is he's done this somewhere else before coming here. The Raleigh office is checking out the national files to cross reference similarities to other killings like this. There's a national case information bank on computer. Every time anybody runs into anything like this, they add it to the file. It periodically cross references itself. It's connected quite a few of these pattern killings in the last couple of years. The killer probably knows about it too. If that's the case, when he feels we're close, he'll just pick up and leave. I know that would be good for Beaufort, but we don't want this to happen anywhere else either. We need to catch him here, hopefully before he kills again or leaves. Let's head over to your office and see if any word has come from the lab yet, if any fingerprints turned up."

They both finished their coffee and went to the register to pay. Sam came over to take their money. This was a task usually handled by Jean, but Sam wanted the opportunity to talk with Morris and Don. He wiped his greasy hands on the once-white apron that rode his pot belly. With his two-day beard and overall appearance, it was hard to face him after you had just eaten his personally prepared breakfast. The thought crossed Morris and Don's mind at the same time and they were glad to know they just had coffee this morning. That accomplished, he ran his huge hands through his equally greasy hair as he spoke. "Bad thing, these killings, Morris. I can see business slowing down a little. Tourists are moving on quicker and I suppose some aren't coming now at all. Are you making any progress? I know you can't tell me much, but are you close to an arrest? Do you have a suspect?"

The lack of a quick response told Sam what he was seeking to discover. "Damn. This is like having Jack the Ripper stalking the town. Do what you gotta, but get this sick monster."

"We're trying, Sam. You can count on that. A lot of good people are working on it, here and in Raleigh. We'll find him before long."

"I hope so, Sheriff. I sure hope so. Forget the coffee, your money's no good here. You know that."

"Thanks, Sam."

Sheriff Stone and Don left, both with a feeling of urgency building in their minds.

8

Several small children accompanied by a parent, were waiting on Sarah's doorstep when she came home from work. They all knew Myrtle was inside, but thought it would be best to wait outside until Sarah got home. The children came from all over town to be with Sarah. This was a very exciting time for them. Several of them jumped up and down on the front steps, trying to go from the bottom to the top and return without a fall or missed step. The less aggressive members of the group crowded into the two rockers and the old wooden front porch swing. It was their favorite. Suspended by chains from the roof over the porch, it would swing out over the rail surrounding the deck, and then back until it almost touched the white siding planks on the front of the house. As it reached its farthest point on either end of its repetitious journey, the children would all squeal with delight, each trying to make more noise than the one next to them. No one ever minded. Though mostly poor and unable to provide them with many of the things children from more affluent areas take for granted, the town loved its children.

Myrtle often thought it would be nice to get to know some of the kids better. She always loved children. But at eighty-four, she just didn't have the stamina she used to and sometimes it caused her patience to wear thin. She did however sit in a lot when Sarah was teaching the kids to paint or especially when she was telling them a story. Today, she was resting in her room waiting for Sarah to arrive and let them in.

Myrtle had always lived in Beaufort. She never had the desire to visit other places. It was as if she knew she was already in the best of all worlds. Most of her youth had been spent outdoors – fishing, swimming, exploring, savoring all that her native coastline had to offer. This thirst for an active lifestyle had made getting old a particularly hard task for her. The increased need for a walker practically made her a shut-in. She was getting particularly frail these past couple of years, bent over and tiring easily. However, her mind, except for a periodic lapse of short term memory, was as sharp as ever and a virtual reference book for the town that she called home.

If someone had to be with her all the time in case of a fall or other emergency, she preferred it to be Sarah or Jean Byrd from the grill. Sarah reminded her not only of herself as a young girl but how close she'd been to Robert, her only son and Sarah's father. He was a hard working waterman, making a living like his father before him. His heart had failed him early on, taking him from her and robbing Sarah of her last surviving parent. Myrtle made up her mind to fill the void for her as best she could. They'd become very close. Sarah not only didn't mind looking out for Myrtle as she got older, but took great pride in caring for her.

Jean Byrd had grown up next door to Sarah. She was twenty years her senior. A delightfully candid person, she was an eternal teenager. With a fanatical obsession for 60s rock and roll, particularly the Stones, she stayed glued to the TV or gossip magazines whenever she had the chance. Sarah and Myrtle loved her company as she added so much life to whatever room she entered. Continually chatting away and chewing gum, she was always in a good mood. She helped Sarah through all the teen years when she needed someone to talk with and had no mother.

On this particular afternoon, Sarah greeted the children as she arrived. As usual, there were smiles and lots of quick hugs from the eight- and nine-year-olds. She unlocked the front door and they poured into the parlor of the old house. Though many of the furnishings were worn, the place was neat and reflected the origins of the family. There were pictures of old men with sailor's garb and families standing proudly in front of white workboats at the waterfront. There were no yachts in these pictures. Beaufort was a working seaport for most of its past, not a tourist haven.

The children found places to sit on the couch, old rockers and even the floor. Their mothers waved and kissed their way out the front door, leaving them in Sarah's charge as was the custom. Everyone knew they were well cared for when she was with them.

She looked at her watch. It was five-thirty on the nose. *Had he forgotten?* She began to get out paints and easels and help the kids get started. Each child fought for her attention as she handed out the supplies.

"Alright now, let's remember our manners. What are we supposed to do? Ellen?"

"Wait for our turn. Raise our hands. Right?"

"That's right, Ellen. Let's all settle down now. I have a surprise for you today."

They all forgot the rules again and proceeded to delightfully quiz her about this revelation.

"What surprise?"

"What are we going to do?"

"Can I be first?"

"No, me! You were first last time."

Sarah quieted them back down. "Quiet, everyone, hush up. It's nothing you'll have to take turns on. We are going to have a visitor, if he shows up. He's an artist and he is going to help us learn to paint better."

"Is he young?"

"Yes, but not a child. He's a grownup."

"Oh good. Is he your boyfriend?"

"You kids are a mess. He's just a good friend."

"Well, if he's a boy and a friend then he's a boyfriend. Isn't that right?"

"If you look at it that way, he would be. But so would my friend David here." She poked a finger in David's side, causing him to double over in laughter.

As she played with the kids, she saw Alan walking up the steps to the door and felt an incredible warmth go through her. This was a special time for her and sharing it with him would make it even more special.

"May I come in?" Alan asked through the screen door.

"Children, this is the man that I told you was coming. Michele, open the door for Alan. Please come in and meet everybody, Alan." He walked in and took a lot of time smiling and greeting each child. He had a good way with kids. They responded immediately to him. It was exciting to the children to have another grownup take a keen interest in what they were doing. He took great pains with each child, helping them get set up to paint. He patiently moved his hand over their paintings, showing them how to put the brush on the paper. He was careful, however, not to actually touch paint to their work as that was taboo in artist circles. He would respect their work and try to encourage them to get better.

It didn't take long for David and Jenny Moore to latch on to their new friend. They were Doctor Moore's children. Jenny was nine and David was seven. Though they were well cared for, the doctor had little time to spend with them. He was one of only a handful of doctors in the area and was on call continually. He loved his kids but like a lot of fathers, it would have to be shown in what he did for them, not with them. This time with Sarah was good for them, he believed, and he made sure they had a way to each of these sessions they loved so much. Jenny and David couldn't get enough of Alan. He was not only a grown up, but a man as well. There was not enough exposure to one in their lives. Alan would have to break away from them periodically just to make sure all the kids got equal time. He was having a good time. Sarah took notice and thought it a beautiful thing to have a man be so gentle and understanding with kids.

The hour passed quickly. Alan and Sarah hugged all the kids goodbye. Jenny and David pitched a fit to stay longer but all were soon gone. Sarah turned to Alan and kissed him gently on the cheek.

"Thanks for coming. I knew you would have a good time. You did, didn't you?"

"You know I did. I've always loved kids. I even used to be one."

"Guess what? Floyd said he would love for you to stay upstairs over the shop. He would feel better knowing somebody was there at night. I've got a key for you right here in my bag." She found her purse and handed him a key.

"That's great. I'll clean it out tomorrow and bring what little bit of junk I have and set up shop. I really appreciate your doing this for me. Hey, what about going on a sail with me this Sunday?

The dock master has a daysailer he said I could borrow. I would love to sail over to the lighthouse at Cape Lookout. How about it?"

"If Jean will watch grandmother for me. She's going to think she lives here if I don't quit asking her so much. I really don't think she minds though. She loves to tell her all the gossip that's going around town."

They were interrupted by Myrtle entering the room. She was leaning on her walker as she shuffled across the floor. She had on her long, worn, pink housecoat that was a perpetual fixture on her. She smiled at them as she came over to where they were standing.

"There's nothing wrong with gossip. As long as it's about somebody else, that's what I always say. And is this the young man you've been telling me about, Sarah? A fine looking gentleman he is."

"Grandmother, this is Alan. Alan, this is my grandmother Myrtle."

Alan walked over to her and took her hand.

"It's nice to meet you, Myrtle. It's easy to see where Sarah gets her pretty looks from."

Myrtle smiled and replied. "And a flatterer I see. Nothing wrong with that either. Where are you from, Alan?"

"New York. I came down on a sailboat a few weeks back. I really love Beaufort. I was planning on staying for a couple of weeks while we worked on the boat, but now Sarah has convinced me to stay at least for the summer. I'm painting portraits down on the docks for the tourists that don't know any better."

Sarah cut in. "Don't let him kid you, Grandma, he's a very fine painter. The best I've ever seen."

"Well, young man, I've known some pretty good artists in my time. Quite a few have come to town to paint seascapes and the lighthouse over the years. I'll have to see your stuff and judge for myself. Painters always interested me. Seems they see stuff most of us overlook. They take the time to notice, you might say."

Alan was impressed with her observations. "You're right on target, Myrtle. I can tell you know your painters. You've probably seen much better than mine, but I'll bring some over for you to look at just the same. Constructive criticism is always good, they say. Painful, but good. Well, I guess I better get on back. Irving, Sherrie and Jason are leaving early in the morning and I wanted to see them a while tonight before they hit the hay. Thank you both for letting me come over and be with the kids today. I really had a great time. Goodnight."

He walked to the door and Sarah watched as he walked away. She quietly said, "Goodnight," as he walked up the street and out of sight. Sarah closed the door and locked it behind her. She started back toward her room.

Myrtle said as she walked by, "You found a real fine young man there. He paints, likes children and flatters old women. Better not let him slip by."

"Oh Grandma, behave."

"Dear, it's time you had someone special in your life, to share everything with. As much as I love you, I know you'll never have the best life has to offer until you have someone to love. Like I loved your Grandfather."

"Well, how do you tell if someone is that special person? I would hate to pick the wrong one."

"You're right to be careful. But don't let your fears talk so loud that you don't hear your heart."

"Sometimes it all seems so difficult, Grandmother, knowing what's the right thing to do with your life. All the decisions are so important and hard to correct if you make a mistake."

"It's better to make a few wrong ones from time to time than to not make any at all. You know what's the hardest thing you'll ever have to do, don't you?"

"No, what is it?"

"Gettin' old. It's the damnedest thing I've had to go through. Only one thing makes it easier. Having people around you that you love. You can't have too many of those. You should always give love a chance. It's the best thing you'll find in this world. Take it from somebody who's been here a long time. Well, I'm going to go sit down awhile. Remember what I tell you now. That's what grandmothers are for. Goodnight, dear."

As Alan approached *Wind Trader*, he saw everyone on deck sharing a freshly uncorked bottle of wine. "Permission to come aboard?"

Irving responded. "Permission granted."

Sherrie rushed over to Alan and hugged him. "I'm going to miss you so much. Change your mind and come with us."

"I'm going to miss all of you too," Alan replied. "Under any other conditions I would go, but there's too much here for me to leave."

"Like Sarah?" Sherrie teased.

"Exactly like Sarah," he answered.

Irving joined in. "Well, we approve, Alan. She's a doll. I always liked women from small towns. They appreciate the things you do for them a lot more. If we have to lose you, at least we know you're well taken care of here."

"Amen," said Jason, and then Stephen joined in.

"Hey guys, I'll be staying here too. Won't you miss me a little?"

Sherrie moved over and hugged Stephen also. "We just hadn't given up on you yet! We were going to get you drunk and shanghai you tonight. Here, have some more vino." Sherrie refilled Stephen's glass.

He gave her a kiss on the cheek and looked at Irving. "Hey, if there'd been a little more of this special treatment, I might have signed back on. Too late now."

Alan dropped a duffel bag in front of the group. "Farewell gifts to remember me by."

He reached in and grabbed a small box. He handed it to Irving who tore into it immediately. "Alright, a stainless Buck." He showed the knife off to the rest of the group.

Sherrie slowly unwrapped the brown paper off a much larger, thin box. Inside she found a painting that Alan had made for her. "It's *Wind Trader*, with all her sails up. It's so beautiful. Look Irving. I promise you we will treasure this and whenever we see it, we'll think of you." She wiped her eyes.

"It's not real large. I kept it small so it would look okay in the cabin."

Irving had not seen any of Alan's paintings before. He knew he liked to paint but didn't realize the scope of his ability. "This is a very beautiful piece, Alan. You couldn't have done anything to please us more."

Stephen lightened up the moment. "More vino! More, please!"

Sherrie got up to pour more wine for Stephen. Jason came over to Alan. "That was really nice, man. We're going to miss both of you guys a lot. Paintings are great and all, but I'll never forget that night offshore when you jumped in after Irving. That one will be with me when I die. He paused, shook their hands and moved to the companionway where he turned on the stereo. "Let's hear some music while we ponder the future."

As he played with the music, Irving told Alan, "We might have stayed a few days more, but this morning we heard that there are several tropical depressions forming south of the Caribbean. If a cycle gets started, it could mess up our whole weather window. We need to have a lot of miles behind us before a hurricane starts taking aim at us. It's probably best we get off in the morning. Besides, as beautiful as it is here and as much as Sherrie is going to miss you guys, the longer we stay, the harder it'll be to leave. So, in the morning it is. You gonna come help us cast off? We're going to try and shove off at sunrise."

"You can count on it," Alan replied.

Sherrie disappeared below and returned with something for Alan and Stephen. It was a small, framed picture of the whole crew, taken the night of the party on *Wind Trader*. She handed one to each of them. "I didn't paint it, but I did get the dock master to take it. And I framed it. So there, I'm an artsy type, too."

"It's beautiful, and it will always be special to me. Hey, when you guys get out to sea tomorrow, do me a favor."

"Sure, what do you need?"

Alan reached in his pocket and pulled out a small box. He opened it to reveal a beautiful stainless steel watch with marine pendants for the hours. "I didn't want to embarrass the old man of the sea, so give this to Jason tomorrow. Tell him it's from me and Stephen. And you guys better drop us some postcards with pictures of exotic places on them from time to time."

Sherrie hugged him again, this time with tears streaming down her cheeks. "You're so sweet. I'm glad you found Sarah. You deserve someone special."

The sun, which had burned brightly all day, was turning a sultry tangerine and extinguishing itself in the dark blue water. There was a gentle breeze snapping at the rigging of the hundreds of boats in the harbor. The people on board *Wind Trader* were good friends, made closer by their journey. Soft music and a gentle wind blew over the deck on what they all realized might be the last evening they'd ever see each other.

Alan walked alone across to his room above the gift shop. He hadn't cleaned it all up yet but he had stored his gear there. He'd bought an old hammock and swung it between two beams in the loft. He liked the place and was looking forward to his first night there. As he approached the rear entrance, someone was leaving the shop. The lights were off and he called out to the silhouette before him, "Floyd? Mr. Thompson, is that you?" There was no response. Thinking Floyd might want to talk with him, Alan briskly walked after the visitor. "Hey! Hang on a minute. Are you looking for somebody?" The man finally slowed and turned around. It was Eddie Fitch, the dock master. He seemed to stagger a little and was glassy-eyed.

"Hey man, thought you might want to hit a few bars with me. I've been making the rounds a little already. Haven't got a broad yet tonight. Lots of 'em around here by themselves. You'd think they'd be too scared to be out by themselves, what with all these killings goin' on. You wanna' do a little serious party'n? Let's do it, whad'ya say?"

"I appreciate the offer Eddie, but I just can't do it tonight. I've already had several glasses of wine on the boat and I'm beginning to get tired. Try me again some other time. All right?"

"Hey, I see you been hangin' out with Sarah. Kinda had an eye on her myself. Good lookin' broad, just a little strange, huh?"

"Not to me. Do you need some help getting back to your place? I'll walk back with you."

"Hell no! I could walk these docks in my sleep. I'll see you later, man."

With that, he continued his shaky walk. Alan turned and went back toward his room. When he got back to his door, it was still locked. Not knowing Eddie that well, he hoped that a drinking partner was all he was looking for. With all the problems in town right now, it would only make sense to be a little more careful. Everything inside was as he had left it earlier in the evening. There was nothing worth taking from his small corner of the world. At least not here. Alan cut on his portable radio, tuned it to a soft, late night channel and settled into his hammock. He fell quickly into a wine-induced deep sleep.

The alarm on the radio had been on for a full thirty minutes before the irritating blare woke Alan. His first taste of conscious thought was of the dry, bitter taste in his mouth and his immediate need for the toilet. Just like a night at college he thought, as he forced himself awake and downstairs to the bathroom in the gift shop. The bathroom mirror revealed the shaggy head of hair and dark lines under the eyes that the late night had left him. Thoughts of the past evening quickly caused the clock in his mind to have its own alarm go off. *Wind Trader* would be leaving early. He finished his toilet visit and made his way to the rear window. *Wind Trader*'s slip was empty. He unlocked the back door and stepped out onto the dock. There was a soft, early morning light and a fresh breeze mingling to stir a bright ripple across Taylor Creek. He looked to the mouth of the creek where it joined the inland waterway, and then followed it to the Atlantic Ocean, just beyond the Beaufort Inlet. There, with hundreds of square feet of bright sail reflecting the orange glow of morning, *Wind Trader* heeled to leeward as she gracefully slid toward the open sea. Though no one could hear, Alan waved and screamed goodbye. He was glad he had spent the night before with them and had made his goodbyes. He would miss them and yes, even *Wind Trader*. There is no question to a sailor that a beautiful vessel has a bond with those who get to sail on her. The sight and majesty of her leaving would remain in his mind long after she had sailed out of sight.

* * *

Sarah had been at the Water Dragon for several hours, busy with customers and displaying new merchandise. She wondered why she had not seen Alan as she knew he was an early riser. She presumed he'd been up late saying goodbye to his friends on *Wind Trader* and slept in. By lunch, her curiosity could stand no more. She closed the shop, put the "out to lunch" sign in the window and proceeded up the stairs to the loft. There was music coming from inside and she could hear movement. She knocked on the door once, then again. There was no reply. After awhile, the door opened. Alan, covered in dirt from head to toe, smiled through his almost black face and said to her, "I'm not ready for guests yet. Sorry, but you'll have to come back later." He didn't move from the door so she could look inside.

"You're serious?"

"Absolutely, do I look like a man who would kid about such things?"

She looked him over slowly. Every inch was dirty except for his beautiful smile.

"No, I can see a very determined person here. And when will I be able to see the results of this massive effort?"

"Here, this is for you." He reached in his back pocket and pulled out an envelope. He blew the dust off it.

"Sorry, guess I should have put it in a drawer while I was straightening up. See you later." He gently closed the door in front of her, smiling all the time.

Incredulous, she opened the smudged envelope where she stood.

"You are cordially invited to a dinner party at the highly stylish Kelly residence, this evening at seven o'clock. RSVP. PS. Bring something to eat."

She carried the envelope with her back to the shop. Throughout the day, Alan would come down the stairs, still smiling, still dirty, disappear, then return with a box or bag and disappear back up the stairs. No words, only smiles passed between them. Around five, Sarah began to close up the shop. She heard the door open upstairs. Alan's voice yelled out.

"'RSVP' You do know what that means?"

"I'm coming. I'm coming. What a pushy character you are."

She heard the door close and the upstairs music increase in volume. She could hear his off key voice accompanying the radio through a medley of old rock and roll songs as she cleared the register and locked up.

As she walked home, Sarah thought back to the night she had been raped. She remembered the terror of the moment when she realized what her assailant's intentions were. It was a sickening memory and filled her thoughts for many months thereafter. And yet, as bad as it had been, how could it possibly compare to what these unfortunate women had just gone through in her tiny little town. By the time he left them bleeding to death, unable to summon help and knowing their life was flowing out of their body, they probably wished they had been raped. At least they'd be alive. That was the realization that brought Sarah back into the world. An understanding rape crisis counselor explained to her that more important than anything else, she was alive. She could put it behind her and try to enjoy the good things that were still all around her. She thought she understood her then, but now with the example of these women, it was all very clear. She had her life and she would make every day count.

Sarah excitedly got dressed and rushed around her house like a crazed person. Myrtle would occasionally turn the TV down and listen to Sarah singing to herself, opera, of course. Shortly, she came in to speak to her.

"Grandma, I'm going to go out for a couple of hours. Do you need me to get Jean or are you okay for a while?"

"Sweetheart, you go see your young man. I'm just fine. Just don't stay too long, and make sure you don't walk home alone after dark."

"I won't. Bye Grandma." Sarah kissed her grandmother and quickly finished the final touches on her hair and clothes. It had been quite a while since she was this concerned about her appearance. She even used a small amount of a pale pink lipstick. It had taken her ten minutes to find a single tube of it in the house. It just hadn't seemed important until now. There was a knock at the door.

"Please, no company," she thought. In her stocking clad feet, she ran down the old, heart pine floors to the front door. She opened it apprehensively, as she was not expecting company and didn't need a surprise visitor slowing her down, not this evening. There, behind a freshly picked bouquet of wild flowers was Stephen. He had a fresh scrubbed look about him and for the first time, she perceived a distinct air of sophistication that she had not really noticed before, one that all his joking and teasing could not hide.

"Your escort has arrived. Flowers courtesy of the gentleman. He thought you should not venture out alone in the late afternoon and thus sent me, Madam."

"Well, I am very flattered."

She ran to the bedroom, slipped on her shoes, then went quickly to the refrigerator, grabbed a bucket of chicken she had

had Sam's Grill fix during the afternoon. She returned to Stephen, locked the door behind her as they left for the short walk to the Water Dragon. Bye, Grandmother. I'm leaving now." This is very thoughtful of you, Stephen. I appreciate it so much. Alan has certainly made a big production out of his loft-warming, hasn't he?"

"The way I see it, you are both pretty special people. Maybe a little off plumb, but special nonetheless."

"Off plumb?"

"Just a little, enough to be interesting. Believe me, I don't escort just anyone to dinner. I'm a very busy guy. My social schedule is absolutely grueling."

"Oh I'm sure. By the way, where are you staying now that your home has left without you?"

"Over at Agnes' Bed and Breakfast. I already feel like a full-fledged Beaufortite. Probably won't be long and I'll start to smell like Zed."

"You're so cruel to poor old Zed."

"I know, but there's so few things that give me this much satisfaction."

"How long have you known Alan? Did you know him before the cruise on *Wind Trader*? You seem to get along so well, I sort of guessed you must be old friends."

"We have known each other for quite a while. We met in school."

"Boston College?"

"Cedar Hill Academy. He was one year ahead of me. He was so shy that I used to fix him up with dates. And, after all these years, here I am, still bringing a date home for him. Who ever said some things never change?"

"What was he like in school? Did he play sports? Was he drawing things back then?"

"He was a brain. On a grade scale of four, he was a six. He's been painting and drawing as long as I've known him. Only back then, he was drawing super heroes or his rendition of a centerfold. I think I have one of those back home, Miss February if I remember correctly."

"You're joking?"

"Hey, you asked. And as far as sports were concerned, he was captain of the swim team in high school and in college. He's the strongest swimmer you'll ever meet."

"And you both have been running around together ever since you got out of college?"

"We see each other at work a lot."

"Work? What kind of work do you do?"

"I handle financial affairs for people, sort of an investment counselor."

"That's sounds interesting. And Alan? What does he do?"

"That's interesting also. But that's something you'll have to ask him."

"Why is that? He's not CIA or in the witness protection program, is he?"

"Both good guesses, but no. However, if he's told you he's an astronaut or something glamorous and I spill the beans, you two might get mad with each other and I would be the one to blame."

"He hasn't ever mentioned anything about it to me."

"Well, I'm sure it will eventually come up. It's not my place. He has to get his own women now. I strictly handle the long walks down the waterfront for him."

"Okay, we're here. Give me a kiss for my effort."

Sarah obliged Stephen with a quick peck on the cheek. "Stephen, thank you for your kindness."

"Anytime. You kids have fun now. I'll see you tomorrow and you can tell me what you thought of Alan's handiwork. Goodnight."

As she approached the top of the steps, the door opened for her. Alan greeted her as he flung the door open to its widest point. The only light was a candle burning on the small table in the corner of the room. As she entered, he gave her a gentle hug and kiss on her forehead.

"You look… stunning. You are beautiful; you know that, don't you?"

"Stop it. You're embarrassing me."

"Well, if telling you that you're beautiful embarrasses you, you're going to be blushing whenever you're around me, because you are beautiful. And, you smell great."

Alan shut the door behind them.

"Ready?" he asked.

"As I'll ever be." The lights came on. Alan had lighted the loft with just a few small directional spots on a metal pole and a couple of strands of the small white Christmas lights from the boat. When her eyes scanned the room, Sarah was amazed at the transformation. With a quick glance you would swear you had entered an artist's loft in some metropolitan artist colony. There were many paintings hanging on the walls. Yards of sheer, brightly colored material hung from the ceiling that reflected colors throughout the room. Furniture was sparse with only a card table, four metal folding chairs and a few nautical props that would have been considered junk by anyone else on the waterfront. There was a definite feeling of design and purpose to everything in the room.

"A parachute. Kinda sets it all off, doesn't it?"

"It's beautiful, Alan. I'm glad you didn't let me in 'til you were finished. This is so unique." Her eyes began to gravitate to the paintings around the room. She recognized a couple she had seen him working on at the dock, but most she'd never seen.

"Are all these paintings yours?"

"Yes, I hope you don't think I'm an egotist for hanging up my own paintings. I just didn't have anything else to brighten the place up. To tell you the truth, there's a couple of them I like."

"A couple? They're all beautiful. Have you done all these since you came here?"

"Some. The rest I had in my trunk on *Wind Trader*. Do you like them?"

"Let me look at them all." She slowly made her way around the room, looking carefully at each painting.

"Take your time. I'll pour you a glass of wine and put the radio on a channel you'll like. I'll just change channels until I hear songs with words I can't understand. Right?" As she made her way around the room, a soft operatic music began to fill the space.

Alan soon handed her a small glass of wine in a paper cup. "No crystal yet. I guess I could try and fool you, say that paper-ware is very 'in' in the Big Apple."

"I think it's sweet. At my house you'd probably be drinking out of old peanut butter jars. Now, be quiet and let me look at your paintings. You're worse than the children."

He didn't speak but stayed close by as she inspected his paintings. After she finished examining the last one, she moved over to his side. "You are a talented man."

"Thank you very much."

"I'm not just saying it. I've only seen paintings like these in museums. Why aren't you pursuing it more?"

"I am. That's what I'm doing here."

"Your work is good enough now to hang in galleries. That's what I'm saying."

"Some of it is."

"Where?"

"Back home, in New York, and some in a couple of galleries in Boston. Once they're finished though, I lose interest in them. It's painting I love, not selling the finished work. Money doesn't mean a great deal to me in case you can't tell."

"What does mean a great deal to you?"

"I'm not embarrassed to say. You do." He walked close to her and embraced her. She wrapped her arms behind his waist.

"I'm glad."

They kissed more passionately than ever before. They realized at that moment they were in love, that they were supposed to be together. After a very prolonged moment, Alan suggested, "Let's sit down and see what you brought for us to eat. Strange dinner party, huh? I knew there wouldn't be time to fix anything after I got the place ready. To be truthful, I'm not real sure what all can be fixed on a hot plate."

"That's right, I hadn't even thought about there not being a stove up here. Look, I brought some fried chicken from Sam's."

They dove into the food. Alan ate as if he were starved. When they were done, they poured more wine, then danced barefoot on the rough wooden floor. Finally, they laid down together in Alan's hammock. Their intense attraction and growing desire found no resistance, only encouragement from both. Like birds that fly thousands of miles each year to the exact same location to mate, they found each other, far from the beaten path and in spite of the different worlds from which each began their journey.

* * *

The town council's meeting room in the courthouse was packed with representatives from practically every investigative branch of police in the state. There were professionals from the crime lab in Raleigh, homicide detectives from Charlotte, and even a couple of investigators from other states, trying to find links to cases they were working on back home. Reporters were camped out on the courthouse steps, waiting for any sort of news related to the killings. Sheriff Stone had barred them from the meeting to avoid unnecessary leaks from damaging the investigation. Some had gotten so persistent in the last few hours that he was considering clearing them off the grounds entirely. Only when he realized it would mean a ton of bad public relations did he decide against that course of action.

Morris and Ellingwood entered together and went to the podium where the mayor normally conducted the town's affairs. Ellingwood walked up to the front and confidently asked the group to quiet down. Morris stayed several feet back, not overly anxious to take questions from so knowledgeable a gathering of experts. He removed his hat, held it in his hands and leaned back against the wall. This promised to be quite interesting.

"Good morning, everyone. For those of you I haven't met, I'm Don Ellingwood, a forensic specialist, with the State Bureau of Investigation. As you know, the state is providing assistance to Sheriff Morris Stone as his staff and resources are limited. Most of you have been lent to us from your various agencies and we need as much expert help as we can obtain. We're dealing with what is, in most expert opinions, a pattern killer or, to use the more current terminology, a serial killer. Here's what we know or suspect about the case. The suspect is most likely male, not just from the strength required to act in the manner that has accompanied both killings, but from the size of the bruises on the neck of the second victim. His hands are strong and proportionately male. The pattern of the killings, the area of knife wounds, disposal of the bodies, and ritualistic carvings on the victims indicate traditional psychopathic motives associated with a serial killer. He probably feels he has a purpose, a reason mind you, for what he is doing. He is definitely a sociopath. The sheer brutality of the killings indicates he feels he has a calling to perform these murders and in no way does it bother him. In his own mind, he is not only blameless but should be commended for his actions. He's a very sick individual.

"Intelligence. Both killings were reasonably close to crowded areas. The victims were in both instances close to their destinations, allowing only a short window of opportunity to grab them. He has left no prints; most likely he's wearing gloves. The locations where he left the bodies indicate he planned most of his actions beforehand, maybe to the extent of observing his intended victims for several days before making his hit. I, for one, believe he has relocated here for whatever reason, and that the cross referencing, which is being done as we speak, will find a match or maybe several. We can't sit back and wait for him to screw up. We're about to go on the offensive. If we wait, there's a good chance that someone else will die or, even worse, he'll feel we're getting too close and he'll move on to begin all over again somewhere else – probably as he has done here.

"I caution you, this is a smart individual. He knows there's a lot of people looking for him now and he'll be watching what we do and say. The strategy I'm about to brief you on will not leave this room. You should not discuss it or any facet of this investigation with reporters, or even each other in any public place. We need surprise on our side. You've all been sent here because of your expertise in these matters so I'm sure that will not be a problem. Here, in a nutshell is what we are planning. Consider this an overview. We'll get more specific with you later in the day.

"Each of his victims had just left a crowded, tourist-filled nightspot. Both had consumed some alcohol, at least enough to take away any measure of caution. There were enough tourists in the area so that a stranger wouldn't stand out. He'd obviously been waiting for them to leave the crowd. Both were young, single females leaving alone. Working with these facts, we'll present him with not just one, but several potential victims. Would you please stand? Sgt. Virginia Davis from the SBI and Deborah Beekins from the State Police's Special Operations Office. These lovely young women will be bait for this operation. They are both, I assure you, highly skilled officers and know full well the risks involved. I commend you both for your courage and you can rest assured we will be supporting you every moment. Please be seated. These officers will be acting in keeping with the pattern our perpetrator has been looking for.

"Beginning this Sunday night, they will frequent the two most popular spots on the waterfront. Both will stay several hours with supposed dates who will be male officers. Other officers will be in the crowd. We will stay in contact with all parties via radios, and continuously monitor the surrounding areas. As each target leaves, even though they'll appear to be alone, they'll follow a predetermined route. In apparently empty, parked cars along the way, we'll have our people stationed. The State has generously lent a chopper equipped with spots and infrared detection capabilities should a pursuit situation develop.

"On each end of town will be four patrol cars, tucked away but on full alert. The targets will be 'miked' and also have a high frequency location indicator built into their clothing. If and when, and I hope when, he strikes, he won't know what hit him.

"We'd like to apprehend this individual alive so we can possibly retrace his movements and link him to any other killings he may have committed. However, the safety of these officers is our top priority and you should not hesitate to shoot to kill if there appears to be any indication they are in imminent danger from the suspect. Okay, enough from me. Let me introduce Sheriff Morris Stone to those of you who haven't had the opportunity to meet him. He is a fine, very capable individual. He immediately spotted the indicators of a pattern killer and got on the phone to our office. He has a small staff and they've slept very little in the past couple of weeks. Let's give them all the help and courtesy they deserve. Sheriff."

Morris Stone walked to the podium in the center of the room. He knew the people in the room all had more knowledge than he did in matters such as these. He wanted them to perform their best work and catch the killer quickly, but he also wanted them to respect his town and office in the process. It would be inappropriate to be a bystander in the investigation. He would watch and learn, and put in the effort required to earn their respect as well.

"Thank you all for coming to Beaufort. As Mr. Ellingwood said, we're a small town and not equipped to handle an investigation such as this. However, I and the six other officers on my staff want to assist you as much as possible and make this investigation go as smoothly as we can. You may use the office space here and also in the courthouse across the street where we've commandeered one entire hallway of offices for the purpose of this investigation. One of my officers will be stationed at each end of the hall twenty-four hours a day. No one will be allowed in without proper identification. Our neighbors in Morehead City have lent us four additional officers during the daytime to spell our guys so that they can rest occasionally. I, of course, will be available to each of you around the clock. Just call the station and they'll find me. Thank you all for coming to our side during this time. I'll turn you back over to Don Ellingwood who is, I'm glad to say, in charge of this investigation."

He put his Texas Ranger style hat back on and returned to his position against the wall. Don took the meeting back over. "Alright, question time. After this, we'll break up into operational groups to work out the small details. Let me throw this out at you for thought. Serial killers seem to inherently believe that their plan is foolproof and overconfidence is often their undoing. This investigation's best hope is that he will feel infallible in his undertakings and leave just one stone unturned. If he does, with luck, one of you in this room will find what was left under that stone."

The next ten hours were spent covering every possible variation or problem they could think might arise in their planned trap. No one present underestimated the gravity of what they were doing. Even though optimism would be needed to carry out such a venture, the odds still favored the killer. He certainly was smart enough to know such an operation was a possibility and he had, after all, survived the hunt to this point. He could just leave if he felt too much heat. They were betting he might try to strike just once more.

9

Sarah hated to ask Jean to stay with her grandmother on a Sunday, especially for the entire day, but she didn't know anyone else she felt would give Myrtle any real attention while they stayed with her. Jean was in her late forties and knew many of the same old timers that Myrtle had grown up with. She seemed to have a genuine interest in Myrtle's stories of Beaufort before the tourists found it. Back then, it was a real seaport, full of sailing ships and characters that Myrtle's tales made bigger than life. Jean said that one day she'd write a book about the history and people of her small town. She'd written a column for the local paper for many years and could always be counted on to be the voice of the community in letters to the editor. Basically, she reflected the opinions of most people in the town. Her graying hair still pushed high on her head in a 1960s style, wire rimmed glasses and no makeup, made her appear to be a prime candidate for librarian of the year or the proverbial school marm. Were it not for her quick wit and willingness to exchange words with the locals, she could easily have been mistaken for a person who might be hard to get to know.

There had been one episode twenty years earlier, when Jean tried the patience of almost everyone in the small, tightly woven community. She had what she would later call her religious period. Through a mountain of correspondence with an evangelical preacher, who the community would later call "The Inquisitor," she convinced him to conduct a revival in the town square. Even though the town was pretty well-known for its hard working, hard drinking watermen during that time frame, they were still, by anyone's standards, a very moral group. There were certainly plenty of examples of wild women and fast living present on any Saturday night, but on Sunday morning, everyone was in attendance at the local Baptist church. However, the moral standards of their home grown religious upbringing, paled by the rigid conduct expected by this fundamental, right wing zealot. If he'd had his way, stocks would have been erected on the public docks, and violators of God's Laws would be publicly humiliated as penance for their sins. If that wasn't enough of a strain to put the citizenry through, the high minded, idealistic Jean would relay every sordid detail she saw, heard about, or even suspected, to this black-suited tyrant. She even repeated names! More than one marriage fell into a state of war after some of these highly publicized revelations. After two weeks, the town had had enough. It took only one late night visit to the preacher's motel room by a contingent of the town's more vocal residents, to convince him that Beaufort would appreciate his moving on to more receptive and appreciative grounds, say, Old Salem.

Jean, though not understanding of his quick departure at the time, forsook her overly virtuous ways shortly after her first late night romp with Lenny Moore, the area's most famous fancier of young women. He had such a way with them that he'd grown infamous among the parents of all the young females along the coast. Jean was no exception. Thirty days, and many evenings in his company had a definite effect on her outlook, demeanor and appreciation for some of the finer points of sin. It was about this time that she developed her taste for an occasional shot of hard whiskey and loud music. Several years in the fast lane convinced her to end her affair with the bottle, but she remained a devout follower of rock and roll to the present day. At least once a week, one old timer or another would jokingly remind her of her journey from saint to sinner. There were also rumors that poor old Lenny had accepted a cash donation to lead her down the winding road that led away from such fanatical devotion to a higher calling. All unsubstantiated, of course.

Sarah heard all the stories and loved Jean's enthusiasm for life. It was not only her interesting past, but because she also liked her, that Sarah never felt she was imposing when she asked her to visit with Myrtle. Jean enjoyed Myrtle's tales as much as Myrtle appreciated Jean's. However, today she would most likely be gone all day and she'd been using her services a lot since she met Alan.

"Please, Jean, won't you let me pay you something for staying with Grandmother? I feel so guilty."

Her grandmother's voice came from the bedroom, "Don't you dare offer her money. She should pay me for giving her all the stories for that book she's writing. She's going to get rich off it and I'll be dead and forgotten. So she can stay with me now when I need the company. That right, Jean?"

"Exactly, Myrtle. You just go on, Sarah, and have a good day. I didn't have a thing I had to do today and I would just as soon babysit."

"Babysit!" Myrtle fired back from her room. "If anybody's babysitting here, it's me. Go on, Sarah. Get out of here before you see me go at it with this smart thing here. Go on. Have a nice time. Tell what's-his-name..."

"Alan."

"That's right, Alan, that I said to take care of my baby. Now git on outta here"

"I love you, Grandma. Jean, thank you. Don't put up with too much grief from her now."

Jean loved them both. "I can handle her. See you tonight. Stay as long as you want, dear."

Sarah closed the door behind her. Even through the old framed walls she could hear them playfully bickering with one another. Myrtle was always in a good mood when Jean spent some time with her. She got her going.

Alan was coming up the street to meet her as she stepped onto the sidewalk. "Well, good morning. You certainly look beautiful today, not that you could look any other way. Did you bring a bathing suit so that we could get in the water?"

"Of course. I come fully prepared for you to flip that sail thing and dunk me in the sea."

"Hey, have a little confidence in me, will you. You're in expert hands here. I wouldn't risk a bone or even a soft spot on that pretty body."

"I've seen those things turn over a lot, from the dock, mind you. That's one reason I only go out in motorboats. I can't believe I let you talk me into this. If you drown me, I'll come back and haunt you. That's a promise."

"No one entrusted to me will ever drown. I have magical powers when it comes to the sea. I have an agreement, you might say, with old King Neptune."

"An agreement? How's that?"

"He won't ever let me drown in the ocean and in return, I never take ugly girls sailing."

"Not even this one time?"

"Especially not this time. We're here. There she is."

The boat was about fifteen feet long. It was an old, wooden daysailer. The sides and bottom were basically flat and the deck was covered with plywood and a layer of gray canvas to keep it from getting slippery once it got wet. There was a small cockpit about two-thirds of the way back, just big enough for two people to sit in. More often than not, it was used to dangle feet in, as the captain and crew would sit on the side decks that ran along the cockpit. That was much more comfortable except for an occasional bottom soaking from the waves. The mast was wooden, unlike the modern boats that used aluminum. As far as Alan was concerned, just being made of wood, was a big plus in his fondness for the boat. He loved the feel, the warmth and even the smell of a wooden boat. He was well aware of the increased maintenance required to keep these older boats looking bright, but he thought that a small price to pay. Besides, he enjoyed working on them just about as much as sailing them.

"It's so small, we can't possibly take that all the way to Cape Lookout. What if it gets rough?"

"It's fifteen feet long and very seaworthy. People have crossed the Atlantic in boats smaller than this. I'm serious."

"Nobody in their right mind would try and cross the ocean in a boat this small."

"Is that so? Answer one question for me, will you?"

"Of course."

"You're at sea. A terrible storm catches you. You're on a four hundred foot long ship. She starts to break up and you know she's going down. What would you do?"

"Abandon ship?"

"Exactly, and into what, a freezing winter sea?"

"No dummy, a lifeboat."

"Correct. A twenty foot cork to ride out a storm that tore open holes in your huge ship. I rest my case. Now hand me your bag and let's get going."

Sarah thought she could swim to Cape Lookout if Alan went with her and truly had no reservation about taking the sailboat. She still thought there could be the possibility of having to do exactly that. This was her first trip in a boat under sail. Even the party on *Wind Trader* was under power. She anxiously awaited the moment when the thing would start to tilt.

"Okay Sarah, just get comfortable. I'll push us out into the creek and raise the sail. Do you know how to steer with a tiller?"

"Of course, lots of fishing boats have tillers."

"Then steer us into the wind toward the far bank on the other side of the channel. Watch out for the boats anchored out there. Here we go. Watch your head when the sail goes up. The boom, that stick on the bottom of the sail, might swing across the deck."

He quickly raised the mainsail with the halyard and tied it off to a cleat on the mast. The sail fluttered in the wind as the boat was headed directly into it. Next, he raised the jib, a small sail on the bow of the boat. After cleating it off, he carefully moved to the stern of the boat and took the tiller from Sarah. Alright, we're underway. Watch what happens when I turn on an angle to the wind."

As he moved the tiller, the boat swung around and the sails filled with the light morning breeze. Quickly, the boat reacted by leaning in the direction the wind was blowing. The little vessel began to glide effortlessly across the water. Being on board, it seemed to be going much faster than they did when watching them from shore.

"Take the radio from my bag and find us some music. There's sodas in there, too, if you're thirsty. Just relax. Get comfortable. Get some sun, or take a nap if you want. I can sleep like a baby when a sailboat is in sync with the rhythm of the waves. It's like being in a rocking chair while someone else is rocking you." The boat gently rose and fell as if keeping time with the music on the radio.

"You're not still nervous are you?"

"If I can see shore, I can swim to it if I have to. And, if you dunk us, you'll ruin the sandwiches I packed. So exercise prudence. Actually, it feels pretty nice so far. I could see how an older person, such as you, might get into this."

"I'll bet you age into it today. It grows on you. Look at the dark shadow on the water ahead. That's wind coming at us. Watch what happens when it hits us. Don't panic, we won't turn over, I promise. It's fun."

Soon the sails were rigid with a twelve knot breeze powering them. The boat jumped ahead as it lay over on its side. The narrow, white hull leaned over even further and effortlessly picked up speed.

"Are we okay?" Sarah asked.

"That's as far as she's going to heel, lean that is. Relax and enjoy. Look how fast we're going. Want to steer her awhile?"

"No. You handle it. Maybe later when I feel more at ease I'll try it. We are really flying, aren't we?"

"Not in land terms, but for a sailboat we're doing pretty well. People take motorboats because they want to go somewhere in a hurry. When I'm on a sailboat, there's no need to hurry because I'm already where I want to be. On the boat. Understand?"

"I think so. You're taking the back way to Cape Lookout Bight, aren't you?"

"You do know your way around out here, don't you?"

"When you grow up here, this is like your backyard. I've been all over this area, in a fishing boat, of course. How long will it take to get to the bight this way?"

"Three hours, maybe four, by lunch if this wind holds. The weather forecast said it would be steady most of the day so we'll have plenty of time to mess around at the Cape when we get there and still be home by dark. See if you can find the weather on the radio. Sarah changed channels until she picked up a weather forecast. The information was alarming, not for the present, but for what the future might hold. The tropical depression that Irving had spoken of earlier had become hurricane Emily. The projected course was for landfall in the Mid-Atlantic States, most probably North Carolina. Sarah did not appear that concerned about the forecast.

"They predict every single hurricane is going to wipe out Cape Hatteras. We haven't had a direct hit in over thirty years. Not since Donna or Hazel has there been any water in the streets. I wasn't around then, but the older folks who were said they almost wiped out the whole town. Since those two, we've had more trouble from winter storms than hurricanes. They call them nor'easters. They can last a whole day with high winds and waves. I've seen plenty of them. They scare me more than hurricanes."

"Well, neither would be just fine with me. I'm a fair weather, light wind sailor, like today. This is perfect. You know what I want to do when we get to the bight? I want to climb the lighthouse. Will you go with me?"

"Of course. You'll need somebody to administer mouth-to-mouth resuscitation when you get to the top."

"I like the sound of that. The mouth-to-mouth part gets me particularly excited. I promise you I'll need it when we get to the top."

"Men. Don't you ever think about anything else?"

"No, not that I can remember. Why do you ask?"

The boat was skimming along quickly by this time. Sarah was beginning to realize the boat was stable when it leaned or "heeled" as Alan called it. It was very pleasant. Without the noise of a motor, the small waves could be heard slapping the bow and the water passing under the boat occasionally made an interesting gurgling sound. It was like being part of a painting she thought. Perhaps that's what attracted Alan to it so much. A pair of porpoises came alongside and kept pace with the boat. They'd rise, blow, and submerge, only to reappear a short time later. They were definitely following the boat. They were very common in the sound this time of year and one of the favorite sights of the tourists who delighted in watching them play. Sarah thought if she had to be an animal, a porpoise would be the best choice. They were always swimming in warm waters, playing and seemed to have a distinct intelligence. Of course, they were beautiful to behold.

As Alan had predicted, by lunch the lighthouse was looming large ahead. They were in the bight now, only a short distance from shore. Since there were no docks or piers to tie up to, boats visiting the area had to either anchor out or nudge up to the bank.

"Take the tiller and steer straight toward shore," Alan directed Sarah. "I'll get out and take the anchor up on the beach. That way, she won't drift out when the tide gets higher."

The craft gently bumped the shore, and Alan did as he said. "Okay, we're here, and all in one piece. Beautiful and unspoiled,

isn't it? I'm glad they haven't put in public docks or services. If they did, you wouldn't be able to get in here on a pretty day like this."

As they looked around, there were several other larger sailboats anchored out. Their crews were either swimming beside the boats, sleeping under awnings over their cockpits, or exploring the beach and lighthouse as Alan and Sarah were about to do. Alan grabbed his bag. Sarah carried her wicker picnic box and they started up the beach toward the lighthouse. They kept stopping along the way to look at any interesting flower or sea creature they passed. Any unspoken-for glances, they gave to each other.

"You know, the lighthouse is so tall that you feel like you're right under it until you start walking toward it. It must be a mile or more from the boat. Myrtle says it's almost two hundred feet tall. She's usually right about things like that. It's funny how people, when they get old, can't remember what happened yesterday, but can remember everything that happened fifty years ago. Why do you suppose that happens?"

"Could be they enjoy the old times better and those are their most important memories. I don't know."

The lighthouse had been for many years manned by a caretaker who lived in a small frame house, similar to those in Beaufort, standing beside the base of the lighthouse. The lighthouse itself was white with large black diamonds whose points touched the one next to it. If the conical pattern was spread out flat, the result would look like a black and white checkerboard. The lighthouse and caretaker's cabin were now set up as a museum with a park ranger supervising them in-season. The light was still functional, but electrically powered now. Its high-powered beam was amplified many times by the prism glass surrounding the lamp room at the top of the lighthouse. Only a periodic check from the Coast Guard was required to keep it functioning. Alan and Sarah approached the door, which opened up to the hundreds of wooden steps that wound their way up the inside of the structure.

"Well, we're here. Let's climb to the top and get started with the CPR."

"Alan, I hope you know how far it is to the top. It really takes a lot to reach the peak."

"Hey, I can take it. You're going, aren't you?"

"If you can take it, so can I. Let's go."

They spent the next twenty minutes climbing steps and both were breathing hard by the time they reached the light at the top. After catching their breath they scanned the horizon. Sarah pointed out the landmarks she spotted. "There's the water tower back home and that smoke is coming from the menhaden processing plant just east of town."

The menhaden plants were old, unpainted wooden buildings with corrugated tin roofs where each day, weather permitting, the large commercial fishing boats would bring their day's catch. They were located at the northeast end of Taylor Creek, several miles upstream from the tourist section of Beaufort. As sanitary and clean as any other seafood operation, they still carried the strong odor indicative of an occasional misplaced fish rotting in the sun. Working there required growing accustomed to the smell. Menhaden, a small, yellow-tailed fish found in tightly-packed schools in warm, shallow waters, were primarily used for fertilizer, though sport fishermen valued them highly as bait for the larger and more desirable game fish, such as king mackerel. Nonetheless, they were a highly profitable venture and supported a large industry in the back waters of the community.

Alan's perspective of the coastal area was oriented much differently than Sarah's. "Look how insignificant it all looks compared to the Atlantic. The ocean is so immense. It always leaves me wanting to see what lies beyond the horizon."

"Well, for two thousand miles beyond, it looks just like what you see right here. Blue and wet. And most of the time, not nearly so smooth. I've heard fisherman talk about seventy foot waves just a couple of miles offshore. You have to be very careful when you go offshore here. A thunderstorm or squall can sink you."

"Tell me about it." Okay, time to see if I'm breathing all right, nurse."

"Your breathing seems fine, but I do detect a rapid pulse and perhaps a heart palpitation. Fortunately, I know just how to cure it."

They kissed, slowly and tenderly, then embraced and spent an hour snuggling, watching the ocean and ships entering the port at Morehead City. Sarah watched as Alan walked on the platform surrounding the lighthouse prism. He was wearing cut-off jeans and a sleeveless Boston College tee shirt. His sandy hair was getting a little shaggy and he'd developed a deep tan during the summer. His slender, wiry frame could by no means be described as muscular, yet his drive and sense of competition had always made him a threat in sports while he was growing up. His hazel eyes darted when he spoke and his enthusiasm and desire showed clearly through them. This zest and fire coupled with his sensitivity and artist's flare were irresistible to Sarah.

"I hate to even suggest this, but we better eat lunch and head back down to earth. You want to eat up here or on the beach?"

"The beach sounds good. Lead the way."

They proceeded back down the circular stairways. Alan put his arm around her as they reached the bottom. They started walking toward the ocean side of the barrier island, opposite where they docked their boat. The island was in reality, just a narrow sliver of land, no more than a mile wide, separating the ocean from the sound and then the mainland. Other than an occasional outcropping of sea oats or driftwood, there were only sand dunes and shells for the entire length of the small Island. The lighthouse was very much like a skyscraper in a desert. They waded out into the calm water of the ocean. There were no breakers. It was unusually calm and serene.

"This is really quiet. Usually the waves are crashing like crazy out here. Look, about a mile offshore you can see the breakers on Diamond Shoals. That's why they had to build a lighthouse here. They had to keep ships sailing down the coast from running aground, thinking they were safe because they were so far offshore. It's really scary."

Alan loved her knowledge of the coastal waters. He playfully pushed a handful of water on her. She backed up to avoid the spray. With just shorts and a tank top on, her small frame revealed how beautifully proportioned she was. Her olive skin and dark brown eyes were very unusual in contrast to her dark blonde shoulder length hair. Her slim, angular body and beautiful face made her the most beautiful person he had ever met. And he had met plenty. Alan continued their conversation. "If there's that much white water out there when it's calm, I'd hate to see what it's like when it's really blowing a gale.

"One of the most amazing things about the ocean is when it runs over a shoal area like this. The breakers can get fifteen to twenty feet tall and crush the hull of a ship like it was made of cardboard. And yet, if the ocean were calm, you could actually wade there. Sometimes the water is only a couple feet deep over the shoals. That always struck me as odd. You were practically ashore, and yet you were in more trouble than if you were a hundred miles at sea in a hurricane. Do you know what I mean?"

"I sure do. You've obviously never been out at sea during a hurricane."

"Okay, wise guy. You know what I mean. Give me a little poetic license here, won't you?"

Sarah shined with delight as she bantered with Alan. "I'm a very literal person. If I see a shell, I call it a shell. If I see a fish, I call it a fish."

"You're a mess, that's what you are."

He playfully hugged and kissed her. She knew as well as he did the dangers of the shoal. They walked back to the beach, holding hands and kicking water on each other.

Sarah reached into her picnic box and pulled out a small blanket. She spread it out on the smooth white sand. "Lunch is served. Do you like the chicken salad or the peanut butter and jelly special?"

"They both sound superb. I'll have one of each."

They sat on the blanket and started to eat lunch.

"Sarah, you've lived here all your life. Is this as beautiful to you as it is to me? I've been pretty much everywhere and this has to be one of the most spectacular places in the world. It's still so unspoiled. It couldn't have looked much different here when the first settlers arrived. Have you ever traveled?"

"That was my plan when I went off to college. I would study during the school year and travel each summer. I figured I'd meet people from all over the country at college and I could visit them at their homes while I traveled. It was all going so well, then..."

"And then what?"

"I was walking from my dorm to the library on campus one evening and, got attacked. He forced me into the trees, away from the lights and sidewalk and then, he raped me." Sarah paused and took deep breaths as she described the attack, not so much from any lingering terror of the night, but because she felt she had to tell Alan and was concerned about how he might react to the revelation. "I thought he was going to kill me. After that, I just didn't feel safe anywhere except here. Everyone I met, I was suspicious of. I didn't want to walk anywhere by myself. I was a nervous wreck. It kind of killed, or maybe just overrode, my interest in the plans I had. I finally just gave in to all my fears. I quit school and came home. I didn't feel safe anywhere for a long time. Then after I'd been back for a while, I realized how good I feel here, how I knew everyone and felt safe. I haven't left since. I guess I'll be like my grandmother and die in the same house I was born in. It's not bad. To answer your question though, yes, it's very beautiful to me. Until I met you, I hadn't gone out with anybody since I came back. I guess I feel safe with you, too."

"I'm glad. I want you to feel that way. I wouldn't hurt you for the world. And I won't let anyone else hurt you either. I hate to see you not finish college though. You're such a bright person. You need to continue to expand your view of the world. No place is really any safer than another anymore. Just look at what's happened here. It could happen anywhere. You'd be safe enough back at school, especially if you had someone there to kind of watch over you."

"Anyone particular come to mind who'd volunteer for the job as my watchman?"

"Well, I am between jobs right now, so to speak. I'd look out for you like nobody else in the world. I hope you know you can trust me. You're the real reason I stayed here instead of going on with Irving and Sherrie. It just felt right; you, Beaufort, the season, everything since I got here. Kind of like destiny I guess. Can you tell I'm a hopeless romantic?"

"That makes two of us.

They watched the breakers roll in for an hour saying very little, just embracing, touching and daydreaming. "I'm going to try and remember this spot and paint it tomorrow."

"You're going to come back and change the color? It's so pretty like it is."

"No, you nut, a painting on canvas, you know, like Rembrandt, Da Vinci, Monet."

"Van Gogh?"

"Are you a Van Gogh fan?"

"You should be, you have the 'Van Gogh Touch.'"

"I'm touched, am I?"

"If my grandmother is right, you definitely are."

"How does Myrtle know I'm touched? I wanted her to think of me as normal. I was on my best behavior every time I was around her."

"She thinks you're wonderful. So do I."

"Just a little touched, huh?"

"I'll explain it to you later. We better start back. I don't want to be out sailing with no lights after dark. Somebody like Zed in a big trawler would think it was great fun to run over us."

"I promised to get you home safe. I'm a man of my word. Let's go."

They gathered up the picnic remnants and their clothes and started back to the sound side of the island. When they got back to the boat, the tide was out and the boat was resting on soggy sand, twenty feet from the receded water.

"This is great. I've got to push it out to the water. Between the lighthouse and this, I won't be able to bend over tomorrow."

The sun was starting its decline in the western sky. The boat was heavy and the moving slow. They'd be lucky to get home before dark. He grabbed the anchor line and secured it to a cleat on the bow of the boat. He then put the anchor back up under the deck, looping the rope over his shoulder. With much strain, he pulled it forward while Sarah pushed the craft from behind. Foot by foot, they slowly progressed toward the water. It took them almost an hour to get it in the water again.

Once the boat started floating, they got in, raised the sails and pointed toward Beaufort. The wind was brisk and they moved

WIDOW WALK 137

quickly. The sense of urgency excited Alan and he continuously trimmed the sail to keep the little boat at maximum speed. The heeling didn't bother Sarah by now and she coaxed him to make as much time as possible.

"I'm so embarrassed that I keep asking Jean to watch Grandmother and then come home late. We're going to be two or three hours late. If this was a fishing boat, we'd have a radio and the marine operator could call the house for me. I hope they're not worried about us."

"If this wind stays with us, you'll only be an hour late. They'll think we got back before dark and stopped for a little adult entertainment before going home. I guarantee you Myrtle was a real pistol in her day. She won't be worried. Relax. Enjoy the view. There's nothing prettier than watching the sun go down from the deck of a boat."

Sarah slid in close beside Alan and got comfortable. "I'm a worry wart, aren't I?"

"You're perfect."

Through the darkening water and sky, the little ship took its crew home. An approaching ship at sundown was a sight Taylor Creek had witnessed a thousand times before and yet each was more beautiful than the one before.

The freshening breeze, coupled with the withdrawing light, was adding a chill to the evening. He pulled Sarah close beside him, cradling her head against his shoulder. He watched the lights of shore grow larger and brighter as they progressed toward their destination. As they got a mile or so away, he could see the anchor lights of sailboats in the harbor, and occasionally the red and green running lights of a late arrival coming into Taylor Creek. Boats making harbor late at night had to anchor out, then wait until morning to get a slip assigned to them by the dock master. Before long, the docks loomed large as they hit the last stretch of water before completing their day's journey.

"Sarah, we're home. Wake up, we made it."

She was sound asleep. The time had passed in the wink of an eye. It was dark. A light fog was starting to form. Alan was glad that it waited until they were back before appearing. Without instruments, a fog could make navigation almost impossible. Their only course would have been to anchor out all night. Otherwise, they could strike a piling or even get disoriented and head out to open water. "Let's hurry, I know they're worried."

Alan tied up the sail on the boom and secured the boat to the landing dock where they had boarded that morning. They walked quickly down the street to Sarah's house. As they approached, they could hear Myrtle and Jean inside teasing and laughing like two teenagers. They eavesdropped at the door for just a moment. "I know where they are too. The darkest spot on the dock. If I was twenty, that's where I'd be. The last time I was down there, I found where my name was carved into the pilings in more than one spot."

"Myrtle, you're a card. I wish I could've seen you then, I bet you were something."

"I was indeed. I knew every back road, dirt lane, dance hall and beer joint in the county by the time I was seventeen. Those were great days, Jean. I still remember them, just like yesterday. They're some of the best memories I have. And don't think I've forgotten about you and that wild Lenny Moore you went with. Your mother almost died that time you stayed gone for two days."

"I almost died when I got back. You're right though, Myrtle. Those were the days, just like the song says. You know something though? I didn't ever feel like we weren't safe then. Today, I worry just crossing the street. And all this recent mess here, what's the world coming to?"

"I'm glad I won't be here to see, Jean. I just don't know where it's all going, but it sure doesn't look very good now."

Alan nudged Sarah and whispered. "Sounds like they're really missing us, doesn't it?"

"They get along so well, I just feel bad about not doing what I say, even if they don't mind."

They knocked, then Sarah quickly unlocked the door and they entered. "I'm sorry, I'm sorry. Jean, I just can't be trusted, can I?"

"Your grandmother and I were just saying you should enjoy every moment you can when you're young. These will be the good old days for you one day. Appreciate it while they're here. You haven't kept me from a thing. When I get home I haven't got

a thing to do but feed the cat and get ready to go to work in the morning. Did you have a nice time? The weather was gorgeous, wasn't it?"

"It was a beautiful day. Sailing was fun. He didn't turn us over like I thought. We spent the whole day on the sound and over at the bight. It was wonderful."

"Sarah, we've all spent days over there with boyfriends when we were young. The hardest part is leaving to come back home. I certainly made many a footprint in the sand on the beach there. I think one day, I might even get one of the boys at the grill to take me back over there on a shrimper; let me spend the day there while they work. Then they could pick me up on the way home. I haven't been there in years. I'd like to go back and look around. Lots of great times over there, yes sir. Well, I'll run along now. Get Myrtle to tell you how she cheats at rummy, will you? I don't know how she does it; I just know she's cheating."

Myrtle spoke up. "Jean, I never saw such a poor loser. Next time, you can shuffle and deal every hand. I'll still whup you!"

"Goodnight, everybody. See you tomorrow." Jean left Alan and Sarah in the front room with Myrtle.

Alan felt a little guilty for keeping Sarah out so long. "Myrtle, you know Sarah fussed at me all the way back for making her so late again. It's all my fault. I accept the blame and the responsibility. If someone has to suffer, let it be me."

"Sarah, where did you say this fella was from? I haven't heard such malarkey since Herb Peterman got caught in bed with that sissy little guy that used to deliver the mail." She laughed out loud just remembering what had occurred many years ago.

"He's from up North, New York, Grandmother, and I'm afraid you're right. He's subject to say or do 'most anything."

"That's good in a man sometimes, Sarah, but a smart woman can always tell when her man isn't being straight with her. You just remember that, young man."

"I promise. Next time we go sailing, you're coming with us. Then we can stay as long as we want."

"Over my dead body."

"Well said, Myrtle. I guess I better be leaving. I want to go back and straighten up the boat a little before the dock master sees it. I left the sails just lashed to the boom. He might not let me use it again if I don't get it shipshape before morning. See you both tomorrow. Breakfast at Sam's, Sarah?"

"Seven o'clock. Don't be late."

"You can count on me."

Alan left into the night. Sarah went over to her grandmother and gave her a hug. "Thank you for being so sweet. I know it's pretty late."

"Baby, there's nothing you will ever do more important than finding the right man, if you want one at all. A little getting to know each other now can save years of getting away from each other later. Take your time and find out what he's really like. As I recall, getting to know your grandfather was quite a bit of fun. Come on. Play me a couple hands of rummy before bedtime. I'll show you how to win every time. You mostly need quick hands."

"Myrtle! You don't really cheat?"

"Don't have a conniption fit! We were only playing for pennies!"

10

Dark was the only word to describe the night. There was an occasional burst of light at sea beyond the horizon. It could have been the reflection of the powerful beams from the lighthouse or summer lightning offshore. There was a slight mist in the air. The cool nights often resulted in a fog by morning. Throughout the night it would build. Sometimes you couldn't see ten feet in front of you. By late morning, the sun would burn through and the process would start over again.

Only the most observant passerby could notice any difference along the waterfront. The contingents of police and detectives had taken positions along the roads and alleys leading to the two most frequented taverns on Front Street. The trap was set. Many hours had gone into setting it up and all those involved awaited the approaching nightfall with nervous anticipation and some queasiness. They were professionals and prepared to face whatever was required, but even professional ballplayers get butterflies before a big game. What they hadn't planned for, was the thick covering of fog settling down on the entire town. It was so thick that a street light less than a hundred feet away was invisible. Such a cover would hinder the apprehension of a suspect should he sense a trap and start to run. Along the west end of Front Street, at the farthest checkpoint set up for the night's business, two barely visible figures leaned back against the side of an unlit shop. They waited in the alley separating it from the next store on the waterfront.

Don Ellingwood lit a cigarette as he spoke with Sheriff Stone. "Don't smoke do you, Morris? I didn't either 'til I got involved in things like these killings. The waiting bothers me more than anything. Waiting for a clue, a tip or, God forbid, another victim. I hope the son of a bitch goes for this. We've covered everything I could think of and some things I didn't. We're about as prepared as we can get. If he strikes our target, we'll get him. I feel certain of it."

"I hope you're right. I would just as soon have the town back the way it was. Quiet is fine with me. I don't like all this. You people up in the big cities are probably used to it, but it burns my ulcer. I never even wanted to be in this whole line of work."

"That right? What did you want to do?"

"I always thought I'd wind up running a charter boat like my old man. I used to work as crew for him during the summer. Take the rich folks out fishing. The ones that didn't get drunk got seasick, and plenty got both. But then some days the ocean would be calm, the kings would start hitting and let me tell you, those were special days. Not just because we got big tips and caught a lot of fish. I guess it was just because I was with my old man, helping him do what he loved. Anyway, he started drinking pretty heavy as he got older. He lost the boat and my mother just got tired of it all and left one day. I've had a bunch of different jobs, but in the back of mind, I just knew I'd get me a boat one day and be just like my old man. I wouldn't drink it all away though. I've seen enough of that to last two lifetimes. Anyway, I signed on as a deputy thinking I would stay just long enough to save money for a boat. I've stayed too long I guess. Cost me my wife and the boat.

You know how you start driving and looking out the car window and wind up somewhere? That's how I got to be Sheriff. I get along well with most folks and they keep re-electing me. Guess I'll retire doing it. I'm only a few years away from it now. Maybe I'll get a boat then. I know one thing; I don't want to get shot by some wild man, not with just a few years to go. I want this maniac out of my town. Let's get him tonight. I could shoot the bastard myself for what he did to those girls."

"It's nine-forty. Everybody's in place. The decoys have been in the bars for two hours. If our guy is watching, they should have established themselves as legitimate by now. One will leave at ten and head our way. If no one approaches her, she'll go back to the tavern like she lost her keys. She'll remain there 'til she gets a signal that the other female officer, who'll leave the second club at ten-thirty, has made it safely to her checkpoint. Either gets approached, we watch for several minutes to make sure it's a hit, and we move in. We'll try to get him before he can get a firm hold on the officer. Their first move will be to get clear so we don't wind up with a hostage situation. These officers know their stuff. If he gets tough with them, he's liable to wind up with his nuts in his throat. You okay, Morris?"

"Yeah. Give me a cigarette."

"You don't smoke."

"I do now."

"Just stay calm. This is a well set trap. We're in control here."

"I wish I was as sure about it as you are. This damn fog bothers me. Can't see your hand in front of your face. How in the devil will we see anybody following them?"

"It's certainly not what I'd hoped for, but the women are miked. We'll hear anything that happens immediately. They'll never be more than a few yards from help. It makes it just that much harder for our man to spot us too. That could be to our benefit. There's a lot of people out here with our team.

The first female officer, Virginia Davis, left the bar at exactly ten o'clock. Using the concealed microphone, sewn into her blouse, she indicated to the backup crew she was preparing to exit the club so they would be ready. At the door, she made out with the male officer working undercover with her.

"You sure you won't come home with me, baby?" she asked him. "I'll be so lonely and cold without you."

"I would if I could, doll. My old lady is at home waiting on me. She's already gonna kill me. How 'bout next Saturday night? I'll meet you here at nine next Saturday."

"No promises, lover boy. I get a better offer, I'm gone. Night, night." She swung her purse over her shoulder. With her overdone makeup and tight skirt, she had certainly dressed for the part. She made her way slowly from the club toward the street. She walked behind the cars parked with their front bumpers into the curb. This meant she was partly out in the street. There was no traffic, other than an occasional car leaving a nightspot. The parked cars all appeared to belong to revelers remaining in the bars. It was also a little darker on that side of the cars, as it was further away from the fog-encased street lights at the end of each block. The darkness would make it more tempting. With the fog that had settled heavily on the town, her backup was straining to keep a close eye on her. She pretended to stagger as if she'd had too much to drink. Occasionally, she whispered into the hidden mike in her blouse, so they'd all know she was still alone. Morris nervously looked at his watch. Through the fog they couldn't see her at all. There were others much closer to her, as he and Ellingwood were at the far end of Front Street.

"How far has she gotten?" he asked Ellingwood.

"About half way. No action yet."

The minutes ticked by like hours. Finally, they heard the click of high heels as she made it to the end of the street and turned into the parking lot by the bank, where they were waiting.

"Trawler is docked," Ellingwood whispered into his mike.

"Five minutes 'til the tide turns." The nautical jargon had been decided on in case anyone's dialogue was somehow overheard. It would sound like a marine radio with fishing boats communicating to each other. Morris asked Ellingwood, "You know, don't you, shrimpers and fishermen don't use all that formal talk on the radio? Half of what they say is cursing and the other half is about how much beer they have on board."

"It's still better than police call numbers; I don't know what half of them mean. I can understand 'the tide turned' better than 'the seven-o-two has ten-ninety-nined.'"

"I see what you mean. How long have you been doing this?"

"Believe it or not, this was my first choice. I was a psychology major in college. Got my Master's at Duke. Did my thesis on deviant behavior. I was always fascinated by the criminal mind. What makes them do the horrible things they do? What causes them to start these bizarre acts? These types of individuals have been around a long time, probably as long as man has. It just seems that in the last twenty years, there's been an explosion in their numbers. If we can understand where they're coming from, maybe we could get a handle on preventing some of them. I've worked on some cases that would make this guy look like a Sunday school teacher. No matter how different the crimes they commit are, all serial killers have common stimuli they work from. That's why they send in somebody like me to help catch them. We understand their mindset to some extent. Not totally, but enough to give us an edge in dealing with them.

An officer's voice came over the radio. "Last boat underway." Morris felt his ulcer heat up. His pulse was racing and he wished he were doing anything but this. Officer Beekins did a similar version of Sgt. Davis' club departure. Backup thought she put more into it than Davis. As she exited the club, she turned in the opposite direction and walked away from Morris and Ellingwood toward the other end of Front Street. Less than a block from the club, she heard footsteps behind her.

"Fish on line," went from radio to radio. Backup officers steadied themselves and prepared to move. Nervous fingers checked the snaps on holsters.

"Twenty feet and on course."

"Ten feet and on course."

"Approaching target."

Deborah felt his hand on her shoulder. She turned to face her intruder. He was larger than expected. Her mind raced, concluding quickly that she could not handle him on her own.

"What do you want?" she asked him.

"I want you to stop and spend some time with me." He reached out to put his arms on her shoulders. She could see he was strong. Deborah waited until she was sure he had a firm grasp on her. Instinctively, she kneed him in the groin. He moaned and released his grip, doubling over.

"You stupid bitch. I'm gonna kill you." But, before he could move a muscle, there were police officers all over him. Squad cars sped in with blue lights flashing. Several large, well-trained officers pulled his arms behind his back, shoved him on the ground face first and cuffed him. An immediate frisking produced no weapon. This fact put a cloud over everyone's optimism as it was a break in the pattern of the previous attacks. They all knew it was a bad sign. In short order, he was read his rights, shoved into a squad car and hurried to the police station.

Morris and Ellingwood were waiting in the lobby when officers brought him in. As they walked the prisoner past him, Ellingwood looked him over. He turned to Sheriff Stone. "It's not our guy."

"How can you tell?"

"Dressed wrong. The biggest thing on this guy's mind is making sure his clothes all have the right labels on them. He's wearing beach sandals. Our man would never wear anything that he couldn't get away in. Can't run in those. He's even got his sunglasses on a neck-cord and he reeks of alcohol. Couldn't be him."

Notwithstanding Ellingwood's appraisal, he was printed, strip searched and taken into the booking room for questioning. Ellingwood fired questions at him.

"Your driver's license says you're Frank Underwood. That correct?"

"Yes, sir. What did I do? I swear I didn't hurt that girl; I don't care what she says. Hell, you guys were on me before I could even think of what to say."

"How long have you been in Beaufort?"

"Since yesterday. I came with a group from Winston-Salem, to fish and party a little. I ain't done nothin' wrong. Hell, I didn't get back in from fishing 'til dark and I was at the club ever since then, drinking beer and dancing. Ask anybody there."

"We will. Have you been here before yesterday?"

"Last year, we went fishing here then. The same guys were with me. Ask them."

An officer walked into the station with two other men in his company. They weren't police. They spotted the suspect. "Frank, what's going on?"

"You tell me. I think they had a fake whore or something to catch guys with. But I never propositioned her or nothing. Next thing I know, she kicked me in the nuts and these guys pinned me to the ground. I'm never coming back to this fucking place."

Morris looked at Don and both shook their heads.

"You can go. I'd be real careful about approaching women after dark though, Mr. Underwood. You could wind up a victim yourself."

"Would I be treated any worse than this?"

"I could take you to the county morgue and show you, but you probably wouldn't get the point. Go on home."

"You'll see me again, with my attorney. You're not going to get away with this."

"You do that, Mr. Underwood. The twenty or so undercover officers that were watching you would probably be glad to corroborate the charges of public nuisance, assault on a female, public intoxication, insulting an officer and, with the mood we're all in, probably jaywalking. Now get the hell out of here before you wind up spending the night behind bars."

Morris was more than a little dismayed at seeing this side of Ellingwood for the first time. Underwood left quickly with his friends, mumbling about what a shitty town Beaufort was.

Morris questioned Ellingwood. "What now? If the real killer was watching, I'm sure he knows what the score is. He'll probably just leave and I can't say I'd be unhappy about it."

"Let's get the crew tucked in and go get some coffee. Anything open all night around here?"

"There's several places in Morehead. Only takes a couple minutes to get there."

"Fine. I'll walk back down to Front Street and let everybody go home except your on-duty guys. You mind picking me up down there?"

"Be there to get you in a half hour. I'll pick you up in front of Sam's."

Ellingwood hustled out the door. Morris radioed to the officers still in the field that all were dismissed except those on night duty. By the time he arrived to pick up Ellingwood, both were tired and as frustrated as they had been since starting the chase for the killer. They drove silently through the fog enshrouded streets, over the Beaufort Bridge, to Morehead City. Morris turned into an all-night diner he knew. Inside were a few tourists, either coming or going from the beach at a late hour. As they entered, a Morehead cop passed on his way out. "Sheriff Stone, sorry about tonight. I heard it over the radio. You guys will get him. Don't let it get you down. See you later."

"I wish I were as confident of that as he is."

They found a booth at the rear, sat down and Morris ordered an early breakfast.

"The food here is always good, Don. Try the breakfast special."

The waitress stood by as Ellingwood pondered.

"Alright, you talked me into it. I didn't feel much like a meal, but maybe it will pick me up a little." The waitress turned silently and left them alone.

"There's one thing all these serial killers have in common, Morris."

"What's that?"

"They are forced by the compulsion that drives them to start with, to virtually re-enact their methods every time. Usually, it's their downfall. The bad news is sometimes a lot of people die before the pattern works against them enough to solve the puzzle."

"You think this guy is out of here after tonight?"

"Either that or he may flaunt his success with one last slap in our face. He feels invincible. In his sick mind, he feels he's doing something worthwhile to start with, and the virtue of his actions, if you will, protect him. To him, we're the bad guys."

"You really believe all that?"

"As weird as it seems, it generally turns out to be the case."

After a few minutes, the waitress brought their food out. They continued their discussion while they ate. Neither felt like sleep right then, anyway. "What now? Do we send everyone back to their home offices in the morning, or wait a while to see if it's over?"

"I think I'm gonna hold everyone for just a couple of days. He knows we've got help now, so that's not the issue. We can get more people checking out virtually everyone in town. We can pinpoint any possible suspect as being here throughout the time period of both killings. I'm gonna call Raleigh in the morning and see what progress they've made on similar killings elsewhere. Maybe something will turn up. I sure don't want to give up on this yet."

"One thing's for sure, if it happens again, the people in town are going to be on my ass and I really don't blame them. We're supposed to prevent this shit from happening."

"You know as well as I do, Morris, that's a lot easier said than done. Until we get some solid leads, we're depending on luck. Bad luck for him; good luck for us. You about ready to get back? I think I could sleep a couple of hours now. I'm beginning to wear out. You could use some too. We'll start again in the morning. Come on. Let's head back."

They walked out of the diner and got into Morris' squad car. They said very little on the way back to Beaufort. Both men were deep in thought and fatigued from a long, disappointing day. As they drove back into Beaufort, the fog was literally blanketing the town. They were the only ones still out that late. Morris pulled into the lot beside Ellingwood's car and he slid out the door slowly. "My back is killing me. Guess I'm not as able to stay out all night as I used to. My age must be showing. Thanks for all your help, Morris. I'll see you at the office at seven tomorrow morning." He fumbled for the keys to his car, finally getting the correct one in the door and opening it. He sat down and decided to contact the State Police office on his car radio.

"State regional office, this is Don Ellingwood in Beaufort. Was there any late word left with you from the Raleigh office for me? They said they would leave a message with you if they had worked up any leads."

The desk sergeant answered back negatively. "Thanks anyway, Sergeant. If anything breaks, have someone come wake me. I don't care how small it is. I'll be at Sheriff Stone's office by seven."

"Yes, sir. Will do. Desk watch, out."

Don leaned back in his seat and stretched his aching back. He was so tired, he contemplated sleeping where he was. It was then he felt the presence of someone in the back seat. His mind immediately pictured the killer, pissed off and ready to slit his throat. He swallowed hard and then turned to confront his fears. Seeing the shadow in the back seat, he virtually screamed, "Who are you? What do you want?"

No reply, no movement. In semi-terror, he opened his door to get the overhead light on and himself out if necessary. There, propped up against the rear seat window was a woman, her face lifeless and ashen white. Her clothes were torn enough so that he could see the mutilations on her chest. She was bloodied and bruised. "That low-life bastard."

He picked up his radio and switched to the local police channel. "Sheriff Stone, do you read me. Are you there, Stone?"

"This is Stone. That you, Ellingwood? You too tired to..."

Ellingwood cut in, "Get the hell back here quick. The son of a bitch did it again. He left the body in my car."

Morris wheeled his car around and floored it. He didn't use the siren or lights as the town was asleep and the streets empty. No need to alert the town to what they would all know by sunrise anyway. In seconds he was back beside Ellingwood's vehicle. He jumped out and ran to the back seat. Ellingwood asked him. "This one looks familiar to me. You know her?"

"My God. It's Jean. From the grill. She doesn't fit the pattern at all. Why her?"

"We messed up his plans. He's showing us he's disgusted with us. He knew this was my car. He knew I left with you. He watched everything. He must have thought I was leaving the car here overnight. Hell, he's probably watching us now for that matter."

Morris knew Jean well. He reached to her forehead carefully and brushed the hair out of her eyes. He thought how badly everyone in town was going to be hurt by this. She was a good and well-loved person. He started to pull back when he heard it, a faint breath, a slight gasp.

"Jesus, Don, she's not dead. Get help here quick!"

Ellingwood grabbed his car mike.

"Highway Patrol, Highway Patrol, this is Ellingwood, answer me, damn-it!"

"Yes, sir. This is Sgt. Worley. What can I do for you, sir?"

"Did the chopper crew return to Raleigh this evening?"

"No, sir. They got fogged in. They're at a motel just down the road. You need them? I can have someone wake them."

"Listen to me. Wake them up and have them call me on the radio immediately. Do it quick!"

"Yes sir. There's a car on the way."

The minutes ticked by like hours. Suddenly, the chopper pilot was on the radio. "Ellingwood, this is Captain West. What's the problem?"

"Captain, we've got a critically wounded woman over here on Front Street. He got her after we shut down. If we can save her, we might have a witness. Is it too fogged in to try it? We don't want a chopper crash too. What do you think? It's totally your call. I understand if it's too risky, but I need an answer right now."

"I understand. Do you have any flare guns over there?"

Ellingwood looked at Morris for this information.

"Tell him we will before he gets airborne."

"Affirmative, Captain West. Are we a go?"

"We'll be overhead in ten minutes. Stand by on this channel."

"Will do. Morris, let's get a rescue unit over here on the double to stabilize her. Also, we'll need at least four guys with flashlights to give them the corners of a clear landing area. Where are those flare guns?"

"I've got a key to the marine hardware store. Here, you run down there and get what you need. I'll stay here with Jean and get up with everybody."

"Okay. I'm gone. Back in one minute."

Morris looked into Jean's eyes. They were dilated and trying to roll back into her head. Her breathing was so faint that it seemed that any breath would be her last. There was already a huge amount of blood on her clothing and on the seat of the car. He and Ellingwood had only been gone for about an hour. If the chopper could just get her to a hospital quick enough, she might stand a chance. Her color was fading and he felt that her odds were diminishing quickly. "Hold on, Jean. Can you hear me?"

There was a slight groan. Maybe she knew he was with her. "Help is on the way. You hold on, Jean. You're going to make it. This is Morris, Jean. Just hang on a little while."

The radio frequency came alive on the waterfront as officers were called in to the scene, as well as the calls requested by Ellingwood. In spite of their wishes, the dock was crawling with locals and tourists. Soon the chopper could be heard overhead. Sheriff Stone directed his men to outline the landing area by standing outside of it with their flashlights. Other officers did their best to clear the entire area. The rescue vehicle came screaming up at almost the same moment. Morris was hoping the extreme measures might save her. Not only was she a friend, but hopefully a witness. This horrible act could be their break. The ambulance crew rushed to her. The crew chief looked her over quickly and yelled to his two assistants. "IV gear, plasma, compresses. At least six stab wounds. Move!"

Morris couldn't help but ask. "Does she have any chance?"

"Until they stop breathing, they have a chance. Depends on how long she's been bleeding and if any organs were cut."

"Ellingwood from the SBI office said the killer's pattern is to avoid quick kill wounds. He lets them bleed to death."

"If that's the case, she may have a chance. Move away. Alright, let's lift her carefully to the stretcher."

That done, they strapped her securely onto the stretcher and waited for the helicopter to attempt the blind landing.

Captain West's voice came over the radio. He was asking for Don Ellingwood, who had already returned, flare gun in hand.

"This is Air Two. Do you copy, Mr. Ellingwood?"

"I do. We're standing by at the landing area. We've got officers standing at each corner with a flashlight. I've got the flare gun. What do you need me to do?"

"We're really landing blind here. I won't see the flashlights 'til we're almost down. You get in the dead center of the landing zone and fire the flare gun twice. Make sure you aim it straight up. I'm going to follow that path back down. Wait ten seconds between shots."

"Affirmative, Captain West. Are you ready?"

"We are standing by. Fire when you're set. After the second shot, get the hell out of there 'cause I'll be coming straight down on top of you if you don't."

Ellingwood fired the first flare. He waited the proper length of time and shot the second straight into the fog shrouded sky and quickly moved back out of the way.

"We have you spotted. Clear out of the zone. Have your corner people pull back as we get close."

"I copy. Good luck."

The noise from the chopper grew louder and stronger. Before long, the glow from its red lights was radiating throughout the foggy parking lot that had become an airfield. As if there was nothing out of the ordinary involved, the chopper set down gently. There was no time for celebrating. Captain West exited the craft and jogged over to where Ellingwood and Morris were waiting. Ellingwood spoke first. "Captain West, that was an amazing landing. How bad will it be getting out of here?"

"Compared to that, a piece of cake."

"That's good news. Are you ready to put her onboard?"

"Whenever she's ready. We're taking her to Greenville, the Medical Center. Right?"

"That's right. They have a helipad there."

"Used it many times. We'll have her there in thirty minutes. Have the staff at the hospital ready for her."

"You can count on it."

They walked over to where the emergency crew was treating Jean. She had been stabilized for the flight. They moved her into the side door of the helicopter. The pilot had not shut down the engine. It was ready for departure, its blades still turning. Two rescue EMTs got in with her. One held the IV bag over her; the other secured an oxygen mask to her face. An officer shut the door to the chopper and in rapid order they lifted off, flying to the University Medical Center in Greenville. The Medical Center was one of only a few in the state to have a trauma unit. They thought Jean's chances would be greater there than at any closer hospital. The time needed to get there, by air was not much more than it took to get to the smaller hospitals. The chopper's lights and droning motor disappeared quickly in the foggy mist. Morris was proud of the courage his fellow officers from all over the state had shown. On a clear day, such a rescue would take great skill and expertise, but at night and in such a fog, it was nothing short of miraculous. The already-long night was about to get much longer. Ellingwood organized the crew. "Listen up. Seal off two blocks around the vehicle. I don't want to see anybody, and I mean anybody, in this area 'til dawn, and then they better be wearing blue. Get a generator and some portable floodlights out here now." He called to a particular officer he knew well and trusted. "J.D.?"

"Right here, sir."

"Call Greenville PD. Tell them we want two uniformed officers by the victim's hospital door around the clock. You get in the car and get up there now. We'll send your stuff up tomorrow. Call Stone's office at seven and tell Esther what you want. This woman can possibly identify the man we're looking for. He's

killed at least two others, so there's a good possibility he might try
to go after her. See to it that's not possible. Do you completely
understand the situation?"

"Yes, sir. I do."

"Then get on the road. Call me on the State Police frequency
when you get her secured, or, if there's any problem at all. Now
move!" A new sense of hope was present in Ellingwood's voice.
They would work around the clock, as long as necessary to follow
up on every possible lead. Even Morris, who already liked
Ellingwood, could not help but admire his drive and dedication.
He was certainly the right man for the job. Morris approached him
and put his arm on his shoulder. "You're going to get this guy. I
really believe you are."

"We're going to, Morris. We're going to do it together. Listen,
how about first thing in the morning, try and backtrack Jean's
whereabouts for the last twenty-four hours. As friendly as she is
and as well known, there's a good chance someone might have
spoken with her, or seen her prior to the attack. I'm pretty certain
she was not his intended victim, just like you said. Try and find
out what she was doing out alone that late, and who saw her last.
Someone might have noticed somebody watching or walking
behind her."

"I'll handle it myself first thing in the morning. What can I help
you with now?"

"Let's just go over to my car. Shit. Do you believe that? My
car? Whoever this guy is, he's a brazen son of a bitch. I'll say
that."

Both men worked until sunrise. The car was dusted as carefully
as possible for fingerprints. Investigators vacuumed it several
times and saved the contents of the bags to be examined by the lab
in Raleigh. Blood samples were taken, to make sure that all that

was found belonged to Jean. Perhaps she cut or scratched her attacker. No evidence would be overlooked. Ellingwood was extremely thorough. He personally supervised every aspect of the investigation. Morris could see that not only was he an expert in these matters, but he had the look of a driven man. This was more to him than a way to make a living. Maybe it was the challenge. Maybe it was the hunt. Whatever the reason, he was becoming obsessed with finding the killer. It might be, he reasoned, this was just what it took to apprehend a criminal of this nature.

As in the previous attacks, no clues were found at the scene. If Jean didn't survive or couldn't remember what occurred, they'd be no closer to solving the case than they had been. Ellingwood couldn't get one thought off his mind. Did the killer really know this was his car? He felt certain he did. If that was the case, what should that tell him? How much about him did the killer know? This meant, at the very least, he'd made contact with the killer at some point. But where? How? His mind would be dominated by these questions until the puzzle was solved.

They decided to go home for a couple of hours of sleep and clean up. The next twenty-four hours would be rough and without some rest, they knew they'd be too exhausted to be as thorough as was needed. With the events of the evening still rambling around in his brain, Morris couldn't help but feel someone was watching him as he got into his car and drove to his house. Even when he arrived and got out of his car, he couldn't shake this feeling. He began to feel he must know the killer. He felt too close to the matter to disregard the feeling. He couldn't if he tried.

* * *

Sarah was in the shower and Myrtle still in bed, when Sheriff Stone began knocking on their door. "Just a minute, please. Just a minute. I'm coming." Still in her housecoat, hair dripping wet, she answered the door. She was surprised to see Morris standing at her door. She could see the exhaustion in his face. The dark circles under his eyes and the worry on his brow spoke loudly of fatigue. "Sheriff Stone, what's happened? Is everything all right?"

"No, it's not, Sarah. Jean Byrd was assaulted late last night."

"Oh no! Is she okay?"

"She's just barely alive. She's in critical condition at the University Medical Center. We're all pulling for her, but it was bad. She was stabbed several times and lost a lot of blood. The next twenty-four hours will tell if she's going to make it or not."

At this news, Sarah felt too weak to stand. She grabbed hold of the doorknob to help balance herself. Her mind was in a panic trying to grasp what had happened. "Let's stay out on the porch, Sheriff. I don't want my grandmother to hear this yet. I'll think about how to tell her later. Do you think it was the same person that attacked the other women?"

"We're fairly certain of it. All of the basic details are the same as in the other cases. I'm not able to tell you what they are but, trust me, it's the same guy. Sam said Jean told them at the grill she'd be spending Sunday with Myrtle. That right?"

"Yes sir. I spent the day with a friend. We sailed to Cape Lookout. Jean stayed with her for me. I feel awful. If we hadn't been so late getting back, it would never have happened."

"You don't know that, Sarah, and if it hadn't been Jean, it would've been someone else you knew, more than likely. What's important here is that we find this person quickly, before it happens again. Who were you with yesterday?"

"Alan Kelly."

"Isn't that one of the men from the sailboat that Zed's had so many problems with?"

"All because of Zed. Sheriff Stone, you know how he can be."

"I do. Did Jean stay here until you and Mr. Kelly returned from sailing?"

"Yes sir. When we got back, she was in a good mood and said she was going to go straight home. She left just a few minutes after we got back."

"Did Mr. Kelly leave with her?"

"No sir. He stayed here with me for a while after she left."

"How long is a while?"

"Probably five, yes, at least five minutes."

"I would like to talk with Mr. Kelly. Will you see him today?"

"Yes sir. Do you want me to tell him to go to the station and talk with you?"

"If you don't mind."

"I'll tell him, but Mr. Stone..."

"Yes?"

"I've gotten to know Alan and I promise you that he had nothing to do with hurting anyone. He's a very kind, decent person and I know he couldn't do anything like this."

"I'm sure that's the case, Sarah, but we have to talk with everyone in the area, just a necessary precaution. Did he know Jean?"

"They had met and spoken to each other a couple times at the house and she waits on us when we go to the grill. He likes her. He'll be very upset when he hears what happened."

"Well, have him come by if you will, Sarah. I'll be at the office after lunch all afternoon talking with people. Thanks a lot."

"If you hear anything about Jean, let me know right away, please."

"You know I will, Sarah. See you later."

"Thank you, Sheriff Stone."

Morris left the house and Sarah walked back inside. The only thing that could have bothered her more than the terrible news about Jean was that Sheriff Stone considered Alan a suspect. She knew he couldn't have any connection to the attack and put it from her mind. She turned and there was Myrtle. "What did Morris need, Sarah?"

"Oh, Grandmother." She embraced her. This would be hard for Myrtle. Jean was almost like a daughter to her.

"Jean was attacked when she left here last night. She's in the hospital."

Myrtle, stunned, placed her hand over her heart, let go of her walker and dropped to the couch.

"Not Jean. Who would hurt her? Everyone loves her."

"They don't know who did it, Grandmother. They said it was the same person that stabbed those other two women."

"She's not going to die…"

"No. Morris said she's going to be okay."

Sarah overstated Jean's condition. This might give Myrtle time to be prepared in case she didn't make it. Her age seemed to show more after this shock than anytime Sarah could recall. She repeatedly kept asking the same questions.

"Is Jean all right? Did you say she would be back tomorrow? How did you say she got hurt?"

Each time, Sarah would patiently answer her grandmother. She went to the kitchen and fixed her a cup of hot tea. She gave it a small shot of the peach brandy that Myrtle sometimes used to help her sleep. Perhaps it would settle her nerves. She stayed with her for a while and comforted her. Floyd would understand under the circumstances, if the shop opened late.

Sarah went through the motions all morning at the shop. She was there but her mind and heart were elsewhere. Customers came and left without so much as a "may I help you?" from her. All the events of the day before, followed by such a tragic turn that night, left her dazed. She remembered that Myrtle always told her, "Everything works out for the best," and it would be the case this time. She would steel herself and what would happen, would happen. By lunch time, Alan still hadn't shown up. She put the "gone to lunch" sign in the window and decided to try and find him.

After a short while, she noticed him on the far end of the boardwalk. He was painting a portrait of Joan Moore, Dr. Moore's wife. As he was painting, David and Jenny, who were there with their mother, kept teasing him. They were picking flowers from the planters located between the boardwalk and the town's parking lot. They were bright yellow and plentiful. Jenny would pick them, run up to Alan and try to stick them in his hair. As Sarah approached, she could see several that had found their mark still sticking in his hair. The children were laughing and Alan and Mrs. Moore were enjoying watching them play. She saw Sarah approaching. "I can see why the kids love your friend here so much," she said to Sarah.

"How he can even concentrate enough to paint I'll never know. They've been picking at him for thirty minutes."

"Hi, Sarah. Sorry I couldn't go to breakfast this morning. I couldn't see well enough after dark to get the boat cleaned up like I wanted. I got up this morning and finished it."

Sarah didn't respond immediately. "Are you okay, Sarah?"

"You haven't heard about Jean then?"

"Is she mad at me for making you so late?"

"She's in the hospital. She was stabbed by that creep who's been attacking people. She's in critical condition, according to

Sheriff Stone. They're not sure if she's going to live." Sarah started to cry. Alan got up and hugged her.

"I'm so sorry, Sarah. Can we do anything to help her? Does she have any family? We could go to the hospital. Will they let people see her?"

"I don't think so. Not yet."

Mrs. Moore came over to them. "Sarah, I hadn't heard. Can I help you? How is Myrtle taking it?"

"I couldn't tell her how bad it is. I just hope she pulls through, so that I don't have to tell her anything worse."

She broke down and had a hard cry on Alan's shoulder. Mrs. Moore grabbed the kids. "You take care of Sarah, Alan. We can finish this another time. Sarah, let me know if I can do anything. If you need to go to the hospital, call me and I'll watch Myrtle for you."

Sarah, sobbing, replied. "Thank you. I will."

After a few moments, Sarah composed herself. Alan asked her, "Are you able to talk about it?"

"I don't know anything. Sheriff Stone said to ask you to go by his office this afternoon. He wants to talk with you. He said it was just a formality. He's talking to a lot of people to try and find any clues."

"I certainly can't help him. I don't know anything except what we all heard about the killings at Sam's. When did he want to see me?"

"Anytime today. He said he'd be talking with people all afternoon."

"Let me walk you back to the shop, then I'll go right over to see him. Would you like a drink, a sandwich or something before you go back?"

"No thanks. I couldn't eat anything. After you talk with Sheriff Stone, come straight back over and tell me what happened. Promise?"

"You know I will." Alan escorted her back to the shop. He watched her open back up and made sure she was under control before he went to see Sheriff Stone. Since he didn't have a car, he walked the four blocks to the station. He very rarely went to this part of town but it was apparent there were a lot more cars and people than was customary. He found the police station and walked in. It was small and crowded. Esther noticed him as he entered.

"Over here, sir. Over here. Who did you need to see?

"The Sheriff. He asked for me to come over and talk with him."

"Your name?"

"Alan Kelly."

"Okay, Mr. Kelly. There's quite a few ahead of you. If you can find a place to sit, I'll put your name on the list. He's seeing people in the order they came in. You can sit on the steps outside if there's no seat left. I'll get you when he's ready for you."

"Thank you. I'll be on the steps." He went back into the warm sunshine and sat down. It was becoming apparent; this would take the better part of the afternoon. Alan got a comfortable spot on the steps and laid back. His thoughts went back to the previous day at Cape Lookout with Sarah. He couldn't remember a better day in his life. It caused him to think seriously about their relationship. Was he ready to settle down? Would she want him to stay with her? What would his family think of her? He hadn't thought much about how things he did affected his family. Something this important would have bearing on them all. He loved his parents, though he'd seen very little of them since he'd gone away to school. He felt he should call them and make them aware of this turn in his life.

"Mr. Kelly. Mr. Kelly, are you awake?"

Alan had fallen asleep while waiting. The station was considerably less crowded than when he had arrived.

"The Sheriff can see you now. Follow me."

He stood and followed Esther to Sheriff Stone's office. Morris, looking more exhausted than before, was seated at his desk. As he spoke, his voice cracked and he took deep breaths, as if he'd just come back from a workout. He was a man in need of rest.

"Sheriff Stone, I'm Alan Kelly, Sarah's friend. You wanted to see me?"

"Yes Alan, I remember you. Come in and sit down."

The office was small and crowded. On the wall were several pictures of state dignitaries that Alan didn't recognize. The furniture appeared to be all military surplus, gray metal with Formica tops. This was not a big city operation. Alan sat in a metal folding chair, one of three placed in front of Morris' desk for the purpose of these interviews. "Thank you for coming over. I hope you haven't been waiting too long."

"No sir. I'm fine."

"How long have you known Sarah?"

"About a month. I came here on a sailboat and liked the town. I decided to spend the summer here."

"You're a painter, I understand. Quite good she tells me."

"I don't know how good, but I am a painter. I've been doing portraits and seascapes and selling them to the tourists."

"Where are you from? That is, where were you living before you came here?"

"I was born in New York City, but I went to college in Boston, and lived there for several years before I came here."

"Do you know Jean Byrd?"

"Yes, sir. I heard what happened and could hardly believe it. I just don't understand why anyone would hurt someone like Jean. She's such a sweet person."

Morris studied the young man carefully as he talked. He was seated quite erect with his hands resting on his lap while he talked. He was very forthright and polished, an intelligent individual. He was not large, but looked fit and athletic. He seemed sincere and unfazed by any of the questions. "Okay, as I understand it, you and Sarah spent the day sailing and Jean watched Sarah's grandmother while you were gone. That correct?"

"That's right. We got back about nine fifteen and she left about five minutes later. I probably should have walked her home but I just didn't think about it. I feel bad about not doing it."

"After Jean left Sarah's, how long before you left?"

"I guess a couple of minutes." For the first time, Alan sensed that he was being questioned more about himself than what he knew about the events surrounding the attacks.

I'm not a suspect, am I? You don't think I could do something that horrible do you?"

"I have to ask, Mr. Kelly. Somebody did it, and we can't afford to rule out anyone until we know for sure what happened. Do you have relatives still living in New York?"

"Yes, sir. My parents live there. Pearson Kelly. Here, I'll give you their phone number and address." He took a pen and paper off Morris's desk and wrote the information down.

"I realize you don't know me but I can tell you, I'm the last person you'd have to worry about hurting anyone."

"I hope that's the case, Alan. How can I get in touch with you here?"

"I don't have a phone, but I live upstairs above the Water Dragon. You can call Sarah there during the day, or come by after they close and knock on the back door. If I'm not there, I'll be at Sarah's."

"I'm certain you're smart enough to realize we'll be doing background checks on just about everyone around here we don't know. But just for the record, have you ever been arrested before? Do you have any prior convictions on anything besides traffic offenses?"

"My past is no secret, Sheriff Stone. I am certainly not a saint, but I've never been arrested at all, for any reason. I would be delighted for you to check on my background. You might find a surprise or two, but nothing of a criminal sort. I promise you."

"You understand that I have to ask everyone these questions, Mr. Kelly; I'm not singling you out at all. We're leaving no stone unturned until this case is solved. It's as simple as that."

"I understand completely, Sheriff. I would request that when, and if, you decide to single me out, you will give me a chance to call my attorney?"

"Of course. That's the law."

"That's correct, Sheriff Stone. It is the law. Is that all?"

Alan had gotten upset by the direction the questioning had taken. His abrupt replies showed this to Morris.

"Yes, that's all. For now at least. Thank you for coming by. By the way, you have a driver's license or picture ID?"

"Sure, I have a Massachusetts license."

"Give it to me for a moment so Esther can make a copy."

Morris left for a moment to make the copy. Alan gathered that because he was a stranger in town, he was automatically a suspect. Morris returned and handed him his license back.

"Thanks, Mr. Kelly. That's all for now. By the way, should you decide to leave town, you will see me first?"

"Absolutely. Believe me; I want to find the person who did this as badly as you do."

"Let's hope we do. Thank you for your time. Tell Sarah thank you for asking you to come by."

Alan left the station. He was upset over the notion that someone would suspect him of such a violent crime, especially of a friend. He reminded himself that Sheriff Stone really had no choice except to interrogate him. He would have done the same. Alan walked back to Front Street and over to Sam's. As he entered, he saw a hurriedly drawn poster and a jar sitting on the counter asking for donations to help Jean. He dug into his wallet and dropped ten dollars into the jar. It was already full and he had to push the folded bill in.

"Thanks, son," said Sam from behind the counter. She hasn't got any medical insurance. None of the girls here do. Neither do I for that matter. We're going to have to raise the money to pay her bills for her."

"That's okay," Alan said quietly. He walked over to an empty booth and sat down. Maureen came over and took his order. He could already feel the place wasn't quite the same without Jean. The grill was almost full, the customers all having the same conversation; speculating about the killer and his motives. Having struck such a beloved person in town, the locals were working themselves up into a furor over this most recent event. One voice started to drown out the others and Alan began to feel it being directed his way.

It was Zed once again, spewing his hatred for anyone not of his kind. He was talking louder than usual, trying to take advantage of the emotion of the moment. He wanted to help sway those within hearing range to his point of view about Alan. Undoubtedly some would be influenced, but most knew Zed. To most of the locals he was just a troublemaker. Zed got up from his booth and sauntered over to where Alan was sitting. With his hands on his hips and his head reared back for effect, he attempted to provoke him once again. "You see me. You know I'm talking about you, don't you, smartass? It's taking Sheriff Stone and those folks from Raleigh a while to figure this all out, but you and I know who killed those girls and stabbed Jean, don't we?"

"No, Zed, I don't know. Why do you think I would know anything you would know? I suspect the only common reading material we have is the tide chart and the funnies. What's your point?"

"That's right, try and smart mouth your way out of it. Where were you last night when Jean got stabbed? I know you were right there, weren't you? You reek of a weirdo."

"Zed, if I didn't know that everyone here realizes what a redneck idiot you are, I'd be offended by your stupid accusation. Just for the record so you'll know, I like Jean and if I knew who hurt her I'd go after him myself. So how about just turning around and minding your own business?"

Zed moved a step closer to Alan. His fists were now clinched; he was begging for any aggressive gesture from Alan, any indication he was ready to go at it. Sam stepped from behind the counter and in front of Zed. "I'm only going to tell you one time, Zed. You take another step toward him and I'm personally going to bust your thick skull open. You know, I was doing that around here while you were still pissing in your diapers. Now back up, go finish your coffee, or get out."

"Well Sam, it's real plain you're taking sides against the rest of the local folks here. I guess you got more to lose than a bunch of poor fishermen. But you hear what I'm saying. I think he did it and you'll see I'm right. You're taking up for the one that got Jean and them other girls. You'll see."

He turned and walked back to the two men he was sitting with when Alan entered. "Let's get out of here; the smell is getting too strong."

Sam held his position until they left. He turned to Alan. "I'm sorry about that. Don't worry about him. Nobody puts any stock in what he says. The rest of us here know you and Jean got along real fine. Folks from up north just set off some of the fisherman like Zed. They don't have much and resent the people who come here to have a good time. I guess it's just pure old jealousy."

"Thanks, Sam. You're a very wise man. If you hear any word about how Jean is doing, please tell me. I'm just as upset about all this as everyone else here."

"I don't doubt it for a minute."

Alan finished his meal. He was already too disturbed about the day's events to let Zed cause any further grief. He rested in the booth and had a refill on coffee. Stephen came in looking for him. A quick look around the place and he spotted his friend. He walked over to his booth and sat across from him. Maureen came over and to take his order. "Just a coffee please. And how about a piece of Key Lime pie? Any left?"

Maureen looked over to the dessert rack and nodded affirmatively.

"Okay sweetheart, go for it."

As she turned and walked off, Stephen spoke quietly across the table between them. "Alan, Zed and his sidekicks are outside. They're brandishing your name around pretty thick. Are they messing with you again?"

"He tried, but it's okay. There's a lot of Zeds in the world. With a little education he would have made a great attorney. I try not to think about people like him any more than necessary. What are you up to?"

"I just came back from talking to the Sheriff. He asked me a few questions about how long I'd known you and what I thought of you. He said he'd spoken with you earlier. Did it go poorly? The way he talked, it almost sounded like he suspects you. I couldn't believe it."

"What did you tell him?"

"The usual. I met you at Bellevue in New York. That as far as I knew, none of the charges against you had ever been substantiated. At least, none other than that time with the sixteen-year-old girl who later recanted her testimony."

"You nut. Please don't encourage any of these people. Zed has already said enough crap to get them thinking twice about me. If someone keeps saying the sky is falling long enough, some people will eventually start looking toward the sun."

"You know I'm just kidding. I told him you were a great guy and that you wouldn't harm a kitten. I think he believed me. So, guess what I'm doing?"

"What, I'm not up to twenty questions today."

"That storm is bearing down on the coast of North Carolina. The forecast predicts a straight path in this direction and it's picking up strength as it moves. I'm getting some plywood stored up and some power tools. If it keeps moving this way, in about two days they'll be boarding up this whole town. Some of the old timers say that when Donna and Hazel hit here years ago, it just about wiped out the whole county. All the streets were under water. The Atlantic went right over the barrier islands and started crashing in on the docks, like it was the ocean front. They say if it continues like it's doing now, all the docks on the waterfront will be unsafe. The yachts out here will have to be moved back to the creeks and anchored to weather the storm. There'll be plenty to do and some money to be made. You want to help me? We'll be partners."

"Let me get this straight. You're going to do physical labor for money? What's the punchline?"

"Hey, I enjoy working with my hands; you know, the feel of a stout board, a strong hammer and all that."

"You have been breathing the salt air a little too long. I could make more money selling pictures of you doing the work, than you're going to make doing it."

"Nevertheless, I'm going to try it for a while. Just blame the adventurer in me. Care to join me?"

"I appreciate it, Steve. Let me think about it overnight. I'm really in a rotten frame of mind today. I think some rest would make me feel more like talking about it. I'm going to go over and see Sarah before she gets off work. She's not likely to be going out in the evenings, at least until all this is over. If I want to talk with her, I'll have to catch her at the shop or at her house later. All this hit her pretty hard. She feels guilty because we were out so late and Jean walked home in the dark. I do, too. Look, I'll see you tomorrow morning. I'll meet you here for breakfast. Thanks, Steve."

"I hope you feel better, Alan. If I can help, let me know."

Alan got up and left. He walked down the street to the Water Dragon. Sarah was inside getting ready to close. His presence brought a smile to her somber face. "How's Myrtle doing?" he asked as he entered.

"I called home a while ago and she sounded all right. She keeps asking about Jean and I don't know what to say. Have you heard anything about her today?"

"Nothing. Maybe you could call Sheriff Stone and ask."

"I've already tried that. They say they can't release any information at this time. The patient information operator at the hospital said the same thing. I'm getting pretty concerned. Do you think she's all right?"

"I just don't know, Sarah. Maybe we'll hear in the morning, they said the first twenty-four hours were the critical part. Let's just hope for the best. Have you heard about the hurricane?"

"Emily? Yes, the tourists have talked about it all day. Storms here are really weird."

"How's that?"

"Just the mention of the word hurricane and a lot of tourists will pack up and leave. Then another batch of them will come down to see the storm as it approaches. It's really awesome here when a big one hits. I've been through several close calls. They really are scary. I don't worry that much about them though. They always say that they're going to destroy us and then they turn at the last second. We haven't been hit bad for almost thirty years. I know they could, but I don't want to worry myself sick about it until I know for sure we're about to get hit. Then I'll probably go insane. I'm much more concerned about the maniac loose on our streets, than a storm two hundred miles away that might hit here."

"You are beautiful. You know that?"

The spontaneous observation brought the smile back to her face. He loved to see her smile. "I guess this was a test."

"What do you mean, a test?"

"Today with Sheriff Stone's grilling me, Zed telling everyone who will listen that I'm a killer, and a hurricane heading my way, I've had a pretty bad day. Just being with you for a few minutes, it all seems just not very important. I hope I don't scare you, Sarah, but I've got to tell you."

"Tell me what?"

"I'm in love with you. Our stars must line up or something. I'm almost overpowered by it. I wasn't trying to fall in love. It just happened. Are you ready to run away from me now?"

Sarah moved over to face Alan. She reached out and took both of his hands in hers and looked him directly in his eyes. He felt something inside both of them touch as he held her hands. "I thought when I came back to Beaufort, after I was raped, that I'd never trust another man. I knew right away that I trusted you. This is meant to be. How could two people from so far apart meet each other and fall in love so quickly if it weren't?"

"You love me?"

"That's a stupid question. This is the last time you'll be allowed to ask me that one. Of course I love you." She tightly embraced Alan and they kissed with the first feeling of mutual acceptance that they were in love. "You don't think I would crawl into just anybody's hammock, do you? Do you think I haven't heard that old line, 'Come up to my place and see my paintings' before? Really. For a big city boy, you surprise me."

"Hey, just because I'm from up North doesn't mean I can't have a moment of insecurity, does it?"

"Come on, walk me home, will you? We can worry about all this other stuff when we get there. Right now, I just want your arm around me and a quiet walk. I do love you."

"What a complicated place this world is, Sarah."

"I know. But it's better tonight."

Together, they walked slowly down the rough, salt treated planks of the boardwalk, oblivious to anything other than how they felt at the moment.

11

Morris Stone arrived at his office much earlier than usual on Tuesday morning after Jean's assault. He'd gotten word from the hospital that she was going to survive. She wasn't conscious yet, but all her vital signs were now stable. He had relayed the good news to Sam and that guaranteed him everyone in town would know by lunchtime. Although deep into the investigation, he now had other things to worry about. Hurricanes on the coast could be deadly. Each threat had to be treated as if it would definitely strike the area. Otherwise, some people would procrastinate or grow complacent. Then, should it actually strike the town, they'd be caught unprepared.

Emily was moving straight toward the coast of North Carolina and was now forecast to proceed in that direction with an expected landfall on the coming weekend. For Morris, this meant days of work to secure the town, on top of the problems already generated by the killings. This he did not need. Don Ellingwood came into the station shortly after Morris for their morning meeting. They'd take the state helicopter to the Medical Center in Greenville to check on Jean's progress and talk to her doctor about her wounds. Morris assembled photographs of the other victims for the physician to examine and compare their wounds with Jean's. They both knew what the answer would be, but all the leads would have to be examined to be certain.

"Morning, Morris. Heard from the chopper yet?"

"Hey, Don. Not yet, but I'm sure they'll be here any time now. How long will it take to get to the hospital?"

"No more than thirty minutes. If she's conscious by the time we arrive and we get to speak with her, we could be back as early as lunch, maybe a little sooner."

"That'll be great. With this storm headed our way, I'm afraid you're going to have to handle most of the work on the assaults while I deal with getting our fine citizens ready for the storm. Every time they say a hurricane is going to hit us and it doesn't, it makes it just that much harder to get folks serious when they say the next one is coming. Most of the people living here today didn't see this place when Donna and Hazel came through. If they had, they'd take it all a lot more seriously."

"I heard they were bad. I remember seeing some pictures over at the museum. You couldn't tell where the land started and the water ended. It looked like the town had been built in the creek. Do you think this one could get that bad?"

"All of them *can* get that bad. It's just a question of whether they come ashore here or not. You have to plan for the worst. We try and evacuate the town as much as possible. We start sealing off the coast at least six hours before a predicted landfall. Buildings can be replaced. People can't."

"You're correct on that, Morris. Hey, I hear the chopper outside. You ready?"

"Yeah, as ready as I'll ever be. Let's go."

Esther was just arriving as they walked out. She relieved the night officer seated by the radio. Nothing ever seemed to faze her.

Morris thought some mornings about coming in and telling her
that Washington D.C. had been completely destroyed by a nuclear
attack just to see her reaction. He was sure it would be no different
than telling her that a dog had gotten run over on Front Street. She
popped the night officer on the back of his head as she passed by
to get her coffee. "Wake up, son. You're in my seat. Go home and
play with the baby's momma."

She then turned her attention toward Morris and Ellingwood.
"Morning, gentlemen. Going to go see Jean?"

"That's right, Esther. Take my calls and tell everyone we'll be
back by lunch if all goes well."

"Will do, Sheriff. Tell Jean we're all praying for her back
here."

"I will, Esther. See you in a while. While we're gone, prepare
the town for a nuclear attack."

"Will do. Want me to have lunch sent over from the grill? You
can reheat it when you get in?"

"Whatever. Back shortly."

Ellingwood looked at Morris as they walked out.

"She's a stone wall, isn't she?"

"That's the toughest old gal you're going to run into. At least
around here."

"She'd get first place in Raleigh too."

They headed toward the waiting helicopter. In a moment they
were on their way. This was very unusual for Beaufort, to have
this kind of support from the State Police. The newspaper accounts
of the killings were apparently making them feel the pressure too,
Morris thought. Otherwise, he'd be making this trip in his worn
out four-by-four patrol car. This was better. He particularly
enjoyed the view of the town. From the air, it appeared to be

completely surrounded by water. It didn't feel like that from the ground, since you were always looking out at the water.

The aircraft was a Bell Jet Ranger. Quiet, reliable and with room for six on board, it was quite impressive with the state seal on the side and Highway Patrol lettered on its tail section. Morris was a little apprehensive about flying; at least until he found out that Captain West would be at the controls again. Morris jumped in the front seat opposite him, and grabbed a helmet with a built-in microphone so he could speak with the pilot. "Captain West, I just wanted to let you know that everyone in Beaufort was proud of you and your crew for picking Jean up in such terrible weather. You probably couldn't pay for a meal or a drink in the whole town. It was the damnedest thing I think I've ever seen. It had to take a lot of nerve to come down blind like that."

"It had its moment, but nothing's ever going to compare to 'Nam. I flew a Huey MedEvac over there for two tours. We set those babies down in rain as thick as waterfalls, picked up six or seven wounded sometimes. Depended on how bad the fighting was, you know, and if they could wait. If they couldn't, we'd grab everybody we could squeeze on board and clip the trees getting out. Just when you felt safe, some VC with a machine gun would open up at you. Sometimes we'd have twenty or thirty holes in the fuselage when we got back. Didn't ever worry about it while it was happening. Middle of the next night, I'd wake up in a cold sweat. Still do some times. Whenever I start to get shook today, I just remember those days. I guess if I was going to go out on a chopper, it would've already happened."

"Well, just the same, we all appreciate your taking the chance for her. When she comes to, I'm going to tell her about it myself. I guarantee you'll be hearing from her."

"I hope I do, Sheriff. Nothing would please me more. We're approaching Greenville. See the Medical Center over there?"

He pointed toward a cluster of large buildings straight ahead. As Don predicted, twenty-five minutes after takeoff, they were setting down in the heliport at the University Medical Center. Morris had been there before but was still impressed by the size of the place.

"This is really a massive complex," Don said to Morris.

"Probably as good as any in the country," Morris replied.

"If I get seriously sick or hurt, I told Esther and the other officers, bring me here first. Don't wait to find out that I should have been here right off. Know what I mean?"

"Exactly. This must be our contact, coming to meet us."

A staff member in a white coat with a name tag came over to meet them. "Hi, I'm Dr. Abrams, chief of the trauma unit. Follow me if you will, and I'll update you on Miss Byrd's condition."

He led them into a side entrance and down several spotless halls to his office. The trauma area didn't have paintings on the walls, any accommodations for guests, or a single magazine rack. This place was all business. There was only one concern in the trauma unit; stabilize the seriously injured so more normal treatment could be initiated. Only the largest hospitals in major cities had trauma units. Morris thought it fortunate to have one so close to Beaufort. Without it, Jean wouldn't be alive. Dr. Abrams escorted Don and Morris into his office. "Gentlemen, please have a seat. How can I help you in this investigation?"

Morris handed him the manila envelope he'd brought with him. "Dr. Abrams, here are photos taken during the autopsies of two previous victims in our area. Would you take a look and see if the wounds are similar to Jean's? We feel certain they are, but we have to know for the record."

He opened the package and studied the photos briefly. "I would say the wounds are virtually identical. If we could have gotten these women in time, perhaps we could have saved them also."

"The killer didn't intend for us to find Jean as quickly as we did. He assumed that Don's car would be in the lot all night. He didn't know we'd just gone out to get something to eat and would be back."

"You mean he put her in Detective Ellingwood's car?"

"That's correct. He knows who we are and wanted us to be the ones who found her."

"Pretty brassy character."

"What's the status on Jean Byrd?"

"Her wounds were, as you know, primarily flesh wounds. They were deep but no vital organs were struck. Whoever did this is knowledgeable in physiology. The wounds were intentionally directed as to their location on the body. They were very precise and clean. The cuts on her chest, as bad as they looked, were not really serious. If they leave scarring, she could consider a skin graft but, at this point, I don't think it's going to be necessary. We see a lot of assault victims here, but this attack has to be one of the most bizarre things I have encountered. You say she's the third victim?"

"That's right. The other two weren't found for at least eight hours after they were stabbed. They, of course, aren't around to tell us anything. That makes Jean very important to this case. Not to mention, we all think a lot of her personally."

"I can appreciate that, Sheriff. You can rest assured she'll receive the best care possible. I'm confident the local police department will ensure her safety. I've worked with them in similar situations before, even with felons who we were treating. They're very dependable.

Now regarding Miss Byrd. She'll be hospitalized for probably three weeks, and then need physical therapy for another six months to strengthen muscles that were severed. The long term prognosis is good. She was lucky. Another hour before you found her and she would definitely have bled to death. Would you like to see her?"

"If you don't mind."

Dr. Abrams showed them the trauma unit as they passed by on their way to Jean's room. With all of the computerized equipment terminals and electronics, it reminded Morris of the control room at NASA more than a hospital. They were impressed with the facility and Dr. Abrams. They took the elevator and rode to the top floor of the hospital. Dr. Abrams explained the significance of the room's location. "Once we got her stable, the officer in charge of her protection, Sgt. Marshburn, suggested that we put her on the top floor at the end of a hall. That way, only those who are actually treating her would have any reason to approach the room. I thought that very crafty on his part."

"They do seem to know what they're doing."

At the end of the hall were two armed policemen. They were alert and watchful. Morris was relieved to see how well guarded the room was.

"Here we are. Please be careful of the tubes and IVs."

Jean was ashen. She had large bruises around her neck. She looked almost like an alien with all the life support systems that fed her and monitored her condition. As bad as she appeared, it was still a relief to the officers to see her and know that she was going to be okay. They had serious doubts when they had first found her that would be the case.

"How long do you think she'll be out? When will we be able to talk with her? She can possibly identify the attacker."

"She should be coming around any time now. Maybe in an hour. Maybe in the morning. I must forewarn you that many times people who are this seriously injured have no recollection of the incident that brought them here. Some do though. Sometimes we can help them along with hypnosis and counseling. I'm just alerting you to the possibility that she might not be of help to you."

"We appreciate all you've done, Doctor. Please remember how important it is that only people you personally authorize have access to this room. Her life depends on it. We are very pleased with what we have seen here."

Morris shook his hand again as did Ellingwood. "Call us if you would the minute she regains consciousness. We'll be here quickly after you call. We'll check back periodically anyway. Thanks a lot for your help."

"Gentlemen, that's our job here. Come with me. I'll escort you back to the helipad. We can use the service elevator and get there a little quicker. Are you in the State chopper?"

"That's right, Dr. Abrams. Are you familiar with it?"

"I believe it's a Ranger. I'm a pilot myself. Always wanted to fly a helicopter but I just haven't had time to get certified in one. I have a fixed wing Cherokee. Every moment I'm not working here, I'm in the air. It's a great escape from all the tension. A trauma unit is incredibly draining."

"I can well imagine."

The elevator reached the ground floor. Dr. Abrams showed Morris and Ellingwood the best way out. They exited through the emergency room doors. They could see the chopper waiting just outside. They trotted back to the aircraft, boarded, and were airborne in minutes. Morris had never been much of a system person. Big government, big institutions and all they represented generally ran contrary to what he stood for. He never wanted more than a quiet, simple life, with as little outside interference as possible. He had to admit that seeing how all these organizations had worked together during this emergency instilled in him a new appreciation of their worth. Here were tax dollars well spent. He was proud to be a part of this operation, in particular. Without all this support, Jean would not be recovering in a hospital room. She would already be in the cemetery. He also realized this same sort of cooperative effort was probably the only way the killer would be brought to justice.

On the approach back into Beaufort, Don asked the pilot to circle the area. He had no idea it was so developed. Morris pointed out landmarks to him. "That's Morehead City under us. Across the sound is Atlantic Beach. It's a pretty big resort area. This whole end of the county is fast becoming just one big city. Each town just runs into the next. Beaufort is actually the smallest. If it weren't the county seat, it probably would have grown very little over the years."

"It's a beautiful area, Morris. I might drive over here later and look around on my own. Let's get back."

The chopper set them down in the municipal parking lot beside the courthouse. The approach and landing seemed to take longer than it did in the fog the night they had picked up Jean. They thanked Captain West and hurried in to see what had transpired during their absence. As they entered, Esther was waiting for them, "How was Jean, Sheriff?"

"Pretty banged up, but the doctor says she'll be good as new in a few months. She's still out, but she'll be coming to 'most any time. If they call from the hospital and say she's conscious, get up with me wherever I am."

"Yes, sir. Here's your messages. There's an overnight letter for you, Don, and a few messages also."

She handed them both their mail. Don opened the overnight package first. "Okay Morris, here's what we've been waiting on. A computer printout on similar cases around the country over the last ten years. I'll start scanning them and meet with you later."

"That's great, Don. I've got to meet with the Civil Preparedness Committee about the hurricane and I've got a bunch of other crap to check on. I'll be back late this afternoon and we can go over them." Morris left the office under a full head of steam and headed to Front Street.

Alan and Stephen spent the day lining up houses to secure if the storm got closer. This was definitely not Alan's idea of a good way to spend time, but his friend had gotten into it and he figured the diversion might do him some good. He'd had a sinking feeling in his gut ever since his meeting with Sheriff Stone. He couldn't get over the Sheriff suspecting him of such heinous crimes.

They'd take plywood and cover all the windows, empty the plumbing lines and cut off water to each house. All power would be shut off as well as gas lines. A major hit would still destroy most of the homes on the waterfront, but anything less than that would be less destructive if these precautions were taken. Burst gas lines were a major concern of everyone involved in the storm precautions. One broken line, a quick spark of any kind and an explosion could devastate a home or a shop. With the buildings virtually side by side, any structure which caught fire could conceivably wipe out an entire block before it could be controlled. If it should occur while there were fifty-mile-an-hour winds, the whole area could be destroyed. No amount of precautionary measures could be too much.

Alan had also promised the dock master and several boat owners in the area that he'd help move their boats to Towne Creek, where they'd be better protected from wind and waves. These precautions had been taken many times over the years. Most of the locals knew where all the best hurricane holes were. Those were places where there was shelter and a shore break of some kind to ease the blow from the storm. Alan had quizzed enough people to find out where the best places were. By dark, both Alan and Stephen were physically shot. Alan suggested a break. "I've had it, Steve. Let's go to the grill and get some supper. If I don't eat soon, I'm gonna pass out. Aren't you hungry?"

"I'm waiting on you, buddy. Let's eat!"

They proceeded down the street. Shopkeepers and homeowners along the way were busily preparing for the worst. "I know these storms are bad, but it's almost exhilarating, seeing all the excitement and feeling the anticipation in everyone."

"You're right, Steve. I'm excited about it too."

For the next several days, Hurricane Emily maintained a straight course, aiming at the Outer Banks of North Carolina. Her strength was increasing every day, with more intensifying expected as she passed over the warm Gulf Stream water just off the coast of the eastern United States. Morris maintained a steady diet of meetings with everyone from the town council to the water department, making sure they all knew the correct emergency and contingency plans for the area. Don Ellingwood continued to research the cases of serial killings around the country hoping to find a match.

Sarah began boxing up the inventory of the Water Dragon. It would have to be moved upstairs into Alan's apartment, the day before the predicted landfall of Emily. The shop was only a few feet above sea level and right next to the water. If the storm surge was great, the first floor of the building would definitely flood and this was a necessary precaution to save the merchandise from water damage. The waterfront shops, if they weren't actually knocked down by the waves, would probably fare better than those farther inshore as the ones built right over the creek were on pilings and had no foundations to damage. Alan had promised when she was ready to help her carry it all upstairs.

By Saturday, a full blown evacuation had been ordered for most of the barrier islands. People who owned vacation cottages were streaming to and from the area with trailers, removing their possessions and especially boats that were trailer-able. The few roads entering and leaving the coastal cities looked like they were having a giant parade. Traffic was backed up in every direction. If they lived inland, it made sense for cottage owners to move whatever they could back home for safekeeping. Emergency assistance from other areas was beginning to arrive. State police officers were pouring in to set up road blocks on roads leading to low lying areas. Only people who could prove residences in the area were allowed access. When the storm approached a six hour landfall, all access would be denied. Even residents would not be allowed back in the area. A few diehard locals were always determined to ride it out at their homes, even though a direct hit would be disastrous. They couldn't be forced to leave their homes. Many years of near hits had caused them to grow overconfident. One experience like Hurricane Hazel would have convinced anyone of the stupidity of staying with their possessions.

On Saturday morning, Alan met Sarah early to help move the Water Dragon's stock. She was waiting at her door when he arrived. "Boy, you're certainly champing at the bit this morning."

"I've got so much to do at the shop and here, I'm just nervous I won't be able to get it all done."

"Do you want to get some coffee before we get going?"

"That's a good idea."

Even though it was earlier than usual, Sam's was wall to wall. Locals, boat-owners and departing tourists getting an early start filled every booth. Alan suggested, "Let's go to Agnes' Bed and Breakfast. Steve says the food there is good and she's never full, since it's mainly people who stay with her that eat there."

"Sounds good to me."

They walked down the street holding hands like high school kids. Alan was actually glad they didn't go to the grill, as Zed's continual verbal assaults were causing other locals to feel uneasy. Lately he could feel a coldness toward him that hadn't been there before. He'd just as soon have a quiet breakfast with Sarah. When they arrived, the last patron was leaving and Agnes, who knew Sarah well, greeted them warmly. "Good morning. I'm so glad you came over, Sarah. How's Myrtle? I know what happened to Jean hit her pretty hard, didn't it?"

"Yes, Agnes. It really did. She's very close to her, more like family."

"I know what you mean, dear. What have you heard about Jean? Is she doing better?"

"The last we heard was a couple of days ago. She's going to be all right, but it might take a while."

"That's just wonderful. Well, are you both hungry this morning? What can I get for you?"

"I'll just have coffee and a sweet roll if you have one. This is Alan Kelly, Agnes. He's a good friend of mine."

"So I see. Nice to meet you, Alan, and what would you like?"

"How about bacon and eggs? I have a feeling Sarah is going to work me hard today, getting ready for the storm. I'll need some breakfast to keep me going."

"Most important meal of the day. I've always believed that. Sure does look like the most serious storm we've had take aim at us for years. Just as soon as I get everybody checked out of here today, I'm going to Raleigh and stay with my sister, at least 'til this thing passes."

"You're not one of the diehards who rides these things out, Agnes?"

"I rode out Hazel, thank you. I won't be doing that again."

"Nothing like the wisdom gained from personal experience is there, Agnes?" asked Alan.

"No, sir. I'll remember that one 'til they carry me away from here. My father went with a group of fishermen to move some boats. My mother and I stayed with my Aunt Libby, about a block farther down the creek from here. Believe it or not, the water and wind picked her house up off its foundation and carried it the length of a football field down the block. With us still in it! I'll never forget it. What's more, the town wasn't as built up back then, so Aunt Libby and Uncle George, her husband, just bought the lot where it wound up. They put a new foundation under it and sold the old lot. It's still sitting right there as sure as I'm talking to you."

"That's an amazing story, Agnes. Are you sure that's not a Paul Bunyon type of hurricane story?"

"Sarah, am I pulling his leg?"

"Not unless everybody in town is in on it. I've heard it just like that since I was little."

"That's a fact. Well, not to be rude, but I'll let you young folks eat in peace while I finish getting my stuff ready to go. Just call if you need me. There's plenty of coffee over on the counter there. Help yourself." Agnes disappeared into the back of the old house.

Alan and Sarah finished their breakfast. Alan poured more coffee for them both and sat back down. He reached over and took Sarah's hand. "You know I love you. Next week, after it settles down, try and get a few days off from the shop. I want you to go on a short trip with me."

"Where to?"

"I'd like for us to fly up to New York. We could see a Broadway play, tour the city, visit a few museums and then, if you feel brave enough, introduce you to my family. They're really pretty nice people. A little stuffy at first, but nice."

"I didn't think you were close to your family."

"For the last few years I've been away a lot, between school and traveling around. I stay in touch to the point that they know where I am and that I'm okay. Believe it or not, my mother still worries about me. I think a lot of them. They've been very supportive of me, even though they wish I was a little more career oriented. My father thinks I'll wake up one morning and wish I'd thought more about what I was doing with my life. He doesn't realize I'm already working at what I want to do, experiencing life and painting what I see. I just feel like I'd like for them to meet you. If you think you might want to be with me on a more permanent basis, you should see what you're getting into."

"What does 'a permanent basis' mean? If that's a proposal, it's going to have to be a little more romantic than that to get me to bite. Call me old fashioned, but that's the truth of it."

"Don't worry, I've got it all planned."

"Is that so?"

"Absolutely. I get you to New York. We spend the day seeing the city. That evening, we go to a fancy restaurant. Later, we take in a musical on Broadway, then finish up with a romantic carriage ride around Central Park. I pop open an expensive bottle of champagne. You have too much to drink. I pop the question and you, in your tipsy state of mind, accept. Fireworks go off, the Goodyear Blimp flies overhead reading "SARAH AND ALAN TO WED," we go to the Waldorf and jump each other's bones. How's that?"

"Go ahead, make the arrangements. This I have to see. By the way, did you carry the bottle of champagne under your jacket all day?"

"That's it, make sport of me, romantic fool that I am."

"I'll tell you this. You ask me that way and your chances of getting a positive reply would be pretty good."

"We have a deal. Let me ask you something. If I wanted to go back to graduate school, how would you feel about going back and finishing your education at Boston College? It's a beautiful place and a great school. I know you'd love it."

"I always thought I'd go back and finish one day, but I just never figured out how, what with Myrtle and the cost and all."

"Details. Let me worry about them for you. Would you go?"

"If everything worked so that I could, sure. But that's a lot of 'ifs' you know."

"Like I said, let me work on it. I have a great friend, Jeff, who is a wizard at getting things done. I'll mention it to him. Well, I guess we better get moving or we won't get everything done today."

He left money on the table and they both yelled goodbye to Agnes. Outside, the sky was beginning to cloud up with angry swirls. The breeze was getting consistently stronger and they could feel the increasingly angry presence of Mother Nature in the air.

As they walked through the breezy mist, Stephen came up from the opposite direction. "Hey guys, you eat at Agnes' this morning? Great, isn't it? I saw you headed this way earlier but I had nails in my mouth and couldn't say hi. I'm putting plywood over the windows of the marine supply shop down the street, and took a break to get some coffee. Sam's was so packed; I thought I'd see if there was any left back at Agnes'. You didn't drink the last cup did you?"

"I don't know, Steve. If you want to get anything there, you better hurry up. Agnes is getting ready to go to her sister's place and wait out the storm. Look, we're going to be down at the Water Dragon moving the stock upstairs all day. Come down later and we'll get a sandwich with you."

"I'll do it. See you." He ran down the street to Agnes' place.

Sarah and Alan continued toward the gift shop. Stephen entered the bed and breakfast just as Agnes was leaving, bag in hand. "Here, let me get that for you. How long will you be gone?"

"I'll be back by Monday evening at the latest. You and the other gentleman, that detective fellow Don, will have to eat down at Sam's, I guess. Just for a couple of days."

"Don't you worry about us. Drive careful and call if you get worried about the house. I'll be here."

"Thank you, Stephen. See you later, dear." She got in her car and left. Stephen went back into the house. As he entered, the phone started ringing. He raced down the hall of the old Victorian home where the phone sat on an antique, cylinder desk, which was backed up under the spiral staircase. He picked up the phone and did his best down East accent. "Agnes' B & B."

"Hi, this is Esther down at the police station. Is Mr. Ellingwood there?"

"Just a minute. I'll check."

He set the receiver down and went upstairs to check Don's room. He knocked on Ellingwood's door. "Mr. Ellingwood, hello.

Telephone." He knocked again and there was still no reply. He apparently was alone in the large old home. He returned to the telephone.

"I'm sorry. He's not here. Can I take a message?"

"If you would. He told the Sheriff he was headed that way about thirty minutes ago. If you see him, can you give him a message from Morris Stone?"

"Of course, let me get a piece of paper to write on." He opened a couple of drawers in the desk under the phone, and pulled out a note pad and pencil. "Go ahead."

"Tell him Greenville PD called. Jean has come to, and the Sheriff wants to fly down there Monday morning. He wants to meet with Don in the morning at the station."

"Got it. I'll leave it on his door."

"Thank you, young man. Bye."

Stephen proceeded to his room and put a few items in an overnight bag. The howling wind, blowing from the ocean against the face of the old home, was initiating all manner of creaks and groans. In rapid fashion, the beautiful gingerbread-styled home that seemed so warm and friendly when Agnes and the other guests were present had become rather cold and sinister feeling. He wouldn't stay here by himself during the storm. Perhaps, he'd wait it out with Alan.

Sarah and Alan finally got all the stock moved upstairs. It had taken the better part of the day. They were both extremely tired but Alan knew that any other preparations that were necessary needed to be done that night. The weather was rapidly deteriorating as Emily continued her approach. "Okay, now to your place. I'd like to get the plywood over your windows tonight. It's liable to be raining hard by morning and it would be a mess to do it then."

"You sure you're up to this tonight?"

"Lead on."

They locked up and headed to Sarah's.

Morris Stone was making a late night check of the town. With a lot of the stores boarded up and the owners gone, an extra thorough check was in order. Almost all of the boats that normally stayed docked at the municipal docks were gone. There were less than five boats where there were usually two hundred. There were none anchored in the creek. All had been moved to more protected waters. Most had moved to Towne Creek but some had gone as far upriver as New Bern.

Morris felt somewhat relieved that the taverns and restaurants were closed and the streets empty. This would probably keep anyone else from being attacked 'til the hurricane passed. The storm was enough to worry about for the night. He checked the front and rear doors of each store along the waterfront. They were completely dark as the power had been shut off to prevent electrical shorts if they were flooded. Only a few battery powered security lights cast any glow in a shop window. Morris felt uneasy as he continued his rounds. Someone jumping out at him at any moment would only complete the scenarios racing through his mind. He continued until he got to the dock master's office. It was locked also. Morris wondered if the dock master had thought to shut off the water at the public dock facilities. They were on the wharf at the end of the dock area. There were men's and ladies' rest rooms and showers. People docking there were given a key. A lot of boats didn't have showers aboard and it was a very attractive courtesy to get boaters to use the public docks. He checked the women's room first. It was locked. He then checked the men's room. The lock was set, but the door was not pulled to completely. He entered and cut the breaker for the lights back on.

The water had been shut off properly. Morris noticed that the room was not as clean as it should be and he determined to mention it to Eddie the next time he saw him. The toilet supplies were exhausted and the waste paper basket was overflowing. He stooped to pick up the spilled paper and put it in the basket. Beside the toilet, to the rear, a piece of material caught his eye. It was not paper. It appeared to be a small piece of rubber. He bent over and carefully studied the item. A closer examination showed it to be latex, and it had what looked like a smear of dried blood on it. His mind raced and he couldn't help but remember Don Ellingwood's thought that the killer probably wore gloves. What about surgical gloves? This appeared to be the same sort of material used for them. It was only about an inch square and looked as if it had been cut into this small piece with scissors. Morris took several folds of toilet paper and carefully wrapped the item without touching it, in case there was a fingerprint on it. He looked thoroughly, but could find nothing else out of the way. He eventually cut the light back off and locked the door.

He continued his late night check for several hours before leaving the waterfront for some sleep. He could hardly rest for all the turmoil in his mind. As he tossed, thoughts of the killer stalking women in houses with the power out and the storm raging plagued his mind.

12

Dawn arrived with Morris in the office, still tired due to a fitful sleep. He watched as a sullen gray daylight appeared through his office window. He fixed coffee and checked in with all the civil defense personnel on duty waiting for the hurricane to strike. Emily's winds were now as high as one hundred twenty-five miles per hour and its course was projected to be a straight shot to Cape Lookout and Beaufort. If this held up, it would be a repeat of Hazel or Donna. The damage would be massive. Everyone would be required to evacuate, though he knew there would be diehards who would refuse to leave their homes.

Even with all this going on, he felt he had to talk with Don Ellingwood before he got started with anything else this morning. He scanned the morning paper as he drank his coffee and waited.

The Beaufort paper was only printed twice weekly so Morris read a large statewide paper. He was impressed with the coverage given the impending storm and the repeated references to Beaufort. The concluding paragraph mentioned the fact that as bad as the weather could be, Beaufort was probably relieved to have something else to worry about other than its rash of recent attacks and murders. He ripped the page, balled up the paper and threw it across the room. "Damn it, can't they find something else to talk about? A hurricane about to bury us and they use the opportunity to mention the killings again. Damn reporters!"

"You seem a little agitated this morning, Morris."

Don had arrived early himself, and was surprised to see that Morris was already there. "That's about the most upset I've seen you since I got to town. What's happening?"

He had grown to admire Morris for his comfortable blend of warmth, dedication, integrity, and humor. What he lacked in technical expertise, he handily made up for with common sense. "I just can't get here early enough to ever beat you in, can I?"

"Couldn't sleep. Otherwise, you would have got me this time. I've actually been waiting to speak with you. Got a couple of thoughts to run past you."

"Go ahead. I'm almost awake. I'll work on a coffee while you talk."

"Remember when we were flying back from Greenville in the chopper, and you were surprised at how developed the whole area is? It made me think. With all the night spots in Morehead City and Atlantic Beach, why does this guy keep picking his victims from Beaufort? They're only a five minute drive from here and they're a lot larger. There's twice the nightlight in Atlantic Beach."

"He could have a fixation on something or somebody from the town, or he knows it better so he feels his chances of not being caught are better here."

"What about this? It's because he doesn't have a vehicle to get there in. A transient boater for example. He certainly wouldn't take a cab to a murder, or borrow a car and get blood in it."

"Makes sense. Keep going."

"If he stays on a boat at the municipal docks, he gets a key to the showers and restrooms. At night, almost no one uses them. They can be locked from the inside for privacy in case someone did show up. He goes back there, showers, changes clothes and washes any blood off the ones he was wearing right there in the washing machines. It's almost too obvious. Plus, I found this in the men's bath there last night." He unfolded the paper and showed him his find from the previous evening. "Looks like a piece of a surgical glove to me. What do you think?"

"You may have something there, Morris. It looks like he was cutting the gloves in pieces so that he could just flush them down the toilet."

"Exactly what I was thinking. The approaching storm drove a lot of the boaters to leave early. Only a few of those remaining have been here since the first attack. You've gone through the list of similar crimes around the country, right?"

"Yeah, I've picked the most similar ones to show you."

"Were there any in the Boston area?"

"That's right! What made you think that?"

"I have a suspect in mind already. You know Sarah, the girl who works at the Water Dragon gift shop?"

"She's the girl with the friend the redneck keeps going after."

"Maybe Zed was right all along. He's been here the whole time. No car. He'd be familiar with a filet knife. He's plenty strong and smart. He came here on a boat out of Boston. He and Sarah were the last people to see Jean Byrd. He knew she was walking home that night because she'd just left Sarah's house where she'd stayed with Sarah's grandmother because Sarah and this guy had been out sailing."

"Haven't you already had him in for questioning?"

"Yeah, just a couple days ago. He's very cool under pressure. I tried to shake him, but the harder I pressed, the smoother he got. I was just about convinced he was a straight shooter. Now I'm beginning to question everything about him."

"Sarah wouldn't be involved, would she?"

"Absolutely not. She'll be devastated if it's him."

"We better bring him in for questioning this morning."

"I agree, but I want to speak to Sarah first. She's gotten really close to him and this is gonna tear her up. I'm gonna tell her what we think and see what she says. Maybe we're wrong. And so far, everything we have is circumstantial. We need to check his place while he's out. Try and find something concrete on him. I've got a copy of his ID. Why don't you get a background check on him while I go see Sarah? I'll be back shortly and we can decide what to do then. We don't want to spook him too soon either. He might run before we find any hard evidence."

"How about this? We forward the material to Raleigh for forensic to work on. They can do a blood type, a DNA test, and possibly find what type of glove it came from. With that info, we can compare it with Jean's blood samples and, if this guy swears he has nothing to hide, perhaps he'll let us get a sample of his. That might help clear up quite a few questions."

Morris grabbed his hat and headed into what was already a twenty-five mile-per-hour wind. He thought to himself that it was weird to have all this going on, just as a hurricane got ready to hit town. He wondered if it might be best to just let everything stay as it was until the storm passed. Before he could make that determination, he remembered his dreams of the previous night and his visions of the killer. He pictured him, after someone in a house with the power off and no way to call for help or even be heard over the powerful winds screaming through the night. He must take action now. As he walked down Front Street, he looked out at Taylor Creek. A two foot chop was already running across the water. With all the boats gone, the shops and homes covered in unpainted plywood and everything loose removed, the scene was surrealistic. He hated to tell Sarah what he believed. He knew about her attack and the problems she'd had getting to know anyone after that. She had to know. It would be better if she heard it from him first. He approached her home. He knocked several times and finally, heard someone slowly coming to the door. It was Myrtle.

"Morris, what can I help you with? You know I'm not going to leave. Don't try and talk me into it. My mind's made up."

"I'm looking to speak with Sarah if she's home. Is she?"

"No. She and her young man went to Radio Island, to look at the waves out in the inlet. They walked over there on the bridge about two hours ago. They were worn out from working all night getting the store and this place ready for this little blow. If it's important, you can probably see them from the road or leave a note and I'll see she gets it. Is everything okay? It's not Jean, is it? She's still going to be all right, isn't she?"

"Yes, Myrtle, she's doing fine. But it's important I speak to Sarah, this afternoon at the latest. I'm going to drive out toward Radio Island. If I can't find them, please have her call me as soon as she gets back."

"I will. Morris, are you all right?"

"I'm fine, Myrtle, just a little overworked. Have Sarah call me."

"I don't forget things like you might think, Sheriff. Get a few miles on you and everybody acts like you're senile or something!"

"That's not what I meant, Myrtle. It's just important. I'll see you later. Call if you need anything or even if the storm gets too bad and you want to get out. I'll come get you."

"That's not going to happen. I'll be just fine. See you later, Morris."

"Bye, Myrtle."

As he left, Morris thought to himself. That is one feisty old girl. She must've been something when she was young. Morris walked over to the waterfront. Waves were continuing to build and the storm surge was already pushing the tide up under the docks. The waves were smashing against the bottom of the boardwalk's planks. The barrier islands across the channel would soon be covered and then, the big breakers, maybe fifteen or twenty foot tall, could come across the creek and smash into the town, just as if it were built on the ocean front. The noise from the impact of their collisions with the low lying island, just across the creek, could be heard throughout the town. As soon as those outlying islands were submerged, all hell would break loose.

Emily was predicted to come ashore around eight p.m. There was a lot to do before then. He hurried back to the police station and began to make final checks with all the agencies assisting in the evacuation of the town. The streets leaving the entire beach area were jammed with cars. Tourists, home owners, permanent residents and sightseers were all on the road at the same time. The State Police had their road blocks up in force. Once you went through, you wouldn't be allowed back in the area without a civil defense pass. The Front Street vicinity looked like a ghost town. He could see several of his men walking the streets to prevent looting. He was proud of his small force. Even though he was concerned about what might transpire with the arrest of Sarah's companion, he felt relieved to know this might mean an end to the terror the town had lived under for the past month.

Alan and Sarah walked along the beach at Radio Island hand in hand, taking in the majesty of the storm. Alan felt exhilarated with the excitement of the approaching storm. "There is no force on earth greater than nature, you know."

"What about love?" Sarah quizzed.

"It's a part of nature too. You're right; it probably is the strongest single aspect of nature. A mother will lay down her own life to save a child. People go into burning buildings, run in front of trucks, even walk into machine gun fire to save another person. Sometimes they risk their life for a complete stranger. That's pretty powerful stuff. A hurricane or a fire just 'is.' There's no thought there. But when a person does something like that, there's knowledge of the action. It's just that much more powerful an action because it's purposeful. You know what I mean?"

"That's a beautiful thought. When we get back, I'm going to write it down so I don't forget it."

"That good, huh?"

"I expected no less from my man."

They continued walking down the beach, talking and touching. The wind was rising and the sky was growing fierce. As a wave would hit the beach and smash into a ton of white foam, the high wind would lift the crest off and carry it, like an airborne spray of salty rain, far inland from the beach. There were none of the usual seagulls riding the wind over the beach. They'd already moved inland, their sixth sense telling them to get out of the path of the storm. And yet there, just beyond the surf, played three porpoises, riding the huge swells, acting as if they had a free pass for the roller coaster at an amusement park. "Won't the storm bother them at all?" Sarah quizzed Alan.

"I've seen them playing just like that offshore, in huge swells during terrible storms. If they don't like the surface, they just dive down where it's quiet. They're a good example of creatures perfectly adapted to its environment."

"Yeah, wouldn't it be great if we could do that?"

"How do you mean?"

"When things get too rough, just head to deeper water."

"It's funny. When people do that, 'we're running away from our problems.' I guess we're just not as advanced in our thinking as dolphins."

Sarah and Alan got back to the house after lunch. Myrtle called to her as soon as they came inside. "Sarah, Sheriff Stone wants to talk with you. He said for you to go by the station no matter what time you got in."

"I hope the shop is all right. I'm almost positive it was closed up tight and locked. Maybe the high tide is already coming up through the floor. Floyd will be sick."

"If you're going to go over to the station, I'll walk some of the way with you. I'm going to go downtown and see if I can find Stephen. He wanted me to help him with a couple of things he promised to do. He's still closing up cottages and some of the windows were so high, he needed help holding the plywood while he nailed. If you stay at the station long, get somebody to drive you home. Don't walk home after dark by yourself. Promise?"

"I won't. I promise."

"Alright, let's get moving before the conditions get worse. You told your grandmother you were having a man over tonight, didn't you? I'm still going to stay with you and Myrtle through the storm, right?"

"We're counting on it."

"This is terrific, our first full night together. Does this mean that your teddy bear will get the boot?"

"You'll have the couch. Teddy will keep me warm. My grandmother isn't that progressive."

"I bet she'd surprise even you."

"Trust me. She's not that liberated."

Both Alan and Sarah left at the same time. He headed to find Stephen and she went to see Sheriff Stone. They walked toward

Front Street together. Several plywood store signs were already lying on the ground where the wind deposited them after dislodging them from their perch above their respective stores. They stopped momentarily to allow a large metal trash can to go rolling past them. It appeared it was chasing its lid, which rolled on its edge slightly in front of it.

As they approached the street corner, where they would separate to go about their tasks, Alan pulled Sarah up tightly to him. There was a light rain falling on them. The drops of water ran like crystalline beads down her face. Her dark blond hair lay flat against the sides of her face. She felt she must look disheveled and tried to pull several wet strands of hair away from her eyes and the front of her face. "No, don't. You look radiant. I've never seen a face, not on canvas or in person that showed so much emotion. I can read your heart with just one glance at your face."

"Be careful, you know what my grandmother said about being able to tell if a man was being truthful."

"Sarah Turlington, to me you are the most beautiful person I have ever known."

When he kissed her, she could almost feel their souls flowing between them. He was worth all the years she had waited. Things had worked out for the best just as she had hoped.

The parking lot outside the police station was jammed. There were highway patrol and civil defense cars as well as others helping the town through the hurricane. Sarah walked into the crowded lobby. She began to think that with this many people here, the Sheriff would be too busy to see her. At best she would be there a long time. She let Esther know she was there. "Oh good. He wanted to know the minute we heard from you. Just stand right there a second."

Sarah watched as Esther walked quickly to a back office and disappeared. There were police in the lobby from many neighboring towns which had lent their assistance. Reporters and TV camera crews from all over the country were trying to get press passes so they could legally kill themselves to get pictures of the storm. Esther waded through the crowd on her way back to a large room where Morris was in a meeting.

Inside, Morris was seated with a group of officers being briefed on the emergency plans for the county by a civil defense engineer. Esther motioned from just inside the door to him. When she caught his eye he quietly stood up and walked over to the door. Esther whispered to him and he followed her back down the hall to the lobby where Sarah was standing.

He smiled warmly and walked over to meet her. "Hi, Sarah. Come back to my office with me if you would, dear. How's your grandmother? She seemed fine when I was there earlier today."

"She's okay, Mr. Stone. She says we're going to stay put at the house tonight. She's awfully stubborn. I guess if it gets too bad I'll have to get you to help me move her. You'll probably need your gun."

Sarah was beginning to feel a little nervous. What could be so important that the Sheriff would stop what he was doing, in an emergency situation, to see her? Perhaps, Jean had taken a turn for the worse. That must be it. She steeled herself for the bad news. "Please sit down, Sarah." Morris closed the door behind them and pulled another chair up close to hers.

"This is not going to be easy for me to tell you, Sarah."

"It's Jean, isn't it? She didn't make it."

"No. Jean is fine. I'm going to go talk with her on Monday and I'll come back and tell your grandmother what she said. You don't need to worry about her. She's well protected too. There are two police officers at her door around the clock. That's what I wanted to talk to you about. We believe we know who committed the two killings and attacked Jean. The problem is, you have gotten very close to him."

"Not Alan! You couldn't possibly think he would do something like that. He thinks the world of Jean. There's no way he would hurt anyone. I know him better than that. No way. I can't believe your saying this!"

"Well, Sarah, I certainly respect your feelings for him and I also value your opinion. Listen though, if you will, to why we consider him a suspect."

"I will listen, but I'll tell you right now, unless you have a witness or a photograph, I'm not going to accept it at all. I know you're wrong about him."

While they spoke, Alan was looking to help Stephen with the last minute preparations he had contracted from the local shopkeepers and cottage owners. Since he didn't know where to start looking, he figured someone at the grill would have seen him if he was working downtown. He went into Sam's Grill though he dreaded running into Zed and his entourage if they were there. As he entered, he noticed they weren't and he looked around for Stephen. Sam came over to take his order. "What can I get for you, son?"

"Just a coffee, Sam. By the way, have you seen Steve? He's the guy who usually eats here with me."

"He's the one covering up windows, isn't he?"

"That's right. Has he been in this afternoon?"

"Yeah, a couple hours ago. I think he's down at the marine hardware store on the next block. He was with Jeff, the guy who runs the place, when he came in for lunch. You might try there. If you get up with him, you two better start heading to wherever you're going to ride this thing out. The last weather forecasts look real bad for the entire coast here. I guess I should have sold out a few years ago when I had the chance. Maybe you can teach me how to paint. I'll just set up an easel on the sidewalk where the store used to be." He snickered at the thought.

Alan finished his coffee and started down the street. The weather was deteriorating rapidly. Though it was only four p.m., the sky was dark with black, swirling clouds, almost concealing all daylight. Rain was beginning to fall steadily. It was wind driven and stung as it smacked Alan on his face. He looked out over Taylor Creek and saw it as he never had before. The barrier island on the other side was completely covered by water. The creek had become part of the Atlantic. Great swells, foaming white on their crests, were rising up under the docks. As each wave rose up under the planks, it would smash them with a great fury. As the waves broke up underneath, jets of water shot up between the planks and continued many feet into the air. For just a moment he paused and watched the awesome spectacle. With top winds of well over a hundred knots, the center of Emily was still miles at sea. She would not reach land until ten p.m. If these swells were only a small sample of what was to come, Alan thought, the waterfront would certainly be devastated when she came ashore.

He continued on his mission to find Stephen. Just ahead, he saw Jeff standing in front of his store, locking the door. "Jeff, I'm looking for Steve. I promised to help him with a few things before the storm gets here. Do you know where he is?"

"Yeah, he borrowed my pickup to run to Morehead and try to get a few more pieces of plywood. I'm almost certain they're sold out by now. Unless he decides to ride up the road a little farther, he should be back before too long. He's been gone about an hour. The way it's starting to look, I don't think it's going to be very

important whether or not anybody's windows are boarded up. I
don't know; might make the places float better. What do you
think? You ever been through one of these before?"

No, sir, and I'm not really looking forward to it. I'm just going
to find Stephen and get boarded up somewhere ourselves. I think
we're going to stay at Sarah Turlington's house. You think it can
weather the storm okay?"

"Well, as good as any house here, I guess. That place is real
old, must have survived the last couple of bad ones. It'll be okay I
imagine. You just make sure and kill the gas, don't want no
explosions. You hear me?"

"I got you. Will you be here when Stephen returns?"

"No way. I'm gone. Right now. You can check back if you
want. If he's here, you'll see my blue pickup with Shore Marine
on the side. He said he'd park it behind the shop. There's a ridge
back there about four foot above the lot. I'm hoping the tide, if it
comes over the street, won't reach that high. Looks like a bad one
now though, doesn't it?"

"It sure does. Thanks, I'll come back in a while to check on
him."

13

The full force of Emily was now lashing the coast of North Carolina. Power lines were down and the only communication with the area was either on a marine VHF radio or the police channel, both of which were already working overtime. The latest forecasts predicted the eye of the storm would come directly into Beaufort. This was the hurricane they knew would eventually come. They would be spared no more.

Sarah fought back her emotions all afternoon as she waited for Alan to return. She knew in her heart he was innocent. Morris Stone was a good man, but he was wrong. Whatever it took, she'd help Alan clear himself. She'd seen a police car pass her house every ten minutes. She knew he'd be picked up as soon as he returned. She decided to venture out into the storm and find him. If she could locate him before the Sheriff, maybe he could find some way to prove he was innocent. She had to locate him. Her head was spinning with the need to help him solve this dilemma. She hesitated at the thought of leaving Myrtle alone in the house with the storm so close. "Grandmother, do you think you would be okay if I went out for a short while to try and find Alan? I won't stay long."

Myrtle had been watching the concern build in Sarah's face all afternoon. "Dear, I'd be more worried about you being out in this weather. I just looked out the front door a minute ago. The sound is already flooded and the docks are almost under water now. It won't be long and waves will be running across the street. The storm surge can push the water in so quick. You can get caught by it in a heartbeat. It'd scare me to death, if you were out in such a mess as this."

"I've just got to go find him. I'll only go to Sam's and see if they've seen him. Then, whether I find him or not, I promise I'll come straight back and stay put until the storm passes."

"You're all grown up, Sarah. You'll do what you think you have to. I wish you'd just stay here, but if you must go, I'll be okay. Anybody wants to bother me bad enough to come out in this kind of weather, let 'em have me."

Sarah ran over and kissed her cheek. "You are wonderful, Grandmother. I love you. I promise I'll be right back."

"I'm holding you to it. Now get going before it gets any worse."

Out through the back door and into the fierce weather, she half-ran with a sense of desperation tearing at her. The rain was almost horizontal and stung intensely. She turned her face to the side to avoid the main thrust of the wind driven spikes of water. She looked out toward the docks. They were no longer visible! The storm surge had completely covered them. Waves were beginning to cross Front Street. She'd have to move quickly so she wouldn't be cut off from her house. Myrtle would be hysterical alone inside, if she couldn't make it back. She'd have to hurry.

As waves crashed into the pilings supporting the shops on the waterfront, she continued toward the grill. She hoped a few die-hards might be holed up there monitoring the situation. The waves that passed between the creek-side buildings, in what used to be alleys were now crashing onto the street. As they flattened out like waves on the ocean front, a large pool of water would race forward over Sarah's ankles, then retreat. She knew they'd continue to get deeper and larger as the storm surge pushed the tide and waves across the low-lying areas of the town. The wind had increased to the point she had to lean into it to make forward progress as she walked.

Her prayers were answered. A soft, warm light came from between the seams in the plywood coverings on Sam's windows. She raced to the front door and beat on it as hard as she could. She had to be heard over the roar of the wind and crashing seas. The door opened and Sam, shocked to see her, helped her inside.

"My gracious, Sarah, what in the world are you doing out in the middle of this? Don't you know how dangerous this thing can be?"

"Yes, Sam, I do. I'm looking for Alan. Have you seen him in the last couple of hours? It's really important."

"Yeah, I heard. Morris Stone came by several times already, looking for him. Alan hasn't been in here since this afternoon. He came by looking for his friend. I sent him down to Jeff Altman's hardware store. Haven't seen him since. I know, as well as you do, that boy ain't got any meanness in him. I told Morris he was looking at the wrong man, but you know how damn stubborn he can be when he gets his mind made up. Listen, why don't you let me get you back home? He'll turn up soon and I'll get in touch with you right away. If you wait 'til the water gets any higher, you won't be able to get back to your place. That water is rising a foot or more every ten minutes. Besides, if somebody doesn't have any place to go, they're putting them up at the courthouse. He'll probably be as well off with Morris at the jail as he would anywhere. You know, he may already have picked him up."

"I don't think so. Sheriff Stone came by our house a short while ago, still looking for him. God, I hope he's alright."

"I'm sure he is, darling. Don't you worry. They'll straighten this all out tomorrow. Morris will realize he's not the guy he's looking for and send him home to you."

"I want him home with me tonight, not tomorrow!"

"I know how you feel, Sarah, but you can't keep running around in a hurricane looking for him. Come on now, let's go."

He turned to several locals, who were riding the storm out with him, and said to them. "I'm taking Sarah home. Keep a lookout for us as far as you can keep us in sight. Keep watching now, 'cause I'm coming right back. You let me drown and you'll have to cook your own breakfast from now on."

The old fisherman seated next to the coffee pot nodded affirmatively and rose, then followed them to the door. As they exited back into the face of the storm, they saw someone coming at them, just a few yards away. "Sarah! Is that you?"

"Alan!" She rushed to meet him. She embraced him in the midst of the drenching rain.

"I was just at your place. Your grandmother said you were out looking for me. I can't believe you came out in this mess."

Sam saw that she had found him. He knew that Morris suspected the young man but he felt he knew him better than the Sheriff did. Years in the restaurant business had made him a pretty good judge of character. Sarah would be all right with him. "Look, Alan, you get her home quick! This storm is getting worse by the minute. I'm going back inside. Get going now!"

"Thanks, Sam. I'll get her home. Come on, Sarah. Hold my hand."

Sarah felt safe again but the dread of what she must tell Alan now overcame her relief in finding him. As they hastily headed back toward her house, wading through the water, she finally exploded with her fears. "Alan, Sheriff Stone thinks you killed those girls and hurt Jean. I know he'll be at the house shortly if he's not already waiting there."

"Me? Why on earth does he think I did it?"

"He's found some other cases like it in Boston, and several other things he thinks point to you. I told him you couldn't do it but he says he's going to arrest you tonight; just to be sure you don't leave. At least not until he's checked you out."

"Hey, I don't have a thing to hide. Don't worry about it. I gave him my folks' number. I wonder why he didn't just check out my background like he said he would."

"He says he found a piece of evidence that strongly ties you to the case. He's probably just jumping the gun because he's under so much pressure to find out who did kill them."

"I'll go with him. We'll get it straightened out. I'll be fine. Come on now, we have to hurry."

They approached Sarah's house. The water was already knee deep and swirling down the street with a current that was getting hard to stand against. The wind was close to fifty miles an hour with gusts reaching seventy-five or more. Anything that wasn't tied down was either floating down the street, or being picked up and carried away by the wind.

As they started up the steps, Sheriff Stone's patrol car rounded the corner pushing a bow wave in front. As soon as he saw them he hit his blue lights. Morris got out of the car and started to move toward them. He hadn't put on any foul weather gear and his khaki outfit was dark brown with water. Water in the street was already above his boots. He was thoroughly drenched and in no mood to be polite. Sarah couldn't help herself. She panicked and began to cry. The prospect of Alan going to jail scared her much more than the worst the hurricane had to offer. "Please, Mr. Stone, can't you wait until morning, just 'til the storm passes?"

"I wish I could, Sarah, I truly do. Alan, you know why I'm here? I'll read you your rights down at the station. We need to go right now."

"Can't we see that Sarah and Myrtle are safe inside, before we go, Sheriff? I'll do whatever you want."

"Alright, I'll go inside with you. Please don't try and leave though, Alan. I don't even want to think about that happening."

"You don't have to, Sheriff."

They climbed up Sarah's steps and she unlocked the door. Myrtle was standing by the front door, greatly concerned about all that was happening. Sarah ran to her as she entered. With tears accompanying raindrops down her soaked face, she spoke painfully to her grandmother. "Sheriff Stone thinks Alan... Killed those girls and hurt Jean. He's here to arrest him. Tell him that he didn't do it, Grandmother. He won't listen to me or anyone!"

Morris came over close to the two women. He already had handcuffs in his hand. A look of contempt for what was going on came across Myrtle's face as she addressed the Sheriff, "Morris, I've known you all your life, and you know me. I'm telling you, this young man is no criminal. I know it as well as I know you're standing there."

"I hope you're right, Myrtle, but I can't afford to gamble with other people's lives. He's going to have to come in with me tonight. If he's innocent, we'll find that out in due course. You all right here now?"

There was a loud banging on the front door. It wasn't the storm. Sarah rushed to open it and Myrtle sarcastically said, "Like a damn town hall meeting here tonight."

The door opened and a shadow of a woman rushed in. The rain and wind literally pushed her inside. As the light in the foyer of the house fell on her face, they could see it was Joan Moore,

David and Jenny's mother. Her face was red and flushed with anguish. Between gasps and tears, she gestured frantically as she spoke to them. "Thank God you're here. The kids, I can't find the kids. David and Jenny, they..." She was so rattled she was making very little sense.

Morris understood that the kids were not where they should be. "Where are they supposed to be, Joan? Just answer me. Stop crying! Get a grip and answer me."

Alan tried to calm her. "Joan, where were they? Where's Dr. Moore?

Sheriff Stone answered that for her. "He's down at the town shelter, helping take care of the older people who are staying there. He's on a four-hour shift."

Joan took a deep breath and tried to tell them what had happened. "They were in the house. The power went off. And then, back on a couple of times. They started screaming. When the lights came back on, just a couple seconds later, the front door was open and... I can't find them. I can't find them. They're gone! Oh my God, find them, Alan. Please!"

Alan turned to Sarah, "We'll find them. Sarah, keep her here. Sheriff, your arrest can wait a few minutes. Let's go find them. You can just shoot me if you want. I'm going to find those kids." Without waiting for a reply, he started out the front door.

Sarah turned to Myrtle. Myrtle looked at Morris with her you-should-be-ashamed look and said to him, "You better shoot him quick, Morris, before he goes out into the hurricane, to find some children."

"You do know me better than that, Myrtle."

"Watch her, Grandmother, I'm going too!"

"Sarah, don't! It's too bad out there." It was to no avail. She was right on Alan's heels with Morris just behind her.

"Get in the four by four. It's still running. Water isn't over the engine yet."

They all jumped into the old Jeep. Morris turned in the middle of the road and started back up the street. The headlights reflected off the water being pushed aside by the old Jeep. The engine had to be half under water. It would not continue running very long. He knew he should have arrested Alan and then gotten help, but a voice inside his head assured him he was making the right choice. They stopped in the dead center of the road in front of the Moore's house. The water was up to the front porch and rising fast. They could barely hear themselves for the bellowing of the hurricane force winds. "Alright, Alan, I'm risking my neck letting you do this. Don't let me down. Grab another flashlight from the back seat."

"Got one. Let's find the kids. I'll embarrass you for trying to arrest me in the morning after you check me out. You search around back, Sheriff. I'll go in the front and look around the inside of the house. Sarah, come with me. You can wait inside 'til we find them."

Just seeing the swirling, crashing waves, around the house, gave them a sick feeling. There'd be no way the kids could survive outside. The water was swift enough to pull them down and sweep them away. The front door was wide open. Mrs. Moore must have left it open for the children. The house was dark. Power was out in large sections of town. Alan went through the entire house calling the children's names as he went. No reply. Sarah followed him upstairs. She waited on the landing at the top of the stairs while Alan checked the bedrooms. He shined the flashlight into the closets and under the beds. He was satisfied that they weren't in the house. While he was making the rounds upstairs, Sarah looked out the small octagonal window at the landing. Because it was so small and high, it hadn't been covered with plywood like the rest of the windows. She looked at lightning flashes in the sky and the silhouetted outline of the house next door. There appeared to be a flash of light in the window. It happened again. She realized it could only be a flashlight. Had Sheriff Stone gone next door, already? "Alan, come here. Come look at this."

He made his way back to Sarah on the landing. "They're gone. They're definitely not here. What is it?"

"Look out the little window here, at the house next door. Look at the upstairs windows. There it is again. See the light?"

"Sarah, Alan, are you upstairs?" Morris called to them.

"Wait right there, Sheriff. We're coming down." They carefully walked back down the steep Victorian stairs in the dark. Alan focused the flashlight on each step as they descended. As they made the last turn on the steps, Morris shined his flashlight on the remaining steps, to help light their path. "There's a flashlight in the window, on the second floor of the house beside us. Who lives there?"

"Reverend Patton and his wife. They went to Goldsboro to stay with friends 'til the storm passes. No one should be in the house. It's in a low spot and not very safe. Let's check it out."

They went back through the door and out to the front porch. They looked up at the second floor windows of the adjacent home as Morris shone his light on it. There was movement by the window. They could see the outline of the kids in the window. "It's got to be them," Sarah said in relief. "Let's go and get them."

Morris grabbed her by the shoulder to hold her back and called to Alan. The house next door was fifty feet away, with a side street normally running between them. This evening, there was a river there. "Wait a minute. It's not going to be that easy. The street runs downhill several feet there. The water would already be up to your shoulders and you could never stand against that current."

Morris was concerned. A rescue would be difficult and it needed to be done fast. There was a loud crack from the front of the house the children were in. A section of the front porch washed away as they watched.

"We've got to get them now, Sheriff. The whole damn house could go any second. The water is already deep enough to wash it off its foundation."

"You're right. I don't know how to get to them, though. Let's try the radio. Maybe the Coast Guard could send somebody over."

"There's not going to be enough time, Sheriff. Do you know what a man overboard sling is?"

"You mean what they use for taking people off boats?"

"Exactly. Any rope around here?"

"I've got about a hundred foot in the back of the vehicle. I'll get it."

Morris headed back out through waist deep water, fighting the waves and current until he got back to his patrol car. By this time, it was apparent they wouldn't be able to use the Jeep to make their evacuation. The only escape possible would be to seek higher ground behind the houses and make it out on foot. As large waves ran across the water in the street and smashed Morris in the face. Each wave hit him with its crest and literally lifted his feet off the ground, as if to take him with them. He fought to stay upright and moved toward the Jeep. As the receding waves washed back from him, he could see the Jeep move! In moments it too would be a victim of the storm. After what seemed an eternity, he was able to grab a handle on the driver's side of the vehicle. He couldn't force the door open, as the water pressure was too strong. He waded around to the back and got the rear window open, using the manual crank. With the window lowered, the inside of the Jeep quickly began filling with water. He reached inside, grabbed several items and fought his way back to the front porch of the Moore's house. Alan and Sarah were now knee deep on the porch. If it weren't for shops still standing across the street blocking the huge swells coming in from the Atlantic, they wouldn't be able to stand on the front porch.

"Here, this is all I could grab." He gave Alan the rope and one life jacket he carried in the emergency supplies.

"I hope you know how to do this, 'cause I haven't a clue."

"We'll make it work, Sheriff."

"Call me Morris." Whether he was innocent and just wanting to help the kids, or guilty and trying to convince him of his innocence with some contrived act of selflessness, he needed help. It would require both of them if these children were to be saved. That was the only matter of concern for the moment.

Alan handed him one end of the rope. "Okay, you secure this to a column on the porch here. Give me your belt. I'll try to get over to the house and slide the kids back down the rope to you. I'll use our belts to make the slings. Be ready. If they drop off, they're gone. Grab them as soon as they get close."

He tied one end of the rope to his waist. "I'm going to try to make it onto the porch. If it starts to wash me out, pull me back with the rope. The swells are large enough that they might help push me toward the house."

Without waiting another second, he dove into the next wave as it swept toward the house. He swam ferociously with powerful strides developed during years of competition. He tried to ride the waves as much as possible. Desperately slow, and with great effort, he made it to the remaining railings on the front porch and grabbed an armful of column. As the waves pulled back out, he was left safely, for the moment, on the porch. The water was shoulder deep. When he knew he was secure, he called to Morris. "Untie the rope. Let me have it."

Morris got the line free and Alan reeled it in around his elbow. When he had it all, he tossed it over his shoulder and began to fight his way to the front door. The downstairs looked like an unlit swimming pool. All the plywood had been torn free from the windows, as well as the glass underneath. Water was washing in and out with each wave. Alan was ecstatic just to be in the structure. Soon however, he became only too aware of a loud cracking and groaning. The house was not going to be on its foundation, much longer. "Jenny? David? Can you hear me? Jenny, are you upstairs?"

"We're up here in the bedroom. Please come get us. David is too scared to move."

Alan could hear crying and Jenny trying to calm her younger brother. "It's okay, Davey. Alan is here. He's coming up to get us. You don't need to cry. It's all right."

Alan was amazed at how calm the youngster was. If she understood how bad the situation was, she wouldn't be so relieved. He'd try to keep them calm. Carefully, he made his way up the steps. He was halfway up before his feet cleared water. "I'm here, David. It's okay. We're going to get out of here right now."

He surveyed his surroundings and saw the upstairs door leading out to the front balcony. "Alright, kids, come with me." He picked David up. "Jenny, hold on to my belt and follow me." They walked out on the creaking balcony. Alan knew it could go at any moment. This would have to be done quickly. He set David down and secured the end of the rope to a support column that spanned the upstairs balcony and the roof. Looking around, he picked up a ceramic flower pot. He dumped out the dirt, took the other end of the rope and tied it through the hole in the bottom of the pot. He then walked over to the edge of the balcony so he could see the shadows of Morris and Sarah on the porch next door. "Morris, grab the rope. Catch it."

They could see him but they couldn't hear a word over the roar from the wind and sea. They saw him point toward the pot and it was clear to them what he wanted. He threw the pot across the span, toward them. It fell in the water just beside the porch. Not waiting for Morris, Sarah jumped in and retrieved it. Her spontaneous actions worried Morris. "Sarah, damn it! Don't *do* that. You stay on this porch. I don't want to have to tell Myrtle that anything happened to you. Hear me?"

"Just tie the rope, Morris. I'll worry about me. You get those kids."

Morris quickly secured the end of the rope to the same column he'd used when Alan crossed over. When it was in place, he yelled and waved to Alan. "She's tight! Send them to me."

Alan turned to the children. "Okay Jenny, you're first. Show David how easy it is."

"Yes, sir."

He took Morris's belt off his waist and wrapped it under Jenny's arms. He picked her up, then looped it over the rope and buckled it securely. "Jenny, you hold this strap with both hands like a swing 'til Sheriff Stone catches you. Don't get scared. It's fine. I'm going to do it myself as soon as you and David get over there."

She was remarkably calm again. As young as she was, she understood the possible consequences of David becoming panicked while he was making the trip between the two houses. "Don't worry, Alan, I'm not scared. See Davey, it's going to be all right. Watch me."

With that, Alan let her go and she slid quickly across the raging torrent below into Morris's waiting arms. It appeared so effortless it was easy to forget how dangerous the process really was. If they let go of the belt for even a second, they could fall to a tragic ending.

"Hey baby, are you okay?" Morris slid her out of the belt and handed her to Sarah.

"I'm okay, Sheriff Stone. He's sending my brother now."

She was being brave but she began to cry softly as she looked up and saw David and Alan back where she had just left. Sarah held her close. "You're okay now, Jenny. Alan's got Davey. He'll be okay. You just stand right beside me. Hold my hand real tight."

The second story balcony began to sway perilously. It was now only ten feet to the water below. Each time a wave slammed into the front of the home, the deck of the porch would shake and separate a little more from its grip on the home. He must act quickly. He took off the life vest and secured it tightly around David. Next, he took his belt off and repeated the sling maneuver he'd worked out for Jenny. David was crying. He was terrified. He had a death grip on Alan and didn't want to take his turn at the man overboard sling. There was no time to argue or persuade. Alan forcefully pulled David's hands free from their grip on him. He picked him up and stuck him through the opening in the belt as he had done his sister. "Davey, listen to me, pal. You're going to be fine. Hold these straps. That's right, squeeze hard and shut your eyes. Now, count to ten and don't let go 'til Sarah grabs you."

The deck had begun collapsing. It was now a structure whose life had just seconds remaining. The column rail holding Alan's end of the line, began to give. He had to do it now. "Here you go. Keep your eyes shut."

He pushed him as hard as he dared. One, two, three seconds, four, it seemed like an hour. Alan braced himself and gripped the end of the rope in case the railing broke free. He could hold it long enough for the child to make the journey to safety. Finally, he cleared the water and into Morris' outstretched arms. "I got you, David. You're okay. I got you."

Morris freed him from his strap but left the vest on him. There was still a lot of water to cross to safety. He looked up at Alan. He was tying the end of the rope more securely. He would have to hand himself down as there was no sling for him to use. He knew time was running out. He stood on the balcony and yelled to them. "Take the kids now! Don't wait for me. I'm right behind you."

Sarah would hear none of it. "Let's wait, Morris. It can't be but a minute. I can't leave him here."

"I can't either, Sarah."

They watched as Alan began the climb down the rope, hand over hand, swinging above the churning, violent torrent below. The waves were increasing by the second and the wind had to be pushing seventy miles per hour. Halfway across, waves began touching his dangling feet. The balcony began to crumble behind him. In only a second, it was gone. Sarah gasped in horror as she saw Alan fall silently into the water. He didn't scream, he didn't cry for help.

"Alan, swim, swim hard. I'll meet you." Sarah screamed from the deck.

Stroking at the boiling water with all his might, he couldn't hear her. Sarah, Morris and the children receded from his sight quickly, in spite of all his efforts. The strongest swimmer could do nothing against such forces of nature. Sarah watched in shock as the retreating swells ripped him out toward the creek. Directly in his path, were twenty foot swells and currents that would sweep him out to sea. She could see him struggling to catch a piling, then a broken section of pier. It all seemed to withdraw from his outstretched hands. She strained to catch any sight of him, watching him struggle with all his might to swim to anything that he might cling to. As his shadow on the water grew small and she began to lose sight of him, she literally felt a lightness occurring in her breast. It was as though she could feel part of her soul being torn away. A few more seconds passed and then he was gone. For over a minute, Sarah stared at the dark waves trying to catch one last glimpse of him. Maybe he'd grab hold of something before he went too far. Maybe...

Morris began to scream at her. "He's gone, Sarah. He'll have to save himself. There's nothing we can do. We've got to help these kids. A couple more minutes and we'll be trapped too."

Jenny turned to Morris. "Did Alan drown?" It was asked with the innocence that only a child could have brought into such a moment.

"I don't know, Jenny. I just don't know. We have to get out of here though, right now."

The mention of the children brought Sarah around. She picked up David. Morris put Jenny on his shoulders and they began wading to higher ground. The waves and current, pushed by incredibly high winds, kept tearing at their footing. One slip, one foot missing its landing, and they too would be casualties of the storm. For the sake of the children, they couldn't make a mistake. It was over thirty minutes before they reached the high ground around the courthouse, in the center of town.

As they neared the shelter, men standing beside the door saw them. They were approaching slowly as they tried to make the last few yards through the water. One of the men yelled out. "Good

Lord! It's Morris. Some of you men come help me. Let's go get them."

Several men joined forces and waded out to them, relieving them of the children. Sarah and Morris were completely spent, physically and emotionally. They gladly accepted the helping hands to get to dry ground.

Dr. Moore was waiting at the emergency shelter and the kids ran to him. Morris turned to Sarah. "I'm truly sorry, Sarah. I don't know what to say. What he did was unbelievable."

"Did that seem like something your killer would have done, Sheriff? I don't believe so." She was talking between gasps and uncontrollable tears.

"You're probably right, Sarah. I don't see how he could be the man we were looking for. I want you to know that no matter how it seemed, I was only doing what I thought was best for the town. I'm responsible for these things. It's my job. Come on. I'll get another vehicle and get you back to your house. Myrtle and Joan are probably scared to death waiting to hear from us."

Morris borrowed a four-by-four from the county emergency crew and drove her home. They would take the road that led to the block behind Myrtle's house and walk to the back door. The water on Front Street, even on the high end, was now too deep to travel through. She sat in the front seat, oblivious to the storm still pounding on the town. She was too full of grief to cry now. With a firemen's coat draped over her drenched shoulders, Sarah walked to the back of the house and banged on the door until Myrtle and Mrs. Moore opened up for them.

"The children? Did you find them? Please tell me you found them!" Joan Moore had desperation in her voice. Sarah just nodded and Morris assured her of their safety.

"They're at the shelter with Dr. Moore. They're fine. Help get Sarah into some dry clothes. You better stay with her Myrtle. Alan didn't make it. He got carried away by the sea just after he saved the children. I'm afraid she's going to take this badly. Please look out for her. Call me if you need anything. The winds seem to be dying down. Either it's moving away from us, or the eye of the storm is here. Joan, you can come with me back to the shelter and see the kids. Get the jacket that Sarah had on and we'll head back over there now. Myrtle, please look out for her. I'll come back by shortly and check on you both."

"You don't have to worry about that, Morris. Been looking out for her all her life. I'm not about to stop now. You were wrong about that young man, weren't you? Hell of a way to get proven wrong, Morris. You get Joan to her kids before the storm picks back up. We'll call you if we need you."

For the remainder of the night, Sarah sat in the Victorian love seat alone in the dark. She would try to sleep but the moment her eyes closed, Alan would come back into her mind. Then just as quickly, she'd awake with a start, realizing she was just dreaming. She knew she would see him no more, except in her dreams.

The eye of Hurricane Emily passed within twenty miles of Beaufort. Like so many hurricanes before her, she veered off to the north and east before bringing her worst to land. The damage was minimal in Carteret County and the Cape Lookout area. A few miles north in Buxton, it was far worse. Still, nowhere was it as bad as it could have been had the storm maintained its course and come fully ashore. In Beaufort, just a few low-lying homes such as Reverend Patton's and Dr. Moore's were damaged. The flooding messed up the interiors of several shops and buildings. Only one death was attributed to the storm. Alan was its only victim. Had it not been for his willingness to risk his life to save the children, he would have been safe also. The sea had spared him once, but this time, she claimed her rights and took him.

14

The evening had been no less eventful for Don Ellingwood. He was anxious to talk with Jean Byrd. If she was lucid and could remember the details of her attack, she might lead them directly to the killer. He felt useless in Beaufort during the storm. Securing the town had become the necessary focus and he felt Morris would handle that just as well without him. He'd driven up to the Medical Center in Greenville to try and talk with her. He parked his car in the visitor's lot and was more than a little surprised to see that the vehicle next to him was from Beaufort. It was the blue pickup from Shore Marine. It was empty. Ellingwood thought it must be a friend or relative coming by to check on Jean. He wasn't worried about her safety as the Greenville Police Department had shown they knew what they were doing and understood the seriousness of their task in watching over her. The dark clouds and rain, though not nearly so severe as at the coast, had followed him inland. It was raining and windy. With evening approaching, the dark clouds cast an eerie shadow over the surrounding town. He continued to the main entrance of the hospital and to the security desk upon entering. In addition to the hospital visitor's pass, security had to issue a separate pass before anyone could visit Jean. The officers at her door would be checking for both.

"Good afternoon, gentlemen. I'm Don Ellingwood with the SBI. I've come to see Miss Byrd." He pulled out his wallet and the officer at the security desk examined his identification thoroughly.

"Thank you, sir. Put this pass there, on your collar."

"I've got it. I was here before when she was first admitted. Your department has been very impressive in handling this detail. I'm extremely pleased with how well run it's been. By the way, any other visitors up here to see her today?"

"No, sir. Just you." He looked at a chart. No one since yesterday afternoon."

"That's strange. Must be another patient here from Beaufort."

"How's that, sir?"

"Oh, nothing. Just recognized a truck outside. Probably nothing. I'll be with Jean for about thirty minutes. Be back shortly. Thanks."

"Any time, sir. I think she's sleeping right now, but she's getting along just fine. She'll wake up and speak with you though. She asked when someone was coming to talk with her about the attack. She seems pretty anxious."

Hearing that news sparked a new excitement in Ellingwood. She must remember details.

She had another visitor, quietly planning to see her. Even though there were two armed guards outside her door, he wouldn't be prevented from taking this required step in order to protect his actions in Beaufort. They, just like most of the talcum-brained civil authorities that had allowed the country to fall into moral decay, could not possibly understand the deep-seated need for a man of his insight. He was needed to make the public understand what was going on and what must be done to eradicate it. Personal risk could not even be a concern with so much at stake. He was amazed at how easy it had been to grab an orderly's coat out of the closet and take a cart with a stainless tray and medical utensils in it. He proceeded slowly, pushing it into the elevator and then up to the fourth floor. When the door opened, he casually steered the cart up the hall toward her room. People entering and leaving other rooms along the hall paid no attention to him. Impersonating such a low-level employee had its benefits, he thought. I'm almost invisible; might as well be a piece of furniture. So convinced of the believability of his disguise, he approached the guards and stopped directly in front of them.

"Officer, could one of you get the door for me?"

He was equally brazen as he passed them on the way into her room. They'd seen many orderlies come and go since they began guarding her room. He looked as innocent as the rest. He had the proper ID on his smock. No need to suspect anything out of the ordinary. Jean still had her IV monitored and other tasks performed for her many times a day. The door swung shut behind him. What a joke, if this is what you call security, he thought. Taking quick notice of the room, he saw that she was awake and looking out the window. Unfortunate, but he'd deal with it.

"Must keep my back to her until the last second," he reasoned. She might recognize him from their previous encounter. She had many tubes going to her. This would have to be quick and she couldn't jump around much. Movement might knock over some of the equipment beside her bed and set off an alarm. From inside the white orderly's coat, he pulled out a piece of silver duct tape, already cut to the proper length, to secure her mouth. That would be the first order of business. Next, he pulled out his steady companion; a filet knife from a sheath under his pants leg. A quick strike and it would be all over, quickly, quietly, and he'd be gone. He'd considered using a syringe and injecting her with a large burst of air. The resulting bubble in her bloodstream would make a

direct trip to her heart and accomplish the required task. But, it was important to use the same weapon as in the other attacks. They had to know that he could get to her, to anyone he wanted. Once a subject was decided upon, she was his. Nothing, no one, could prevent him from doing what must be done. As he made his move toward the bed, the door behind him opened again. Ellingwood entered. He saw the orderly at work, and backed to the wall, beside the door as it swung shut.

"Good evening. I'll just wait here while you finish up. Will that be all right?"

"Certainly," he answered quickly, careful to not look at the visitor or speak too boldly. The situation had become particularly tricky. He couldn't give either Jean or Ellingwood a good look at his face. Either one might recognize him and sound out to the guards.

"I'll just clean up the bathroom here, while you speak with her." He stepped into the small room. He would wait it out and pretend to be busy while they spoke. The detective moved over close to the bedside. He felt he knew Jean from hearing so much about her. She was someone he would certainly like. As weak as she looked, she still was in much better shape than the last time he'd seen her.

"Hi, Miss Byrd. I'm Don Ellingwood from the State Bureau of Investigation. How are you feeling?"

"A little better, thank you. Is Sheriff Stone with you? I need to talk to him." She spoke slowly, her voice still weak.

"No, he's not, Jean. There's a hurricane heading toward the coast and he had to stay and handle his duties there. I'm sure he'll be coming up as soon as it's over. And everybody in Beaufort said to tell you hello and come home soon."

"I sure miss them all. Maybe I can leave in a few days. I heard about the storm on the radio. I wish I could be there. Are Myrtle and Sarah all right? Maybe I should call them."

"I think the circuits will be pretty tied up now, Jean. They're going to be fine. Morris was going to keep a check on them. You can call them tomorrow after the storm has passed, if the lines are still up. Either way, I'll make sure they get up with you and let you know they're all right. Both of them are anxious to talk with you. And I am too, that's why I came up here. You'll be going home before too long, but right now, you need to stay here 'til the doctors say you're all right."

As he spoke to Jean, Ellingwood walked around her bed to get a little closer. The other side of her bed didn't have the IV stand or a night table.

He waited close by the partially opened bathroom door. Since she would undoubtedly know his identity, there were only two choices. He could attempt to leave the room and most likely the country, or he would now have to kill them both. The latter seemed to be the more desirable of the two choices. If he succeeded, the impact of such a bold move would generate more attention to his personal crusade than anything else ever would. If he failed, at least he would have done his best. In his distorted and perverted world, he was womankind's savior; his mission was dire and mandated by all the evil in the universe.

As the detective came by the door, he grasped the knife tightly in his hand. It was his friend, his accomplice in this quest. Tried and trusted, it had never failed him. He raised his arm to the best strike position. With perfect timing he could take him out in one swift movement. Silently, he stood ready. Seconds went by and the detective did not pass. What had happened? Where the hell was he? He opened the door a little wider for a better view.

Ellingwood had gone back out the door into the main hallway. This was his chance. He'd strike Jean first. He started to back out of the bathroom, his face still hidden from her view; he would turn on her at the last second. He couldn't contain the pounding of his heart in excitement. The terror on her face would sum up all that he stood for, vindication for all that he'd gone through. The door to Jean's room reopened suddenly and Ellingwood re-entered. He spoke to Jean and the would-be orderly quickly turned his head once more.

"Jean, I need to get a statement. One of the officers outside your door is getting me some paper so I can take a few notes. I want to ask you some questions, Jean. Do you feel up to talking about your attack?"

"Yes, sir. I want to. Have you caught him yet?"

"No, we haven't been able to find out who did this and we've been hoping you might be able to help us. Let's let the orderly finish up and then we'll talk."

"Are you about done there?"

Ellingwood had positioned himself on the far side of the room quite by accident. He was staring directly at the impostor. His plan was ruined, there was no way he could take them both out unless he got at Ellingwood first and the needed element of surprise was no longer available. He decided to back out slowly without further delay. She knew who had attacked her, and soon she would tell Ellingwood. He had to leave the room, the hospital, the state, now. As he backed out, he dragged the cart behind him, hoping that the task would make his unorthodox movements look more natural. The cart hit the side of Jean's bed, dumping the tray and all the utensils on it. He tried to remain calm. Too late, Ellingwood was moving over to help him retrieve the spilled contents.

"Let me help you," Ellingwood said.

"No, I've got it, they're sterilized. You'll get them dirty."

"Dirtier than the floor? You can't use them after..."

It was getting too complicated. He made a break for it, never showing his face, not looking back as he ran through the door.

"Stop him!" Ellingwood yelled to the men outside the door. He was too quick. Before they reacted, he was halfway down the hall, at a full run. They struggled to draw their weapons, caught totally by surprise. Ellingwood ran out the door, only seconds behind him. Jean's room was on the fourth floor. It would take him a few seconds to get downstairs.

"Call the main desk. Seal off the building and the parking lot. Get some patrol cars over here immediately. One of you come with me," he directed one officer. The other would alert the officers downstairs and hospital security.

He flew down the corridors stripping off the orderly's coat as he ran hoping to change his appearance. As soon as he noticed that no one was immediately behind him, he dropped the coat and began to walk. Ellingwood turned the corner just behind him. He looked confused at the quick disappearance. There was just the one visitor in the hall. He approached him from behind, calling to him.

"Sir, did anyone run this way?" He just shook his head and continued walking. Ellingwood noticed the white coat lying on

the floor just a few feet behind the man. The stranger picked up his pace. Ellingwood yelled to him this time. "Stop. Don't move."

He drew and pointed his revolver toward the man's back. "Stop, not another step."

At that moment, two nurses stepped out of a nearby room directly in front of him. Sensing the desperation of the moment, he pushed one to the ground, turned the other around, between himself and Ellingwood. He didn't want a hostage to slow him

down. He knew the detective wouldn't shoot at him with the
nurses in his line of fire. He started to run again, this time as fast
as he could go. He turned to the fourth floor stairwell and half
leapt, half fell down the four floors of stairs. His lungs were
bursting and his head reeled from the pulsating pressure in his
veins. As he finished his decent, he exited into the first floor
corridor. Two uniformed officers were already moving his way at
a fast pace, just down the hall. Again, there were too many visitors
in the hospital for them to even consider firing their weapons.
They immediately noticed him turning from them in a fashion that
indicated he was not one of the ordinary visitors that day. Yelling
for him to freeze, they broke into a dead run in pursuit. The large
double glass doors loomed in front of him. Once outside, he'd
have a chance. The parking lot was huge and had thousands of
cars in it. It was raining hard and there was almost no daylight left.
He could make good his escape. Thirty feet to go. Twenty. As he
lunged for the door, a young man with flowers in hand stepped
into his path. Ellingwood, now spotting his target and closing
quickly, realized that if the suspect reached the outside, his
chances of catching him would drop quickly. He yelled to the
flower carrier, "Stop him! Stop that man!"

Dropping his flowers with the fleeing suspect almost in his
face, the young man stepped up and tried to grab him around the
shoulders. He stared into the wild-eyed face. It was like looking
into the eyes of a caged animal. He was filled with rage and panic,
with fear and hate mixed in a single expression. His face was
familiar to his tackler.

"You!" he gasped as he was momentarily held by the young
fool. No sooner had he stopped him, he released his grip and fell
to his knees staring in disbelief at the blood pouring from his
chest. This wild beast stared back for only a second, his knife, still

in his hand. With only contempt for the life that he had just obliterated, he ran from his fallen prey, outside, through the door, which was still held open by the body of the young man. As the dark, open expanse of the stormy night sky and the labyrinth of parked cars loomed before him, two Greenville Police cars screeched to a halt, burning rubber and sliding sideways directly in front of him. Four officers jumped out, guns drawn and yelled to him, "Drop the knife and lie down! NOW!"

He made no movement. He studied the situation quickly, looking for a path to take. He wouldn't stop for them. He'd always made it. This time would be no different. He broke in the opposite direction. There were no bystanders this time. The officers opened fire simultaneously. The bullets ripped through him, carrying with them a deadly fire exploding in his body. He fell to the pavement. Blackness overcame his tormented mind. And he died.

Ellingwood stood over him, his gun still hot in his hand. He stared into the hard, emotionless face. "I recognize this man. He's from Beaufort. Check him for identification. Seal off this area. Don't touch anything."

Don ran back to the door of the hospital where the staff was already attending to the young man on the floor. He was lying on his back, blood covering his chest. His face showed a great deal of pain. An emergency room gurney was already being brought over to transport him. They'd only have to carry him through the doors and down to the trauma unit, just a few yards away. Don walked over to him, wanting to assess his wound and try to determine if he'd be all right. Other emergency room personnel were running to the parking lot to check on the recipient of the police gunfire. They would find him already dead.

Ellingwood knelt beside the young man on the floor. "How is he?" he said to any of the attending staff who might know.

"I'm going to be okay, Mr. Ellingwood. He just got me in the shoulder."

Don was taken back when he realized that he also knew the man who had been stabbed. It was Stephen. "What in the world are you doing up here?"

"I came here to get some more plywood. Morehead was sold out. Everyplace in town was out, so I thought I'd drop some flowers off for Jean and say hi if they would let me see her. Was that the guy who attacked her? You know who it is, don't you?"

"I know I've seen him before in Beaufort. Who is it?"

"Eddie Fitch, the dock master. That son of a bitch. Damn, this is really starting to hurt."

Ellingwood put his hand on Steve's good shoulder. "Thanks man, your quick action probably kept him from getting away. He won't be a problem anymore. He's lying dead in the parking lot. And you don't worry about a thing. You're in the best possible place. I'll tell your friends where you are. You need to go on and let them take care of you now."

Don looked at the doctor who was standing beside them. "Whatever he needs, Doc, the state will pick up his tab. Take good care of him."

15

When Morris Stone returned to the shelter, word of the hospital confrontation and death of Eddie Fitch was waiting for him. With phone lines down, the message had to be relayed over state police radios. Amidst all the confusion and activity in the Beaufort area, it had taken a couple hours for the call to get through. Morris was devastated when he found out. He sat at his desk with his face in his hands and cried like a baby. Thanks to his incorrect assumption, Alan Kelly's last hours were spent being accused of a heinous crime. Everybody who even remotely knew him had told Morris it couldn't have been him. Well, at least he had had the last laugh. He had gone out a hero. He would've gone after the kids and met the same fate whether or not Morris had tried to arrest him. Still, he couldn't shake the feeling of guilt that gnawed at him. He helped people at the emergency command post all night. He figured he might as well be of whatever help he could. He'd never be able to fall asleep with his mind in the state it was in. It made him feel better to see so many of the townspeople pulling together throughout the night. During a quiet moment, he related the facts surrounding Alan's daring rescue and its tragic consequence to any who cared to listen. Giving praise to Alan seemed to ease his mind.

Daybreak offered the townspeople a chance to survey the damage from Emily. Several homes were destroyed. The old timers delighted in finding out that the older houses had fared better than the newer ones, which were built to the supposedly rigid, modern building codes. The same had proven true in Charleston when Hurricane Hugo had hit there. So much for progress, they thought. Several fishing boats and yachts had slipped their anchors and been blown to a watery grave. Some had been found intact many miles away, apparently blown by the storm until they found a quiet resting spot. One small sailing craft was found, south of the storm area, still intact. It was miles from its normal anchorage. The sails were still furled and it appeared to have been beached. This led some to speculate that opportunists were using the storm to abscond with a boat. Numerous shops had suffered water damage to their first floor. Moving the Water Dragon's stock upstairs had saved the business. A few days of cleanup and they could be back in operation. The town docks had lost several sections, but the damage could have been much worse. Even with all the different stories to be heard about the storm, one dominated the talk all over town.

Alan's daring rescue of the children was on everyone's lips. Sam's Grill, after a quick floor scrubbing, was already open, serving breakfast and coffee to the early risers. Most listened silently as the details of the children's plight were related over and over. Morris hadn't shown up yet and no one really expected to see Sarah for quite a while. This would be another episode in a life that most of the townsfolk already considered pretty sad. It was therefore quite a shock when the door to the grill opened and Sarah entered. She said good morning to Sam, went over to a booth and sat down. Coffee was brought to her. She sipped at it slowly and appeared deep in thought. She couldn't sit at home and brood. It would kill her and she knew it. She would go to work and try to carry on as she knew Alan would have wanted her to.

The brisk morning breeze shuffled the newspapers that several customers were reading, as the front door opened again. In came Zed and a couple of the fishermen he worked with. They went over to a booth to order breakfast. Sarah saw them enter. She didn't acknowledge them and continued drinking her coffee. While the rest sat down, Zed came over to her. He took his dirty baseball cap off his head and carried it sheepishly in front of him as he spoke to her. "Sarah, I just come over to tell you that I'm real sorry about last night. I feel pretty stupid. I know I was a jerk to your friend and I was wrong. I just wanted you to know how sorry I am, how sorry all of us are. If we can do anything to help you, just let us know. Anything, you hear?"

"Thank you, Zed. I hope a lot of people learned something from this. You shouldn't assume things about people just because they're different. Alan was a very decent man. It's going to be hard for me to not have him around. I'd like to think that the town and people here are a little better for his having stayed here."

A lot of what she said went right over his head, but Sarah just said what she felt inside.

"Okay, Sarah. I'm going back over to the guys now, but don't forget to call if you need anything."

Sarah decided that if someone as thick as Zed could benefit from this tragedy, others probably would too. She finished her coffee and went down to the Water Dragon. When she walked up to the back door, she noticed that Sheriff Stone was already inside talking with Floyd. She expected Floyd to come by early, to see how much damage the water had caused but she was taken back a little to see Morris inside. She walked up to them.

"Good morning, Floyd. Sheriff. What's going on?"

"Hello, Sarah, I mostly came to see you. How are you doing? I went by the house and Myrtle told me you'd decided to come in to work. I really didn't expect you to be here today."

"I needed to, Sheriff. I don't want to sit around and feel sorry for myself. I was lucky to even get the time to spend with Alan that I had. I'm going to try to look at those times as something good. I need to stay busy and try not to dwell on it."

"I see what you mean. I wanted to tell you how much I admired what you did last night. You and Alan. We have a couple of men searching the beaches and the sound this morning, to see if they can find, well, him." He didn't want to use the word body.

"I put a call in to his family in New York, and told them what happened. They are going to come down for the memorial service."

"Memorial service? What are you talking about?"

"Joan Moore called me this morning and said she wanted to have kind of a ceremony on the waterfront for Alan. She is paying to have a stone marker put up by the docks. I called the town council members and they all thought it was a good idea too. So next Saturday, we're going to get together down at the dock and present it to the town. Of course, we all want you to be there. You will be there, won't you?"

Holding back a river of tears, she put her head on Morris' shoulder and just nodded. He hugged her. There was no way to console her other than show he cared. "I know, Sarah. We all feel real bad for you. You're going to be all right though. You're a strong young woman. You're going to make it."

She regained her composure, stifled her tears and stood back up. "I will, Sheriff. You're right. Yes, you know I'll be there."

"And Sarah, Alan's mother wants to meet you and spend some time with you while she's here. She said to be sure and tell you. Well, I better get going. Lots of reports to fill out this morning."

"Sheriff, is Stephen all right? I want to see him as soon as I can, and tell him about Alan."

"He's doing fine. He'll be back in the morning. He was told what happened already, but I'm sure he'd like to talk with you when he gets here. I'll see you a little later."

"Bye, Morris."

Morris put his hat on and walked back out into the clearing day. Only scattered clouds remained. The sun was breaking through and Morris felt a sense of relief that the town would be safe again, even though it could never be quite the same.

Sarah stayed as busy as she could all week. She threw herself into every task and tried not to dwell on sad thoughts. She determined that when she thought of Alan, she would only think of their pleasant times together. She also felt a special bond for David and Jenny. She'd always loved them but now they were especially close to her as Alan had loved them too, enough to give his life for them. Whenever she saw them, she couldn't help but remember the day at the docks when they were trying to fill Alan's hair with flowers. Just the thought of that time gave her a reason to smile. She'd take a special interest in their lives.

Throughout the week, many townspeople came by to see her. She never had so many locals drop by the shop. She could only conclude they were coming by just to see her and it made her feel a sense of community with the townspeople. They really were a family in a sense. Most told her they would be at the service on Saturday and were happy about the marker being placed there. It was a place of honor to any sailor. Alan would be there to look out over the thousands of visiting sailboats forever. He'd become a part of the history of Beaufort never to be forgotten by the town or its citizens. For this Sarah was happy and proud. She knew Alan would've been pleased.

Saturday came quickly. The morning sun was bright and a soft breeze blew in from the Atlantic. Many visiting sailboats were anchored in the harbor. Word of the ceremony had been passed to all the visiting boats and they were flying their flags at half-mast. The marker, a granite stone, highly polished and already erected in its place of honor, was covered with a flag waiting for the presentation before it would be revealed. It was scheduled for ten a.m. Alan's family would be arriving at the Beaufort airport around nine. Sarah and Stephen, still in a wheelchair and wearing a sport coat with one arm pulled tight against his chest under it, were waiting for their plane to arrive. Morris was there also and would drive them to the docks for the ceremony.

"This is really sad, Stephen. I don't know what to say to his family. I'm not good at this type of thing. Can you help talk to them, please?"

"Of course, Sarah. Just relax. You know that if they are Alan's parents, they've got to be pretty nice people. Just be yourself and you'll be fine. He loved you. They'll love you."

"Here comes a plane. It's probably them." Morris pointed it out to them. "It's a jet! Looks like a Lear."

The airport at Beaufort saw a lot of beautiful, private planes come and go as they brought yacht owners to join their captains on their boats heading south for the winter and north for the summer. Few could match what was now arriving. It was a sleek, fifteen-passenger Lockheed Gulfstream, one of the finest corporate jets made and painted a midnight blue, with *Kelly Industries* in gold lettering on the side. It landed gracefully, needing the full runway to come to a stop. It turned at the far end and taxied to the small terminal where they were waiting. They were in awe of such an arrival. This was not what they were expecting. As the jet came to a standstill in front of them, a side door opened and laid down to the tarmac. It had steps on the inside, creating a gangplank, to walk down.

The staff at the small, general aviation terminal, strained to see who had flown in on such a craft. In recent years, many private jets had arrived there carrying everyone from top business executives to actors and rock stars. Most were coming to meet their yachts, brought to Beaufort by their professional captains. They'd relax onboard the boat for a few days and then have the jet take them back to their world of hustle, while their yachts continued on without them. Today, all were in agreement. This was the most impressive plane they had seen.

The first person out of the plane was a young woman in a uniform. She was a private company stewardess. Next came a slender gray-haired man in a dark suit. Sarah thought that must be Mr. Kelly, as he looked very distinguished. He walked over to Morris. "Sheriff Stone?"

"Yes, please call me Morris. Welcome to Beaufort, Mr. Kelly. Did Mrs. Kelly come with you?"

"I'm Jeffrey Chamberlain, personal assistant to the Kelly family. Yes, to your question, Sheriff, both Mr. and Mrs. Kelly are on board. Do you have a car ready? I understood that there would be a car to carry them to the service."

"Yes, sir, right here. The county let me use one of their Jeeps 'til mine can be fixed. Mine got filled with water during the storm. This one's not as nice, but it runs fine."

Jeffrey looked at the rusting four-by-four. It was not their usual mode of transportation. "Oh dear. I hope it's a short ride."

"Less than a mile. Won't take but just a minute."

"Fine, can you pull it over a little closer to the plane?"

"That won't be necessary, Jeffrey." The voice came from Mr. Kelly. He and Mrs. Kelly were already walking up behind Jeffrey. Mr. Kelly had his hand extended. He was tall and thin, with the same sandy hair and hazel eyes as Alan. He had a much more serious countenance than his son. His suit was obviously expensive, no doubt tailored. He had a commanding presence that demanded respect.

"Sheriff Stone, thank you for your call and your kindness. We appreciate all the arrangements you've made." He looked over at Sarah and Stephen.

"And you must be Sarah."

"Of course she is, dear. She looks just like I expected she would. You're just lovely, dear. I'm Alan's mother. I want to thank you for being so kind to our son while he was here. He spoke of you several times on the phone. I know how strongly he felt about you. I want very much to get to know you better. You come sit by me." She took Sarah's arm as they got in the Jeep beside one another. Mr. Kelly put his arm around Stephen.

"Good to see you again, Stephen. We need to spend a little time together while I'm down here. Don't get away after the ceremony. Stay and have dinner with us."

"Yes, sir, Mr. Kelly. That would be fine."

They all got into the vehicle and took the short trip to Front Street. As they approached, Jeffrey nudged Morris.

"Isn't there something a little newer, maybe larger, that I could rent for the Kelly's for the afternoon? I know they wanted to drive around the area a little. They are very curious as to what

fascinated their son so much about the town. Please don't be offended. I'm sure this is the precisely correct vehicle for the area."

"I'll see what I can find. Dr. Moore would probably be pleased to lend Alan's parents one of his cars. A new Buick, I believe."

"That would do nicely. Thank you so much, Sheriff."

"Please call me Morris."

"Certainly, sir, I mean, Morris."

By the time they arrived, there was already a large crowd gathered at the docks awaiting the start of the ceremony. There were about fifty folding chairs sitting directly in front of the veiled marker and a small podium was set up just to its right. Morris eased the vehicle through the mostly pedestrian crowd and pulled over to the curb, adjacent to where the ceremony was to take place.

"We're here. Told you it wouldn't take but just a minute. I hope you didn't cramp up back there. Certainly could have used a little more room."

"It was just fine, Sheriff. My wife and I are both very pleased with all the kindness you've shown us. There really is a quite large crowd, isn't there? Are there always this many yachts here? This is not the poor little southern port I was expecting."

"Yes, sir. There are always a lot of yachts and commercial boats here. The whole town is built on their business. That and the tourists. Well, they know you're here now. They're fixing to get everything started."

A section of the high school band played the Star Spangled Banner and everyone quieted down. The Mayor, Tom Faison,

gave a short speech. Since he had run unopposed for the past three terms of office, his speech-making ability was not worthy of a politician, even though he gave it his best shot. It was, undoubtedly, hard to talk for several minutes about someone you never met.

Even Morris got up and said a few words. It was not his nature to talk in front of a large group, so he made his remarks brief. "I barely knew Alan Kelly. He was a visitor to our town and was well thought of by those who were fortunate enough to get to know him, especially David and Jenny Moore. I don't know what kind of person it takes to risk your life so quickly without regard to yourself. He had only known these children a short while. I can only assume that Alan Kelly regarded all children with the same reverence and would have done the same had he never met them. We live in a town that has lived and died at the mercy of the ocean and its whims for many years. I have myself seen a number of good people lose their lives pursuing their livelihood on these beautiful, yet dangerous waters. None, even those whom I knew well, affected me as much in their passing as did Alan Kelly. He, without reservation, gave his life for his fellow man. No finer act can be performed. I will remember what I saw and hope that it serves as an example to all of us. I guess that's about all I wanted to say. Oh yes, and I would like to welcome his parents to Beaufort and hope that all of you will take the time to speak with them after the ceremony. Would Mr. and Mrs. Kelly please come up here? And Sarah, you too."

Morris escorted them over to the memorial and Sarah, at the request of Mrs. Kelly, was given the short ribbon to pull which caused the flag to fall off the marker. The audience applauded and Mayor Faison read the words inscribed on the monument. It was a dark, highly polished granite block with a bronze plaque mounted on top of it. It read:

Alan Christopher Kelly
From New York City, NY
Born June 25,1965 – Died August 31, 1993
Lost his life while successfully
rescuing local children from the
storm waters of Hurricane Emily on
the night of August 31, 1993.
The Town Of Beaufort honors his
memory and bravery.

As a special favor to Sarah, the sound of Pavarotti singing Nessun Dorma began to fill the waterfront, its powerful melody adding to the beautiful setting. There, in the midst of all the tears and emotions, one most unusual occurrence began to unfold. As the song began to reach its powerful crescendo, *Wind Trader* re-entered Taylor Creek. She was majestically under full sail, gleaming white and heeling proudly. Jason was at the wheel and her new crew, caps in hand, led by Irving and Sherrie on her rail, paid tribute to Alan and his ceremony. Jason paused and stared at the beautiful watch on his wrist that Alan had given him so recently. With no one watching, he touched his hand to his eye to eliminate the remote chance that a tear might be forming. They had raced for a week, under full sail, upon hearing the news of Alan and the memorial ceremony. They wouldn't have missed it for any reason. They left port in Florida within an hour of hearing the news. Never had a more beautiful vessel made such a graceful and spectacular entry. Not a dry eye remained among those who witnessed the moment. No finer tribute could be paid to a sailor than this. His friends and family had all remembered him. Mrs. Kelly and Sarah embraced and shared their tears. Though touched by the sincerity of those involved, Mr. Kelly remained stoic. His emotions would be dealt with in private, on dark nights to come as he remembered his only son.

Almost in relief of the moment, the band started to play a more up-tempo song and the crowd began to rise and disperse. Many came by and gave their best wishes and condolences to the Kellys and Sarah. Considering the turmoil and confusion of the last month in Beaufort, it was as good a conclusion as the town could have expected to such a difficult time. Sarah turned to the Kellys, "How long will you be staying?"

"Unfortunately," Mr. Kelly replied, "as much as we'd like to stay longer, I have to be back late tonight. I have company briefings tomorrow to prepare for a proxy fight next week. It's never business as usual anymore. Seems like someone is always trying to buy my companies out from under me. I'm spending more time convincing my stockholders to hang on to their stock than I am running the damn business. I had hoped Alan would come home and help me with all the day-to-day operations of the company but... I guess that's not going to occur now. So, I'll have to carry on without him. He is going to be missed a great deal by his family."

Sarah caught a glimpse of moisture in his eye as he spoke. For a minute, she thought he might crack, but he quickly composed himself. "If it weren't for these concerns, I would really like to stay a while. Perhaps we can come back later."

"That would be nice."

"Incidentally Sarah, Jeffrey has some papers to go over with you before we leave. Perhaps Mrs. Kelly and I will look through the town while you and he find a place to sit and go through them."

"Papers? What kind of papers?"

"Jeffrey, why don't you go with Sarah? We'll meet you at the restaurant down the street in an hour. You'll come too, won't you, Sarah?"

"I'd be glad to."

"Fine, now Jeffrey, what about that car?"

Jeffrey spotted Morris standing by a new Buick just down the street, trying to get their attention. "Right there, sir. The Sheriff is standing beside it."

"Tremendous. See you both shortly."

Jeffrey walked over to Sarah. "Where would you like to go? We need to sit for a little while."

"I'll open up the Water Dragon. It's closed, so we can talk there. What's this all about?'

"Let's just walk down the dock and look at the yachts. I'll explain everything to you when we get to the Water Dragon."

"That's a good idea. I want to wave to my friends on *Wind Trader*. After we eat, I'm going to visit with them." Sarah waved and hollered to Irving, Sherrie and Jason until they finally saw her and excitedly waved back. Irving called out to her. "We'll see you after we dock."

Sarah nodded affirmatively and they walked on toward the Water Dragon.

Jeffrey picked the conversation back up, "By the way, what is the Water Dragon?"

"Just a small gift shop, where I work. I met Alan there, the first day he came to town. I remember it so clearly. It's hard to believe he's gone. We spent so little time together. Yet, I felt like I really knew him. You know, he spoke very little of his family. All I knew was that they lived in New York. He did speak of you. He called you Jeff though, not Jeffrey."

"We were very close. When he was growing up, his family spent a lot of time away. I was more like an 'uncle' than an employee. He meant as much to me as if he had been my own son. Had I ever married, I could have asked for no better child."

"You know, he looked just like his father, but his personality seemed to be more like his mother's."

"You are very observant, Sarah, and precisely on target with your observation. Don't think that because they seem so composed and reserved, they weren't upset over Alan's death. It upset them a great deal. He was their only child. They've been in the public eye for many years and are very good at keeping their emotions to themselves. Mrs. Kelly literally doted on him. His father always hoped he would get tired of traveling around the country and come home to help run the family business interests."

"What sort of business are they in?"

"Alan never mentioned to you his family's holdings?"

"No. What are they?"

"They have very extensive stock holdings in several large corporations that were founded by his grandfather, Admiral Randall Kelly. Everyone who knew him said that Alan was the spitting image of him. He was a sailor. He retired after a very distinguished career in the service, then made a fortune supplying the Pentagon with the gears that made the military turn. One of the original members of the military industrial complex you hear so much about but, of course, never any names of the players. He remained well liked and quite the wanderer, sneaking off for weeks at a time, much to the chagrin of his staff. Quite a character."

"I wonder why he never mentioned any of this to me."

"Believe me. You knew the side of him that he wanted you to. He was always concerned about real relationships, not friends of fortune so to speak. Do you understand what I mean?"

"I think so. He always talked about trust. How important it was to him, and how I could always believe what he told me."

"That's a fact. I don't believe I ever caught him in a lie, even when he was very small. It just wasn't his nature."

"Well, here we are." She unlocked the door and they entered. She locked it behind them.

"Very quaint. This whole area reminds me a little of Mystic Harbor."

"I've heard of that. Is it as pretty as Beaufort?"

"Quite similar, actually." Jeffrey pulled a manila folder out of a small leather binder that was tucked under his arm.

"You can use Floyd's desk in the corner, if you need to."

"That would be nice. I have some papers here for you to sign. I'll go over all of that in just a minute. Now, if I get anything wrong, you just interrupt me and tell me how it is incorrect."

"I'll try."

"Okay, Sarah. I understand that you and Alan had talked about going to Boston College together this fall. Is that correct?"

"Yes, sir."

"Jeffrey, or Jeff, will be fine, Sarah."

"Yes, Jeff. We were going to go there together."

"He called me several times and told me to take care of making the necessary arrangements. If you still wish to attend, your tuition and all expenditures for living and transportation are to be taken care of."

"You're kidding!"

"Certainly not. Alan thought it very important that you finish your education. The Kellys have a foundation that gives out a number of scholarships each year to deserving students. One of these has been set aside for you for as long as you wish to continue your education. You could obtain your Ph.D. if you desired. Everything would be taken care of."

"I couldn't do that. It wouldn't be right for the Kellys to spend that much on someone they don't even know."

"I assure you, the amount we're talking about would not even be noticeable to them. And they loved Alan a great deal and would want to do this for you. I've worked for them almost all my life. They are very fine people. They would be more concerned if you did not accept this."

"I'll need a little time to think. Without Alan, it just doesn't seem the same. Do you understand what I mean?"

"Absolutely, take some time. The semester begins in three weeks, so there is a little time."

"I would have to make arrangements for someone to stay with my grandmother, and Floyd would have to replace me here at the shop, not that I would be that hard to replace."

"I'm sure you will be missed by all."

"Okay, I'll call you in a few days and let you know. Should we go eat with the Kellys now?"

"In a few minutes. We're not finished quite yet."

"What else is there?"

"This may be a little hard for you to accept so suddenly, but Alan expressed to me how deeply committed he was to you and I think he fully intended to marry you before you went to Boston."

"Yes, we had talked about it. Gosh, he did tell you everything, didn't he?"

"Alan confided most everything to me, Sarah. I respected his wishes for confidentiality and tried to follow them as much as possible. He also directed me to make you a beneficiary and to provide for you with a portion of his assets and insurance. This was intended to be in preparation for your marriage, not this unfortunate situation."

"What? When did all this happen?"

"Just two weeks ago, when he asked me to make arrangements for you two at Boston."

"What are you talking about? All he ever had was a duffel bag and his paintings."

"Alan, through his participation in his family's holdings, was a very wealthy man. Granted, he never seemed to need a lot to be happy, but his estate, of which you are a beneficiary, is quite large."

"Alan was wealthy?"

"Very much so. He owned over four hundred thousand shares of Kelly Industries. It sells for over fifty dollars a share."

Almost unable to speak, Sarah tried to reply, "That's... That's almost..."

"It's over twenty million dollars, Sarah. Even though the majority of it will go into a trust fund, your portion will probably make you the wealthiest person in this county. The insurance is several million dollars also. Listen, Sarah, no one really deserves this amount of money so don't feel guilty. Alan knew exactly what he was doing. This was how he intended it to be. Not so soon, of course. Please, sign these papers now. I will help you look out for your affairs until you understand all the repercussions of your business activities."

"Repercussions?"

"Yes, of course! You'll have to vote at board meetings and your decisions will affect thousands of company employees. Don't worry; we'll all help you through it. It's a very complicated situation, but we know you'll do fine."

"And how do Alan's parents feel about someone they've just met having a voice in the family business? I certainly don't want his folks mad at me."

"Erase those thoughts from your mind, Sarah. This is how it is. They were quite aware of all this before they came here and I'm sure they only feel that much better after meeting you. This will all work out nicely. Just trust me, if you will. I have only your best interests at heart. I will advise you, as I know Alan would have wanted me to."

In a state of shock, Sarah signed the papers where Jeffrey indicated. As each was completed, he neatly placed them in a manila folder and carefully sealed the entire collection back up. He then tucked the file back under his arm. "Okay, what do you say we go meet the Kellys now for dinner?"

"That sounds fine to me, but you'll have to pardon me if I can't remember the way. I'm in shock right now."

Jeffrey laughed. "Trust me, this is just the beginning. Things in your life are about to be changed forever. Alan knew you were up to it. He trusted you, also. Otherwise, I assure you, I would not be here today. You'll get used to it. I promise you. Life is a very complicated affair, isn't it?"

"That's odd. That's what Alan used to say. I feel so bad, his doing all this for me and he's not even here to know what's happening. It would all be so much better if he were here to share it like we had planned. Of course all I thought we would be sharing was a hammock and walks on the beach."

"Sarah, wherever Alan is, he's undoubtedly looking down on you very pleased. I'm sure of it."

"I truly hope so, Jeffrey. I really do." They exited the Water Dragon and started walking down the street toward the restaurant where the Kellys would be waiting. She enjoyed the evening with Alan's parents, but couldn't wait to go aboard *Wind Trader* to reminisce with the friends she and Alan spent such pleasurable times with. It was a long, tearful evening that would stay in her mind for a long time.

16

Sarah, all bundled up against the New England winter, walked down the common on her way to class. She'd only been at the college for a few days, but already she realized this was the right decision. Alan was in her thoughts continually. Since he died, she'd grown more confident each day. Jean had gotten well enough to return to Beaufort and was staying with Myrtle, a match made in heaven Sarah thought.

It was as if all the events of the past months brought her in this direction on a straight course. This had to be correct. It was all so preordained, she thought. Things just work out like they're supposed to, whether we anticipate or understand them at all.

Each morning, on her way to class, she passed the Art Department. It was in a grand old stone building that was both warm and foreboding at the same time to her. She wanted to go in and see where Alan spent so much time, and yet she couldn't bring herself to enter. His memory was with her so much already. Being that close to his past might unleash emotions she was already fighting to control. She was afraid to go inside the gallery hall. Every morning she'd start to enter and then, at the last moment, turn away and continue to her class.

The same thing occurred this morning. However, after walking past the entrance, she stopped and turned back. She had to put this behind her. It was there and she would, sooner or later, have to deal with it. She'd face it this morning. Slowly, deliberately, she walked up the brick path leading to the Gothic arch under which the huge wooden door swung. Students, smiling and talking, passed her and entered. She fell in behind the next group. The halls were similar to the exterior. There were stone walls with large exposed wooden beams. It was much like she always envisioned an old English castle might look. Her footsteps echoed off the cold stone floor. The entrance hall had tall cathedral ceilings and was dark. Light came from small, shield shaped windows, located symmetrically down the expanse. It would be easy to assume you'd entered an old castle were it not for all the preppie students rushing in both directions to classes. Sarah walked slowly down the hall stopping occasionally to look at paintings; mostly old oils by well-known artists who had attended or taught at the prestigious school. She tried to inhale every detail of the building, the furnishings, and the art. For a moment, she felt as if Alan was walking beside her. There was definitely a part of him there. A feeling of warmth embraced her as she slowly continued down the hall. There were dozens of paintings, some modern, some very old, all along the walls. It was as much a gallery as a school building. Near the end of the hall, she felt a strange sensation pass through her. A chill spread across her skin and she froze. Directly in front of her was a painting that shook her very foundations. She stared incredulously at her own face framed with yellow flowers in her hair. The blue Atlantic was behind her. She was kneeling and there were two small children holding the same yellow flowers in their hands. It was unmistakable. She felt she might faint. Alan had painted this. How did it get here? When? Why? Why didn't she know about it? So many questions raced through her mind that she dropped the books

from her arms. Were it not for a student coming to her side and
catching her arm, she would have fallen to the floor.

"Are you all right?" the student asked.

"Yes, thank you. I'll be fine." She took her books he picked up
for her. She studied the picture for almost ten minutes. Too late
and too unsettled to go to her classes, she returned to her room.
She left only to eat dinner and then returned. She called Jeffrey
and hoped he'd return her call before the day had ended. Fitfully,
she fell asleep around midnight. Pictures of Alan and Beaufort
raced in her dreams. Scenes from their days together seemed to
come in and out like excerpts from a novel. One moment she was
placing flowers on her mother's grave and the next she was sitting
atop the lighthouse at Cape Lookout. She and Alan were picking
out shapes in the clouds out over the sea. There were screams of
children and then, the horrible moment when Alan was swallowed
by the waves as he fought to save himself.

17

The late fall sun warmed the hands of crew members on the trawler *Edna Fae*, a commercial netter out of Charleston. The first mate, Anthony, kept a sharp lookout for any tell-tale signs of fish schooling in the calm Atlantic waters, fifty miles east of Murrell's Inlet, South Carolina. The boat's owner and captain, David Francis steered the seventy footer slowly hoping that the passing of Hurricane Emily and two subsequent Nor'easters would encourage fish to begin feeding near the surface in these waters kept warm by the close proximity of the Gulf Stream.

"Cap'n, there's a hell-of-a-lot of debris out here, enough salt treated wood in the water to build a pier longer than anything on the coast I reckon."

"That's a fact, Anthony. I just don't want to be takin' any pieces of it back stickin' out of the side of our hull. There's more crap floatin' out here than I've seen since Hurricane Hazel went through. We was all just lucky this one didn't decide to cut a bee line through the state."

The morning passed quietly, the ocean almost too calm to feel natural. There was an oily appearance on the surface with occasional whiffs of steam rising as the late sun baked down on the water.

"Captain, does that look like the bow of a boat stickin' out of the water over to port? 'Bout fifty yards out?"

"Ain't sure. Could just be a piece of somebody's deckin' washed out here. I'll head over that way. Keep an eye out for anything under the surface in our path."

The *Edna Fae* eased toward the floating debris. As they got closer, Anthony stared ever more intently, trying to make out the nature of the material.

"Damn, Cappy'! I swear there looks to be somebody on top of an overturned skiff. You see it?"

"You're dead on. What in the hell would somebody be doing out this far? S'pose they must've lost a boat in some of this ungodly weather we've been through. You see any movement?"

"Not yet, get me in closer. Burt, get your ass up here with the rope ladder," Anthony called to another of the boat's crew. Two others on the stern dropped the net they were repairing and followed the crewman forward as he carried the rope and wood ladder to the bow of the boat.

By the time they came alongside and backed off the motor, it was obvious that a ragged looking body was lying on the bottom of an overturned, flat-bottomed boat, about fourteen feet long. The stern was out of her and had the ocean been anything but flat, every small wave could cross over the boat as it floated almost even with the water's surface. Anthony took the ladder, secured one end to a massive deck cleat and tossed the other end over the side. He removed his rubber work boots, straddled the bulwarks on the side of the ship and eased down the ladder. He tried to put his weight on the skiff, but it became apparent the passenger already lying on it was all she would handle without going down deeper into the sea. Without further consideration, he dropped into the water alongside the small boat. Easing himself over to the man, he felt the ankle of his disheveled body.

"He's warm. He's still alive! Hey, buddy, you awake?" There
was no response. He shook the leg. "Hey, you hear me, fella?"
Still getting no answer, he called to the crew back on the *Edna
Fae*, "Throw me a collar with a line on it and I'll hitch him up. He
ain't much alive. I'll swim alongside 'til you pull him up." In just
moments, Anthony had retrieved a floating collar with a line tied
to it and placed it around the chest of the limp figure. That
accomplished, the crew began pulling the line slowly, first easing
the man off the skiff, into the water and then up the side of the
Edna Fae. Soon, they had the man on the steel deck of the
workboat. Anthony followed close behind. The men gently rolled
the limp body over on its back and began to determine the man's
condition.

"His eyes ain't rolled back and he's breathin' on his own."

"Yeah, but none too well and bejesus, he's covered in salt
water boils, and his right arm don't look to be right. My guess is
it's broken. He needs to be in a hospital pretty damn fast or he
ain't gonna last much longer."

Captain Francis took over the situation as all onboard knew
he'd seen many men pulled on board before. If anybody could
handle this situation, it was David Francis. "Burt, get the Coast
Guard on the horn and tell 'em we need a chopper out here in a
hurry. They're gonna try to get us to tell 'em he's alive and they're
gonna say we should just bring him in real fast. That ain't gonna
work. This fella needs a hospital now. You hear me?"

"I know how to handle them, skipper."

"Okay, the rest of you men get him below and see can you get
him awake and maybe a little warm coffee or even sugar water in
him. Mix some Karo syrup with warm water and see if you can get
some down his throat without choking him. That's as close as we
can get to an IV right now."

The men carried the incredibly lucky sailor below to the ship's dining area where they laid him on a settee that ran along the back wall. Quickly, his wet clothes were stripped and they wrapped him in blankets. They understood how easily hypothermia could take a life once someone had been in water where the temperature was in the low sixties. They needed to get his body temperature back up to normal. As the Captain had ordered, a mixture of Karo syrup and water was warmed and the sticky fluid scooped out with a large spoon. One crew member held the man's bearded head up while Anthony slowly dripped the fluid into his mouth. Burt returned to inform Captain Francis of the Coast Guard's response to their request for assistance.

"It was like you said, Skipper, but I told 'em he was going to die in an hour if they didn't come get him. After a little while, they said they was sendin' a chopper out. I gave our position and they said to stand by. I'll listen out for 'em on the VHF and give you a shout when I get up with 'em."

"Good job, Burt. Now, let's see can we get this fella to come around."

Over the next thirty minutes, the man began to moan and grunt as his mouth was forced open to pour in the syrup.

"Man, those sores in his mouth have got to hurt like hell. I hate to pour this stuff on 'em."

"He's out of it, and the Skipper says we got to get some of this in him. It's like glucose, you know, like they give you in the hospital. That ain't nothin' but sugar water."

Slowly, the man's eyes half opened and he started to help in the swallowing process a little. The crew became ecstatic as they watched life reappear in the man's eyes.

"He's tryin' to say something Anthony. I swear he is. I can't figure it out but I know he's tryin' to say something to us."

The VHF radio next to Burt and David crackled with the distant voice calling for the *Edna Fae*.

"*Edna Fae, Edna Fae*, Coast Guard Air Rescue vessel calling. Do you copy?"

David picked up the hand-held microphone.

"This is the *Edna Fae*."

"Switch and answer channel twenty-two, Skipper. That's two-two alpha."

"*Edna Fae* going to twenty-two."

"Yes, Coast Guard, this is Captain David Francis on the *Edna Fae*. We have your passenger in stable condition awaiting your pickup. How do you want to do this?"

"*Edna Fae*, since it's so slick out here, we are going to drop a swimmer who will help you load the victim onto a basket which we'll be lowering. Do you have a ladder to help the swimmer on board?"

"That's affirmative. We will be standing by waitin' for him."

"Very good, Captain. We'll drop down to a few feet off the water and he'll swim over to you."

The chopper maneuvered to within several yards of the calm water and a wet-suited swimmer jumped in and began swimming toward the *Edna Fae*. He made the distance to the trawler where David Francis waited with the rope ladder. As this was happening, Anthony and Carl Sweat, the fourth crewman noticed eye movement in their new charge.

"tah... ah... sehy..."

As quickly as he tried to speak, he would black out again.

"Wonder how long this guy has been out here."

"Weeks maybe, I've heard of people making it up to six months with nothing but a pail to catch water in and a paper clip to use as a fish hook."

"Come on, Anthony. That's a bunch of crap. How you gonna catch food with a paper clip?"

"Forget it. Buy a book. Rub some water on this guy's face; we got syrup all over him."

The eyes opened again, "tey, sey"

"He's trying to talk again. Wish I knew what he wanted."

David Francis and the Coast Guard swimmer approached them. The swimmer, also a sea-rescue expert, examined the man.

"This is one lucky guy, probably wouldn't have made it to morning. Has he come to yet?"

"Yeah, a couple of times, but just for a few seconds. Keeps tryin' to say something."

"How about an ID?"

"Nothin' on him."

"What about numbers on the skiff?"

"I didn't notice, but we can still check it out."

"Wait 'til we get him on the chopper, then you can give the station a shout on the radio."

"Ok, let's get him in the basket. Everybody put their hands under him and make a stretcher. I'll keep his head upright. All together now. Let's do it."

They made their way to aft deck of the *Edna Fae*. The Coast Guard chopper was overhead, the basket was already being moved into position. Quickly the passenger was strapped in. In moments, he was aboard the chopper, followed by the swimmer and shortly after, they were bound for medical attention in Charleston.

Morris Stone had been walking to work a lot since the storm. He'd pass the townspeople putting their homes and stores back together. He was impressed with how the community had again pulled together and how quickly things were getting back to normal, if that were possible. After the bizarre turn of events surrounding the attacks and the discovery that the killer was actually Eddie Fitch and not Sarah's friend, Alan, Morris had become a lot more philosophical in his approach to being Sheriff. He was taking a lot more time with everyone, getting to know them all over again. He entered his office thirty minutes later than usual.

"Morning, Morris, or should I say afternoon?"

"Morning, Esther. It's a beautiful day. I walked in."

"Again, huh? It's time you quit worryin' about things you can't do nothin' about. There's lots of folks here wouldn't trade you for nobody. I know it's none of my business, but there, I said it."

"I'm fine, Esther, just a little down."

"Well, there's no reason for it. By the way, got a Commander Everett with the Coast Guard been trying to get up with you all morning. Number's on your desk."

Morris parked his hat in its usual berth and picked up the stack of notes on his desk. He took the top one and dialed the number. "Yes, this is Sheriff Morris Stone in Beaufort, North Carolina. I'm returning a call to Commander Everett. Thanks, I'll hold." Morris browsed through the other notes while he waited.

"Sheriff Stone. Good morning. Tom Everett here. Got a question for you."

"Good morning to you, Tom. Fire away. I'll answer if I can."

"We've tracked the number on a skiff found off South Carolina to Raymond Caulder there in Beaufort. You know anything about it?"

"Raymond's been dead for several years. I'm sure it was just being used as a flower pot by his wife. They live on the creek and the hurricane probably washed it out to sea. South Carolina, huh? That's amazing."

"A little more than amazing, Sheriff."

LES PENDLETON

"How's that?"

"A trawler found it over fifty miles out to sea with a man clinging to it. His own boat more than likely went down during the storm and he found the skiff floating, used it as a life raft."

"Who is he?"

"Well, we don't know. No ID on him and he's not really up to talking yet. We thought you might be able to help us, but I guess we're not going to learn anything from the skiff."

"He's still unconscious?"

"Most of the time. He keeps mentioning a boat name but we can't find anything on it in our records. Might be a foreign yacht or trawler. We just can't find anything with that name in the records."

"What's the vessel's name?"

"The *Sarah Turlington*."

Morris felt a flush come over his face. He was dumbstruck. "That's not a boat. It's a woman. I know her."

"You're kidding, Sheriff. Is she missing too? Was she on a boat?"

"She's fine. Tell me. Is this person a white male, about thirty, kinda thin, dark hair with fine features?"

"Real thin, right now. But just about like you're describing. Why? Do you have an idea who he is?"

"You won't believe me when I tell you. Where are you now? Where is he and is there a helicopter pad close by?"

* * *

There was a loud ringing in Sarah's apartment, bringing her back to the conscious world, the hard, dark world of reality. A world without her love, her passion. The phone was ringing. "Jeffrey" she thought to herself. It must be him. She raced to catch the phone. How long had it been ringing? Would he hang up, just as she picked up?

"Hello. Jeffrey?"

"No, I'm sorry to wake you so late. It's after two a.m., I know, but it can't wait."

"Who is this?"

"You don't know my voice by now? I'm hurt!"

"Stephen, is that you? What are you doing this late? I was expecting a call from Jeffrey."

"I know, Sarah. It's important we talk."

"You're right, Stephen. I didn't realize you knew Jeffrey that well."

"I've known him all my life, just like I knew Alan."

"When can you come over? Or just tell me and I'll meet you wherever you want."

"Now, Sarah. It has to be right now. There's a lot happening you have to know about."

"What are you talking about? You want me to meet you tonight? Where? How will I find you?"

"Look out your window." Sarah moved over to the window. There was a light snow falling. It was quiet and surreal. There, below her window, parked on the circular drive that wrapped around the fronts of all the dormitories, was a long black limousine. Standing beside it, was Jeffrey. The back window rolled down and Stephen, wearing a tie and dark fur coat and hat, stared up at her. The same feeling that befell her in the hall earlier, came back with a vengeance. She sat down on her bed and picked up the phone.

"Jeffrey is there, with you."

"That's right, Sarah. It's fine. Come down. We'll go for a ride and I'll explain it all to you. Don't worry. I promise it's okay. Come down, now."

Sarah didn't bother to place the phone back on the hook. She walked over to her closet, grabbed a heavy coat, a stocking cap and boots. She threw them on as she raced down the stairs. She stepped quickly in the new covering of snow as she walked over to the back door of the limousine. Snow was beginning to fall harder. There was a brisk wind and the night was cold. She was trying to put the pieces of the day's events together in her mind before she reached the car, but, to no avail.

Jeffrey smiled warmly to her as she approached. It was sincere and reassuring. The door opened and she got in the back. There was Stephen, as she had never seen him before. Well groomed, even polished, he reached over and kissed her on the cheek.

"What is this all about, Stephen? I don't like to be kept in the dark, especially when there are things going on that I don't understand."

He reached past her and closed the door. Jeffrey walked around the limousine, got in and started to drive out of the circle of dorms. Stephen took her hand and said. "You know you can trust me. We'll get you some more clothes in the morning."

"In the morning? What do you mean, 'in the morning'? Where are we going?"

"Right now, to catch a plane."

"To catch a plane! To where? I've got classes in the morning."

"Tomorrow is Thursday. You'll only miss two days; you can call early and let them know you're going to be away 'til Monday."

"Stephen, I'm too tired to play guessing games. What is going on?

"How's school?"

"You got me out in the snow at two a.m. to ask me about school? Jeffrey, what's going on here?"

"I'm sure that Master Stephen was just curious if you were enjoying your new environment."

"So, the stonewall. You're both in on it. Boston College is just fine. It was fine twenty years before I got here and I'm sure that it will be just fine twenty years after I leave. Now, why are we driving around in the snow in the middle of the night?"

Stephen and Jeffrey continued to ignore her questions and change the subject. They continued driving through the snow covered countryside and making small talk. Sarah was too tired to continue being courteous or act pleased with what was happening so she lay her head back on the seat and fell asleep. After what seemed to be just seconds of needed rest, she was awakened by the motion of the slow moving limousine coming to a halt.

"Sarah, Sarah, we're here. Are you awake?"

Sarah opened her heavy eyes and immediately noticed the blur of flashing red and blue lights. They'd arrived at the airport. They were not at the passenger terminal, but at the general aviation area. The limousine was actually parked out on the tarmac, adjacent to several others obviously waiting on their planes. The still falling snow had brought almost all air traffic to a halt. As her eyes opened and she cleared out the cobwebs from them as well as her tired mind, she noticed a familiar aircraft, parked off to the side of the taxi area. The runway lights bounced off the snow and cast an iridescent hue over the polished, almost dark purple fuselage of the Kelly Industries' jet. Its running lights were also on and the overall effect was stunning. Its presence brought more questions into Sarah's already overwrought mind.

Jeffrey picked up the cellular phone in the car and notified the plane they were there and standing by. Before long, the door on the side of the jet opened and set down in the snow.

"That's for us. Come on, Sarah, we're on."

By now, Sarah's adrenaline was pumping, her mind awake. Anticipation was building for whatever her friends had planned for her, but what did any of this have to do with her discovery earlier in the day of the painting? Jeffrey opened Sarah's door and threw his topcoat over her as he escorted her to the plane's companionway. The stewardess greeted them as they entered. Once onboard, Jeffrey turned to Sarah and Stephen, who had followed close behind them to the aircraft. "Is there anything else I can help you with? Sarah? Stephen?"

"No, thank you, Jeffrey. See you shortly."

"Very well. I'll see you both over the weekend."

With that, Jeffrey politely nodded and left the plane.

Sarah looked around the inside of the plane. When she'd seen it before, she didn't get to actually enter it. The interior and the staff manning the aircraft were interesting. There were no rows of seats like one would usually find on a commercial airplane. There were a number of large, permanently mounted, deep cushioned chairs, almost like recliners in a home. The walls contained two television sets broadcasting the news on one and the stock market reader board on the other. There were several framed maps including the United States and a larger world map. Both had colorful spots highlighted on them as if they were of particular importance to the Kelly business interests. About a half dozen uniformed or suited employees were hustling about, each appearing to be busy at some specific task. The lights in the plane were low and there was soft background music being piped into the cabin. A voice came over the intercom.

"This is Captain Wheeler. Welcome aboard. As soon as we can get clearance from the tower, we'll be taking off. The top of the cloud cover is at ten thousand feet and we'll be out of all this white stuff, so prepare for takeoff, if you would please. He called to a stewardess, "Anne, would you please show Sarah to her cabin."

Anne came over to Sarah and gently held her arm as she led her to the rear of the plane.

"Won't you come with me please, Sarah. Your quarters are in the owner's section."

She opened a door to the section of the plane that occupied the back half of the aircraft.

"Right in here, Sarah, use the intercom to call if you need anything."

Sarah entered the dimly lit stateroom. There was a built in desk in the center of the warm, rich looking cabin. There was polished stainless steel and varnished cherry everywhere. Behind the desk was another large chair, apparently being occupied by another attendant who'd be looking out for her needs on this trip to wherever she was being taken. Sarah walked over to the attendant who was facing away from her.

"Hi, I'm Sarah Turlington, have you got a clue where this thing is going? Everyone seems to know except me. Do you have any idea what the destination is?"

The attendant turned and answered, "I know exactly where we're going, to Beaufort, North Carolina, for your wedding."

He turned and the small cabin light exposed him. At the same moment, Sarah recognized the voice that was speaking to her. It was Alan.

For a full moment, she stood frozen, staring in disbelief at the lost love of her life. Completely overcome with emotion she burst into tears and ran to him, embracing him so tightly that he had to call out. "Easy Sarah, you'll break something else, I've got a shoulder and arm in a cast here."

Though still crying, she loosened her embrace and backed up enough to look into his face. It was truly him.

"How is this possible? I, I saw you, the storm and the waves. How did you stay alive? Where did you go? What's wrong with your shoulder and arm? Are you hurt? I'm so happy... I am SO happy to see you. I love you. I love you."

She started to break down again. Alan held her head gently, stroking her hair and kissing her cheek. "I know, sweetness. I love you too. I couldn't wait to see you. I need you. We will never be apart again."

The captain came over the intercom again. "Good news, we're cleared to take off. We only have a small window, so buckle up and let's get out of here."

The engine noise began to grow stronger. Alan motioned Sarah to a seat beside him. "It's a couple hours to Beaufort. Sit down and I'll tell you how I managed to grab a small boat and survive the storm by tying myself to it. Remember what I told you about a cork in storm?"

"I do; I really do. What happened then?"

"I drifted for quite a few days, miles at sea. My shoulder and arm were broken by the boat pounding into the waves. I was in a coma when a work boat crew from South Carolina picked me up. I wound up in a hospital in Charleston. The first two weeks I drifted in and out of consciousness. After about three weeks, I started to come around and gather my senses. I was wrapped up, from my waist to my neck and in a lot of pain. I'm just now able to get around a little. The hospital found no identification on me and didn't have any idea I'd drifted all the way from Beaufort. They thought I was in a boat that must have gone down off their coast and didn't know who to contact. They finally tracked the skiff down to Beaufort and shortly after, good old Morris Stone came by to see me. I finally managed to call home and talk with my folks and Stephen and to check on you. I asked them to not tell you anything until I could do it myself. And, here I am."

"You rat! You let me worry myself sick about you for two months and didn't tell me the minute you came to. I feel like breaking your other shoulder. You should have let me know the first minute you realized what was going on."

"There's a lot more to talk about my beautiful, Sarah. I'll fill in all the details after the wedding."

"What do you mean after the wedding? We can't just run off and get married. I want my grandmother and Jean and all my friends to be there. Call me old-fashioned if you want."

"Hey, ease off. They've known about it all week. And I spoke with Jean. She's doing great. I can't wait to get back there. And then, we can still go back to school together if that's what you want. Whatever you want is fine with me. You're going to have the biggest wedding in the history of Beaufort. It's going to be a very special affair. I've been arranging it all week. All your friends will be there and a few things that will surprise you."

"Such as?"

"Well, as you recall, I made a lot of bold promises to you about how I was going to propose to you, that have not occurred yet and you know I'm a man of my word. And, there's one other thing."

"What's that?"

"You won't believe who's going to sing at your wedding."